EDITING LIFE

EDITING LIFE

SANDY DUGGER

SAPPHIRE BOOKS

SALINAS, CALIFORNIA

Editing Life

ISBN - 978-1-939062-79-6

Editor - Kaycee Hawn
Book Designer - LJ Reynolds
Cover Desingn - Christine Svendsen

Sapphire Books
Salinas, CA 93912
www.sapphirebooks.com

Printed in the United States of America
First Edition – December 2014

Dedication

This book is dedicated to everybody who has encouraged me to follow my dream.

Acknowlegdments

I would like to thank everyone at Sapphire Books who has helped me make my dream come true.To Chris and Schileen for taking a chance on a new author, thank you for the confidence you have in me. Kaycee, my editor, thank you for making this a pain-free experience. To all my Sapphire sisters thank you for the encouragement to keep moving forward.

Thank you to my family for supporting me and pushing me forward. Thank you Mom, Dad, Wil and Tina, Shannon, Gloria, and Lori. Stacy, I want to thank you for the time you have given me to allow me to write. I know you have given up time we could have spent together. To Deborah and Tracy thank you for reading through this before it was ready and pushing me. And Erin S. you stuck through this and gave me so much valuable feedback I can never thank you enough for sticking with me.

And to everybody, or had a family member, who has suffered through cancer.

I would also like to thank the GCLS and their mentor program for their help. I had a wonderful experience with two different sets of mentors and both times I learned so much that has helped me with my writing. I want to thank Jae, Lee Lynch and Ann McMan. This is a wonderful program and I know it will help others as much as it has helped me.

Chapter One

The little steps Bailey Hutsell took made her life her own, but she couldn't help but be frustrated as she stood naked in front of the open closet for twenty minutes, unable to make a single choice. Tonight was a special occasion and she wanted to look her best. It was the first time she would be spending more than just a few minutes with her former best friend. Ten long years had passed since they had spent any quality time together. For the third time, she reached for her dress uniform. It was habit to reach for the dark blazer, white shirt, and black slacks. With a sigh, she shoved the garments into the back of the closet, and continued to search her civilian clothing.

"Are you ready?" Bailey heard Morgan holler from the hall.

"Not yet," Bailey shouted back. Bailey shivered and glared at the old, single pane window. With a huff, she turned to return to the task at hand. She reminded herself she needed to put plastic on the windows before winter set in.

"Shit, Bailey, you're not even dressed. At least put something on or close your door."

Bailey turned to the voice. She looked at her sister leaning against the doorframe. Four months she had been home and the changes in her little sister continued to surprise her. Bailey was amazed at how her younger sibling had grown into a woman while she was away. The light blue sweater she wore made her aqua eyes pop. Black slacks accentuated her womanly curves. Bailey didn't know when she learned to walk in the four-inch heels she was perched on, and wondered where the gangly little girl who used to follow her around in overalls went.

"Sorry, modesty is one of the first things you lose when you enter the military." Bailey turned back to search her feeble wardrobe. "Until a few months ago I only wore uniforms. I rarely wore civilian clothes."

"Pick something. It's just a get together. Something casual is fine."

"But we're going to the club afterwards."

"Just wear what you wore when you went out when you were on base."

Bailey was embarrassed to tell her sister she didn't go out when she was in the service. There was usually a bar on base she frequented, but even then, she was in uniform. It frustrated Bailey that it only took the military two months to break her, before rebuilding her into the perfect soldier. A drone who lived to follow every instruction and started to live her life for the next order. For years, she didn't have to think. Her only objective was what her superior told her. She generally spent her spare time in a classroom, or in her barracks room reading or writing. Now free of the military, she couldn't even decide what to wear to a birthday party.

Morgan pushed Bailey to the side and reached into the closet. Hangers were shifted around before she pulled out a black pair of pants and an old black vest, a keepsake from Bailey's youth. "Here, this is fine. You can wear a tee shirt under it."

Bailey scowled at the vest. It was what she was

wearing when she last saw Shayla, the birthday girl, and her former best friend. "But this is from high school. It's over ten years old."

"Right, and that makes it retro. Just wear it and hurry or we're going to be late. Who knows, you might even bring back an old trend," Morgan said and left the room.

Again Bailey watched, amazed at how her sister could walk on four-inch sticks.

"What time is the party again?" Bailey asked. She walked over to her old beat up dresser, the furniture physically scarred by the stickers of her youth. The top drawer screeched as it opened to reveal her underclothes, still folded per Navy regulations.

"Nineteen hundred hours."

"You can just say seven," Bailey yelled at her retreating sister. She grumbled and slipped into her boxer briefs and sports bra. Next, she pulled on her jeans. She rifled through her shirts, folded identical to what she had been taught ten years ago. She settled on a plain white tee. There was no way should could go wrong with black and white. It was safe. She unfurled the thin cloth. The garment revealed faded black ink on the bottom of the shirt. She remembered back to the first week of boot camp when she had spent hours on her knees stenciling those letters and numbers on every article of clothing she was issued.

Bailey pushed the black writing into her pants. Ten years she walked around with ink covering her clothes, a constant reminder of the lack of control she had over her life. She couldn't see the lettering but knew it was there, a persistent reminder of what the military had taken from her. She stripped off the shirt and tossed it across the room. She dug through the drawer again. A purple tee was pulled over her head and tucked into her jeans.

"Are you ready?" Morgan's voice came from the hall.

"Give me one more minute," Bailey shouted back.

Bailey slipped into the vest and stood before the full-length mirror. What she found staring back surprised her. Bailey's blond hair was still long and pulled back in a ponytail. The hat she normally wore was left sitting on the dresser. A few more freckles dotted her tanned face. Her clothes, plain though they were, hinted at her toned body. It was one thing she planned to retain from her days in the United States Navy. The woman standing in the mirror looked strong and confident even though her insides were shaking at the thought of seeing Shayla.

"Come on," Morgan yelled.

Bailey grabbed a pair of socks from the top drawer and turned off the light before leaving her room. Her naked feet thundered on the stairs, taking her back to when she had lived there years earlier.

"I just need to get my shoes and socks on." Bailey pulled her boots close as she sat on the last stair to finish getting dressed.

"Hurry or we're going to be late." Morgan checked her watched, let out a sigh, and jingled her keys.

"Can't have that now, can we," Bailey said, unable to remember the last time she was late for something. Punctuality was an important part of military life. She left the service to be with her small family and in the past months, it had continued to dwindle until it was only her and her sister. Life had gotten away from her while she was gone and now it was her time to take it back.

"I'm ready." Bailey pulled her pants over the top of her boots. "Let's go."

Bailey opened the door and a gush of icy wind assaulted her exposed face. She shivered as she pulled on her pea coat.

Bailey stared out the window into the dark night. The car sped along the quiet road. Shadows rushed past her window as she continued to gaze into the blackness. She could imagine the streets the way they were when she lived there years ago. For the tenth time in the past few minutes, she moved in her seat. Her nerves were a jumbled mess, resembling a kid at a rave.

"You ok?" Morgan asked from the driver seat.

"Yeah, just nervous," Bailey said.

"Why?"

"I don't know," Bailey said. It hurt to lie to her little sister. Of course she knew, but a short drive into town wasn't enough time to confess why she had left her plans of college to join the military. "The past few times I've seen Shayla there's been tension." A partial truth had to suffice.

"You've barely seen her. I don't know why you haven't spent more time with her."

"I guess I just don't have time right now. It's not easy to acclimate to civilian life after ten years of being told what to do, where to be, and what to wear. I mean, it feels odd sleeping in my old bed. Not having someone telling me what to do every minute of my day. Plus I'm trying to make a good impression at my new job." Bailey fidgeted with the automatic locks on the door.

Again, another lie. She wanted to confide in her sister. It had taken her a long time to come to terms with her own feelings and she still couldn't figure out how to put her feelings into words. Even after ten years, the pain of rejection was as sharp as the finest blade. It was easier letting Morgan believe Bailey had been selfish when she surprised everybody with the news she had enlisted in the military.

"I understand being busy, but you should still make the effort to visit her. She's missed you."

A little fear ebb away, excited her old friend might still want to be a part of her life. "I should, and I will. It's just been hectic. And to be honest, I'm afraid." She had locked away any hope that her friend still wanted her in her life; now she could feel something banging on the door, shouting for someone to unlock it.

"Afraid of what?"

"I'm scared of what she'll say. I didn't give her any warning when I left. I changed every plan we had made. I didn't give her an option. I didn't talk to her, I didn't even say bye. Had it been the other way around... I can't blame her for hating me." Bailey continued to flick the power button, starting to relax in the rhythmic click.

"Oh, she's mad, but it's in the past, move on. She doesn't hate you, but I'm not going to lie, she was upset and still is," Morgan said. Her eyes remained on the slippery road.

Morgan was right. She did need to move on with her life. She lost so much. How much more was she willing to lose before she grew up and started living? Any bit of anger Shayla had for her was justified. Bailey made her bed; now it was time to lie in it.

"Talking has never been my strong suit and I

promise to have that conversation with you about why I left, but not now."

"Will you stop playing with that lock? You're worse than one of my students."

Bailey went back to silently staring out the window. The miles disappeared under the tires. A sharp pinch from her sister pulled her attention away from the window.

"Ow. That's going to leave a bruise." Bailey examined the red mark.

"Don't ignore me. I said, are you going to make plans with her tonight? I'm tired of being your go between. You're home now, you take care of it," Morgan said.

Bailey understood her sister's anger. She should have never asked that much from a then fifteen-year-old girl.

"I did make a quick call to her the night I got back into town. I asked her to start fresh. She agreed, but since then I haven't had time." Bailey turned from the window and watched her sister. A handful of minutes remained before they arrived at the store. There were still things she needed to say. Not giving herself a chance to back out, she continued with a sigh. "Look, we haven't talked much since I've been back either, but I wanted to say thank you. I've asked so much of you over the past few years and I haven't been here for you. I owe you."

"You're right. You owe me, and now I'm going to collect," Morgan said. A red light forced her to stop.

Bailey's mouth went dry when her younger sister turned to address her.

"I want you to promise me something."

"Of course."

"No, say the words 'I promise'," Morgan said.

"What am I promising?" Bailey couldn't help the fear that crept into her voice.

"You'll find out once you promise. You owe me and you owe me big. Now you're going to make me a promise without even knowing what it is."

"But..." Bailey started to protest.

Morgan didn't give her time to continue. Her foot slammed the gas. "Damn it, Bailey, no. You don't get a 'but' in this. You don't have a choice. You owe me. You said it yourself. You used me ten years ago to do your dirty work. You came home early from your summer break, skipped town just as quick, and expected me to clean up your mess." Morgan backed off the gas and took a few seconds before she continued. "You weren't there when Shayla knocked on our front door; you took off and left me the task of telling her you joined the Navy. I was the one who fielded her calls for years. I was only allowed to give her crumbs of what was going on in your life. I did this for you even when I didn't know why you were doing it. Granted, I got a best friend, but I had to muck through a ton of grief to get it. Shayla has always been like family and you not only hurt us when you left, you hurt her too. I can't thank her enough that she was here to help through the time when...."

"Don't say it," Bailey said. To hear the words from Morgan's lips would remind her of how she failed to be there for her sister.

"When I got sick," Morgan said.

Bailey sighed. "I agree I put you through more than any teenager should have gone through, and I can never apologize enough for not being there for you when you needed me."

"Not just me, Shayla, and Grandma and Grandpa too. I don't know what happened over that summer to cause you to change your plans the way you did, but it wasn't fair. What did happen? It must have been major to keep you away from your family for so long."

"It's personal," Bailey said. Tears blossomed in her eyes. She had failed so many people. Morgan's words were just a reminder how she had messed up so many people's lives. But still she could not voice the words. No amount of talking would take back all the hurt she had forced on the people she loved.

"Of course it is. Everything's personal. You need to just open your mouth and allow the words to flow. They're there," Morgan said.

Bailey pressed an imaginary brake, trying to slow their progress toward the person who still haunted her dreams.

"I'll tell you what happened, but not right now."

"Fine, but I'm not going to let you off easy."

Morgan's ability to pester had been something she had excelled at. Life is nothing but constant movement, but Bailey was thankful there were things that never changed.

"Fine."

"Ok, now say it."

"Say what?" Bailey asked.

"You promise."

Bailey was aware of the dangers of giving her sister a promise without knowing what it was first. It was similar to handing a crack addict a blank check. She did owe her sister. Her fears told her to keep silent, but her head recognized that nothing she promised could ever repay her sister for what she put her through.

"I promise. Now just what am I promising?" Bailey asked. Fear planted itself in her stomach like a lead anchor.

Morgan took her eyes off the road long enough to meet those of her sister's. "I want you to promise to never leave again without talking to me first."

Bailey's chest tightened. Morgan asked her for the one promise she didn't think she could keep. Many people believed Bailey had been courageous when she enlisted during the war in Afghanistan. A brave sailor cruising waters to protect the nation, when in truth she was the biggest coward. She ran from her friend's rejection right into the arms of Uncle Sam, a man who had total control over her for at least four years. She had left to protect her heart from Shayla, but she never conceived that another part of her heart would be the cost.

The tires ate up the pavement as they drew closer to their destination. Every time she attempted to form the words to promise her sister, her lips moved, but no words escaped. She didn't know if she could take watching Shayla move on with her life. On the flip side, her sister was her only remaining family. She scrounged up every ounce of courage in her reserve. She owed it to her to be there for her. She didn't know what she would do if she lost another family member because of her inability to protect her heart.

"I promise. I promise not to run again." Bailey forced the words through clenched teeth.

"Good, now we're here. I want you to promise to take time to talk to Shayla. She may not show it, but she misses you," Morgan said and cut the engine.

"I can't promise you that. But I will try. That's as much as I can give right now," Bailey said, fear creeping up her spine as she gazed through the large pane window. Blue eyes searched for the woman she longed to see, but feared to face.

"Then that's what I'll take. Are you ready?" Morgan reached for the wrapped packages in the back seat.

"As ready as I'll ever be," Bailey said. With a sigh, she exited the car. It was going to be a long night and even though she was thankful for the invitation, she wasn't looking forward to the evening and what it might hold.

Shayla listened to her small group of friends argue over whose present was next. The first one hadn't been up for discussion. Six women watched two twenty-one year old girls struggle to drag a cumbersome bookcase through the small glass door. For their present, the youngest of their group had restored an old bookcase. Shayla loved the detail work and the color matched the wood floor she installed in her one bedroom apartment located above the bookstore.

The women continued to argue. Shayla tuned them out, knowing nothing she unwrapped that evening could compete with the gift she received months ago when she picked up the phone to hear the velvety voice from her youth. Shayla looked into sapphire eyes, the same ones that made her heart pound when she was in high school. Bailey's dimples appeared. Shayla returned her smile before Bailey turned away to chat with her sister. Shayla started to stand to talk to Bailey when a heavy box was thrust into her lap.

"Here, this is from Connie and me," Dion said and sat next to her partner of thirty-three years.

Shayla pushed the thoughts of Bailey to the side. She untied the large bow. The lid was set aside. Bright sheets of paper filled the air as Shayla searched for the gift; finally she pulled out two large stones.

"They're lovely." Shayla examined the two large purple quartz bookends.

"If you don't like them, we can return them. I wanted to get you bookends that were dogs. One half was the front and the other was the tail end but Connie thought you might appreciate these better," Dion said. She folded her strong arms over her buxom chest.

"Oh no, these are stunning," Shayla said. She placed the stones on the floor and hugged the two older women. Connie and Dion were not only her friends but they rented the shop next door. Every day one of the women came over for a morning cup of coffee and gossip. She never once regretted renting out the shop to the two ladies.

"They're exquisite." Bailey picked up one of the stones. Her eyes sparkled as she studied the rock. "I look at them and think of a book. On the outside it's just a cover and not till you look inside do you see the beauty."

Shayla stared as her old friend ran her finger along the glass surface of the stone. She couldn't remember a time when Bailey ever said something so thoughtful. It was then that she realized how much her friend had changed in the past ten years, and how much she didn't know about her. She frowned when she thought about the time that had passed without a word. She wanted to get to know her, to pick up where they left off, but she couldn't help the overwhelming feelings of wanting to hurt Bailey as much as she hurt her.

She invited her former best friend to her birthday party because it was the proper thing to do. Morgan was coming, and there was no way she couldn't invite Bailey. She looked at her old friend, and her first love; she wanted Bailey to run her fingers over her body the same way she was touching the stone. Yet she wanted to break every bone in her hand for the pain she put her through.

Before her emotions continued on the path they were on, another smaller package was shoved in her hands.

"Here, this is from me," Wanda said, and returned to her seat next to her younger sister Dion. "I hope you enjoy it."

Shayla removed the shiny wrapping paper and found a leather-bound copy of Romeo and Juliet. "Wow, I love it."

"I figured you might appreciate it. I mean, you have so many copies and I thought this would be a nice addition to your library," Wanda said. The older woman settled into her seat, straightening out her skirt. Her bright red lipstick was still flawless along with her jet-black hair. Everything about the woman was always perfect.

"It's marvelous. I'll treasure it," Shayla said. The shop owner placed the book on her new bookshelf. "It has a new home."

"My turn," Morgan said. She handed over another small package.

"Hmm, I wonder what this is," Shayla teased as she shook the brightly wrapped gift.

"Oh, my!" Shayla exclaimed when the paperback

novel was unwrapped. She turned to the first page, lovingly stroking the inscribed words.

"Read it," Morgan said. The room quieted.

Silent moments passed before Shayla cleared her throat. "'To my biggest fan. I hope this brings you as much pleasure as it was mine to write.' It was signed by Allura Williams." She turned the page and read the dedication. "'For my guardian, my love, my rock.' How did you get this?" Shayla asked as she continued to stare at the printed words. She loved that in all the books Allura wrote, the dedication never changed. Shayla always wondered about the meaning and hoped one day to meet the author and ask her.

"I have my ways," Morgan said. She leaned back in her chair and stared at her sister. Shayla didn't understand why Bailey glared back, but she never understood their competitive relationship. She was raised a single child and couldn't understand the sibling dynamic.

"I can't believe it." Shayla clutched the book to her chest. In that moment, she wanted nothing more than to be able to run upstairs to her apartment and start reading. It was her party and leaving wasn't an option. There were still more presents to unwrap. Plus the women said they were going to drag her to the only lesbian bar in Portland. "This isn't even out yet. I have ten on order and I haven't even received that shipment yet. I just can't believe this."

"Top that," Shayla heard Morgan whisper to her sister.

"I don't think I can," Bailey whispered back. Shayla saw fear and tears blossom in the normally stoic woman's eyes.

"This is great. Now I'll have two things to put

on the fantastic bookshelf Mac and Sandy made for me," Shayla said as she started to read the first page. It hurt to see pain in Bailey's eyes and had to look away. There was only one thing that could draw her from the woman and that was a book from her favorite author.

"Here, I got you this." A package wrapped in the Sunday comics disrupted her view of the book.

Bailey continued to stand in front of her, wringing her hands. The closeness of the woman had started to unnerve her. The silent years that had passed crumbled their one time close friendship. She wanted to start rebuilding it, but she knew there were a lot of hurdles she would have to jump to get back to where they left off. How do you allow someone back in who took your heart and ripped it out? Granted, Shayla was partially at fault since she never told Bailey how she felt, but Bailey hadn't given her the opportunity. The summer after graduation, she worked up the courage to tell her. But when she returned from camp and headed straight to Bailey's, Morgan met her at the door, telling her Bailey joined the Navy, and had already left for basic training. Her first year of college had been a struggle, but Morgan and the little bits of information she passed on had made it bearable.

Shayla ripped through the paper and stared at the white box in her hands. She turned the box over until she found the silver apple. "Uh…thank you." She couldn't help the disappointment that had seeped into her voice. She didn't know what to expect but something electronic was not it.

The smile disappeared from Bailey's face as she knelt beside Shayla. She extended her hand. "It's an iPad."

When Shayla placed the box in Bailey's palm, she

pulled the device from the container and opened it. "Now you can read your books on this." Bailey pushed the button at the top and the screen lit up. "These were lifesavers on the ship. We were able to load a ton of books on just this one device. They didn't take up as much room as one single paperback. Of course, there was the library onboard, but space is so precious and with this little thing, we were able to get any book we wanted. I used one to download my student books and it came in handy to read lesbian novels. I didn't have to worry about someone seeing the cover," Bailey added.

Shayla watched Bailey's long fingers fly over the screen. After a few taps a white screen appeared. Bailey handed it back to her, and through her glasses she made out the title, Romeo and Juliet. She glanced up at Bailey's expectant face.

"That was very generous of you Bailey, but," she waved her hand at the room they were sitting in, "My books mean so much to me. Mac and Sandy just built me a new bookcase. How am I supposed to fill it with one of these? Plus I own a bookstore and read all the books I want right here." Shayla tried to keep her voice appreciative but when Bailey's smile disappeared, she knew she had failed.

Shayla was old fashioned, something about herself she accepted long ago. While attending college she saw how technology was taking over and taking human contact out of life. It was easy for her to decide that wasn't what she wanted. She didn't own a cell phone. She only owned one computer for inventory and work purposes. She may have been a child of the technology age, but her old soul would not allow her to welcome technology without a fight. She held her tongue about how the device she held in her hand was her business competition.

"I know. It's not meant to replace your books. Everybody knows you can't go anywhere without your books, you never have, but this will help. Instead of having two or three books in your bag when you travel or if you're on the go, you can download multiple books. And, if your work computer and this device is connected to the internet I can help you view your inventory here. Plus there are sites that have free stories that you can't get in book form. You'll be able to use this to read them," Bailey explained.

The gift she held in her hand screamed about how much time had been lost, and how different they truly were. Her other friends gave her things to enhance her library.

"Thank you, it's a very thoughtful gift," Shayla said, setting the iPad aside. She watched as Bailey made her way back to her sister's side. Her strong shoulders drooped as she plopped into the battered couch.

"I gave you other ideas. You should have taken one of them." Shayla could overhear Morgan whispering to her sister.

"Shut up," Bailey hissed. "If you don't want it, I can return it," Bailey said to Shayla.

"No, it's ok. It's just I don't travel much. Plus I'm not that good with electronic things," Shayla said in an attempt to dispel her friend's disappointment. The idea of being able to view her inventory from her apartment was very appealing but the other functions held no attraction for her. She enjoyed the sensation of a book in her palm. The scent of a book was better than any perfume to her.

"Well, if you want, I can come over later in the

week. Then we can set it up and connect your devices. You can play with it now. I've taken the liberty of downloading a few stories from online that you can't get in print. But if you find you don't want it, I'll take it back and get you something else," Bailey said. Shayla couldn't help but notice how Bailey would not meet her eyes.

"Thank you. I'll take you up on the offer of merging my inventory," Shayla replied. The idea of spending time alone with Bailey was more of a gift then the tablet. It took Shayla a while to even become accustomed to the idea that Bailey might be back in her life again. It took years to overcome the overwhelming anger and disappointment, but Shayla knew the feelings she held in her heart for Bailey were there to stay.

A few months ago, Shayla's life had shifted when Bailey had waltzed through her bookstore doors and, with Morgan, sat in on one of her book clubs. It was hard for her to get through the session with Bailey across the room. Shayla struggled with her jumbled feelings. She was more than angry with her friend, but she wanted to begin to explore the feelings that hovered around the edges; butterflies had taken flight in her stomach. That had been the longest they spent together since the last time Bailey took her home from the last day of school. She didn't count the funerals when Bailey and Morgan's grandparents passed.

During the months Bailey had been home, Shayla had only seen the woman a handful of times. Whenever Bailey entered her little world, it tilted. She couldn't think straight, her stomach was in knots, and her head felt full of cotton. Her emotions were frazzled and it frustrated her to no end. She wanted to rage at her friend for leaving her and in the same breath she wanted to draw her close and never let her go. Now she was going to spend the evening with her in a crowded, noisy, lesbian filled bar. A quiet evening with Bailey, or upstairs with her new book, was more appealing. She did not relish the possibility of watching Bailey with other women.

"Ok, so are we ready to go then?" Mac stood up. Like a puppy following her master, Sandy followed Mac's lead. The group of women started to break up their little party.

Connie grabbed the dirty plates scattered around the room and placed them in a plastic tote to return to the bakery. She boxed up the remainder of the homemade carrot cake. Dion kept the bakery running, but it was Connie's pastries and cooking that kept the customers filing through their doors.

"So, does anybody want another piece of cake before we take the rest of this home? Are you sure you don't want this?" Connie offered Shayla for the third time.

"Oh, no. I'm sure. It was wonderful but you take it," Shayla insisted.

"Well, if you're sure," Dion said and smiled as she snatched up the cake. It was no secret carrot cake was her favorite. The women laughed as she hefted her full figure towards the door quicker than any of them had seen her move in the past. She exited the building, leaving any protests to go unsaid. Shayla had one time overheard Dion say that carrot cake was the secret to a happy marriage. Even though she could burn water, Shayla would learn to bake if it meant getting Bailey back in her life, if even as just a friend. Possibly Dion could teach her how to bake something easy.

"Are you sure you don't want to join us tonight?" Shayla moved out of the way as Bailey hauled four folding chairs to the back of the store. She couldn't take her eyes off the woman. She appreciated the muscles that rippled as Bailey easily moved throughout the store.

"We're sure. It's getting kind of late and we have to be up early to prepare the pastries in the morning." Connie grabbed the plastic tote loaded with dishes. Her slight frame hid strong muscles honed from years of rolling and kneading dough.

"We old ladies don't need to cramp your style," Dion said. Shayla appreciated the way she relieved Connie of the heavy tote, not as if it was a chore, but an honor.

"Speak for yourself. I'm coming," Wanda said and patted her perfectly coiffed black hair. "So, any cute men at this club?"

"Yeah, but sadly for you, they'll more than likely be looking for other cute men," Sandy said.

"That's ok. I'll find myself a nice young woman."

Dion laughed. "You would never be with a woman."

Red lips pursed, her perfectly plucked brows knitted as she thought about her sister's statement. "You're right. I think I'm too old to be changing teams," Wanda said. She straightened her white blazer. The action was wasted as the garment held so much starch no wrinkle dared crease it.

"That makes you a cougar," Sandy said as she flung her arm around the older woman and escorted her to the door.

"Honey, I'm too old to be a cougar." Wanda tossed her head back and laughed.

"Remember you two, you have to be in at noon," Connie reminded her two young employees.

"Well, we'll leave so you ladies can head out." Dion pulled Shayla in for another hug. The woman took the opportunity to whisper into her ear, "Happy Birthday. And try to have fun tonight." Dion pulled away and gave Shayla a wink before turning her glance toward Bailey.

"I'm only going to ask one more time. Do you want to join us?" Undertones of panic laced her own voice.

"Some other time. I'm tired tonight." Dion hefted the tote onto her hip.

"I understand." Shayla sighed.

"But thank you for the offer." Dion smiled at Shayla.

The jingle of car keys from Morgan propelled Shayla toward the door.

"Do you want me to drive, Morgan?" Shayla asked.

"Nope. I'm fine. You're the birthday girl. It's a requirement you drink," Morgan said as she held open the door. The frigid air whipped into the store.

"I don't have to drink." Shayla pouted, shuffling to the door like a prisoner being led to the firing squad. The thought of sitting in a crowded bar with the smell of stale smoke, music pounding her ear drums, and women clinging to Bailey was not something Shayla was looking forward to. The mere thought of having to watch Bailey interact with another woman made her cringe as jealously and disappointment competed against one another.

"I'm taking my car, too, just in case you guys leave early," Wanda added. Her whole forearm disappeared into her bag as she searched for her keys. "I plan on dancing 'til dawn or until they kick me out. Whichever happens first." After a few seconds, she extracted her arm, holding her keys in her closed fist.

"What do you keep in that thing?" Sandy asked. "It looks like it can hold everything, including the kitchen sink." The group of women laughed as Shayla locked the front door.

"A small kitchen sink maybe, but you never know when you might need something," Wanda said as she hefted the bag onto her shoulder.

"I think you just need your I.D and cash," Shayla said, since she didn't have much more than that in her slacks.

"That might be what you need, but I need powder, a brush, my lipstick..." Wanda continued her list as she walked to her car.

Sandy linked her arm in Shayla's and pulled her to their waiting car. "You're drinking and I intend to buy you your first drink, so you won't need any cash. We're going to get you so drunk you won't know how you got home," Sandy said

"Oh, no you're not," Shayla complained. She hoped that the night would end early enough to be able to start reading her new book, but for some reason she was not counting on it.

Chapter Two

The women crowded around a small table perched on the edge of the dance floor. As the night approached last call, the small stand strained beneath the weight of the empty glasses and beer bottles. The two extremely drunk young women thrashing around on the dance floor had consumed over half of the drinks.

Bailey had taken it upon herself to make sure every empty glass was replaced with a fresh drink. It didn't matter how much it hurt her pocketbook to ensure each women had a drink in hand, she was thankful for any excuse to escape the table. No matter how much alcohol she consumed or how hard she tried to build up her courage mentally, she still wasn't confident enough to ask Shayla to dance.

On the drive to the bar, she hadn't been able to talk to Shayla. Sandy took control of the conversation from the time they left the store until they arrived at the club. Bailey didn't think she ever had as much energy as the butch girl when she was her age. When she arrived back in town, it took a while for Bailey to warm up to the younger women.

They were not at the club for more than five minutes before Mac and Sandy disappeared on the dance floor. The music sounded foreign to Bailey. The beat barely changed, turning the evening into one long song.

She spent most of the night trying to avoid looking at the woman who haunted her dreams. The lady sitting on the other side of the table didn't possess the type of good looks that turned heads, but to Bailey she was the most stunning person in the bar. The few pounds Shayla gained since high school fleshed out her womanly curves. Her chocolate brown eyes were still hidden behind black square framed glasses. Thick wavy locks of auburn hair were captured in a long braid that hung heavy down her back.

Bailey again looked at the women on the dance floor. Even though not one of them held her attention, she feared being caught staring at Shayla again. Even if she wanted to talk to Shayla and try explaining how foolish she had been to run off, the pounding music would make any sort of apology sound angry since she would have to shout. Plus it wasn't a conversation she wanted to have in front of hundreds of strangers.

To avoid the icy looks tossed her way, Bailey paid more attention to her beer. Being a lightweight, every sip that passed her lips upped the chances of her doing something stupid.

Bailey noticed another butch woman approach their table. In an attempt to prepare herself to have to watch the woman talk to Shayla, she took another sip of the warm liquid. She was relieved when the woman strolled past Shayla—until a warm hand fell on her shoulder. Again, she was confused when the question of a dance fell on her ears. Politely she turned the woman away. The only person she wanted to dance with was now glaring at her.

The empty glasses danced when Shayla's hand landed on the crowded table. Bailey jumped, trying to catch an empty bottle from hitting the ground as it rolled off the table. She turned to Morgan for an explanation and her only response was a shrug of her shoulders. Bailey returned her gaze to the women gyrating on the dance floor.

"It's going on two, I'm going to switch to water. I'll be right back," Shayla shouted to the two women who still sat at the table. Her anger bubbled and she needed to escape for a few minutes if she didn't want to cause a scene. For the third time that night, she watched another woman ask Bailey to dance. It was the last straw.

Shayla attempted to skirt the table and found her arm captured by a firm hand.

"Can you get me one more?" Bailey asked. The half-full bottle swung between her thumb and middle finger.

Shayla wanted to ignore the question shouted at her, but since Bailey supplied everybody with drinks throughout the night, who was she to deny her one drink?

"Sure. Morgan?" Shayla yelled to the other woman still at the table. When she shook her head, Shayla dusted Bailey's hold. The table was becoming too overwhelming for her. She refused to take another moment watching Bailey scan the sea of women. Every time she tried to make eye contact with the cool blue eyes, she found them locked on the dance floor. With each passing hour, she became more restless. The booming noise, flashing lights, and strong drinks were starting to give her a headache. She hadn't been to a club since college and now she remembered why.

The last time she consumed alcohol she found herself in bed with her roommate. If she planned to be able to wake up on time to open the store without a hangover, it was best if she finished the night with water.

Frustrated with how the evening had progressed, she attempted to weave her way through the throngs of ladies. As soon as she maneuvered through the women, they closed ranks behind her, but what truly frustrated her inebriated brain was the barricade of women between her and the bar that forced her to zigzag every which way on her small journey. She attempted to slide her way through two women, but tripped on an unknown object. Before she hit the ground, she found herself arrested by strong arms as she hung inches from hitting the sticky ground. When she finally was able to right herself, she stared into strikingly pale blue eyes.

"Are you ok?" The woman asked Shayla as she helped her to her feet. Concern laced her husky voice.

"Oh. Yes, thank you," Shayla murmured, flustered because the powerful hands still clutched her arms. It wasn't until Shayla started to straighten her clothes that the woman removed her hands.

"I'm sorry, I can't hear you," the woman yelled and leaned in closer. Shayla inhaled a musky scent that wafted off the woman. She didn't know if it was the alcohol or the proximity of the bodies, but a flush blossomed on her cheeks.

"I'm sorry, I said yes, thank you." Shayla leaned in closer to the woman.

"I hope you have a designated driver."

Shayla couldn't look away as she watched her eyes travel over her body. She had never seen someone so brazenly check her out and found herself enjoying the attention. Normally Shayla would have been put off, but each glance felt like a caress.

She knew she should continue her fight to get to the bar but something held her rooted to the spot. "Yes, plus I'm not drinking anymore. I was trying to get a glass of water."

"Water is good." Blue eyes crinkled as she smiled. "I'm Dana." The woman held out one of the hands that had kept Shayla from hitting the floor.

"I'm Shayla. Again, thank you." The hand in hers was warm and soft. Flirting was something she didn't do very often, but she couldn't help herself at that moment. "Can I buy you a drink?" Shayla asked, holding the hand a few seconds longer. The liquid courage she consumed earlier had taken over the driver seat in her brain.

In front of her was the type of woman dreams were made of and stories were written about, with short dark hair, eyes as blue as an Oregon summer sky, lips so full Angelina Jolie would be jealous, and curves of a woman who took care of her body. It was her birthday and if she had to watch Bailey checking out other ladies, lingering over every eye-catching woman, then who was she to not to flirt with one of the most striking woman she had seen?

"You don't have to do that," Dana said.

"I insist. If it hadn't been for you I'd be peeling myself off the floor, embarrassed to no end." The wall of women had not moved and Shayla realized she couldn't make it back to her table if she wanted to. Nonetheless, she found herself pointing in the direction she had come from. "Allow me to thank you properly. It's a bonus to spend more time with you." The words poured out of her mouth, bypassing every filter. Shayla wanted to slink off after stating something she would have never said, had she been sober.

"Well, if you insist." Dana grasped Shayla's hand. Shayla allowed herself to be pulled, surprised when the women parted like the red sea.

"If you don't turn around you're going to hurt your neck." Bailey heard her sister bellow from across the table. Tired of looking at the crowd of women who blocked her view of Shayla, Bailey turned back to the table.

"I just want my beer, that's all," Bailey said to her snarky sister. They stayed at the table to allow Sandy and Mac to escape to the dance floor to work off their drunken energy. Wanda hadn't been back to the table since they arrived hours earlier. She found herself a sexy young gay boy as effeminate as herself, and like so many, disappeared into the crowd to never be seen again.

"Right. You still have half a beer in your hands." Morgan nodded at the bottle that swung from Bailey's fingers.

"I should go see if she is ok," Bailey yelled above the pounding music before she chugged the tepid liquid.

"Maybe you should just wait for her to come back. I'm sure she's fine." Morgan glanced at the wall of women separating them from the bar. Moments later, she smiled. "Don't worry, here she comes."

Bailey whipped her head around and smiled as Shayla set a new beer in front of her. A tall glass of water was placed next to an empty wineglass.

"I'm going to dance and I'll be right back." Shayla leaned on Bailey's shoulder. Her warm breath on her ear sent shivers down Bailey's spine.

Yes! Finally she's ready to dance. Bailey thought and made a move to escort Shayla to the dance floor. When she turned, she noticed Shayla's hand captured by a much larger one. Stunned, she finally observed the tall female standing behind Shayla. Her body felt numb and it wasn't from the beer. Bailey ignored the conversation happening between her sister and Shayla. Bailey was too dazed to do more than nod. She picked up her fresh bottle of beer and began an intricate label-picking pattern. As the couple left and moved together onto the dance floor, Bailey lifted her eyes to study the two females. She lifted the beer to her lips and guzzled half the bottle. The whole evening she tried desperately not to stare at Shayla sitting so calmly on the other side of the table. It took everything in her to look away when Shayla shifted in her direction. Now jealously churned in her belly and she couldn't keep her eyes off the pair as they moved on the dance floor. It had been years since Bailey had danced with Shayla. The last time she remembered being in her arms was in the eighth grade as they practiced for an upcoming dance. When Shayla put her hands on Bailey's shoulders and pulled her close, an odd tug blossomed behind her bellybutton. For years, Bailey tried to recreate the sensation with different women; no touch had ever made her feel the way she did that night.

One song merged into another and another. Bailey never felt so alone even though women crowded her. Sandy and Mac danced their way back to the table, but still did nothing to ease Bailey's isolated mood.

"Where's Shayla?" Sandy asked as she searched the empty glasses that littered the table.

Bailey nodded towards the dance floor where Shayla swayed, wrapped in the arms of a woman whom she never wanted to see again.

"Isn't that Dana?" Mac asked Sandy.

"Hey, yeah," Sandy said.

"You know her?" Bailey asked, finally looking away from the couple.

"A little," Sandy replied and continued her search.

Bailey scooted closer to the younger woman so they didn't have to yell over the thumping music.

"Well, details?" Bailey wanted particulars on the woman dancing with Shayla the way she wanted to.

"Not much. I've only talked to her once or twice. We have a few friends in common. I've seen her at a few parties." Sandy shrugged, giving up her futile search of liquids.

"No matter how trivial," Bailey pressed.

Sandy didn't elaborate. She eyed Bailey's fresh drink. Bailey slid the half-full beer across the table to her before she pleaded her case. She hoped the beer wouldn't only quench her thirst but loosen her lips. "Look I'm... I mean, I was her best friend. I'm just watching out for her like you would do for Mac."

Bailey recognized a spark in the younger woman's eyes when she spoke Mac's name. It was a look she had seen many times reflected in her mirror when thought of Shayla.

"I don't know how much I can help. I've never said much more than hello to her in the past. But the few things I do know is she's in her mid-twenties, still lives at home, and recently dropped out of college. That's about it," Sandy said before taking another pull from the brown bottle.

Bailey spent the past few years programming computers for the United States and Dana screamed corrupt code. She didn't know what was off, but she would try to find out.

Jealousy crept up her spine as she watched Dana's hands spread along Shayla's back. Because of her foolishness and bruised feelings, she let Shayla slip through her fingers and into the arms of someone else. Dana's fingers finally settled on the small of Shayla's back.

"Do you think you could ask around about her?" Bailey asked.

"Why? It's nice to finally see Shayla having fun." Sandy again took another pull from the bottle.

Stung by the young girl's words, Bailey grabbed her drink back. What hurt worse was Bailey wanted that for Shayla too, but she wanted to be the one making her happy.

"I've known Shayla for a long time and I guess I just want to look out for her. I may not have been around for the past few years but I still care."

"I can't promise to get much, but I'll do what I can."

"Thank you. I might be new to your little group and you might not trust me yet, but believe me, I only want the best for Shayla." Bailey hoped that Sandy believed her. A moment later, the young woman danced back onto the floor and disappeared into the throngs of gyrating women.

"Do you think we should get going?" Bailey and Morgan found themselves alone once more. She started to pick at the sweating bottle label again.

"No," Morgan said, her eyes never leaving the dancing women.

"But it's getting late. Everybody but you has to work in the morning. And I don't think I have to remind you that you weren't feeling well earlier. That's why you offered to drive," Bailey said. She wasn't above using any tactic in her arsenal to get Shayla away from Dana.

"I'm fine now, thanks." Morgan turned to look at Bailey. She was busted. "When Shayla gets back to the table we can ask her if she wants to go. It's her birthday, let's let her decide when we leave. She's having fun. Plus that woman she's with is easy on the eyes, don't you think?"

Bailey heard her sister's question but chose to ignore it. Morgan caught her red handed and was now pushing her to reveal something she wasn't ready to discuss. She hated the fact she was unable to manipulate her sister like she used to when they were little. Now her sister held the power as long as she had the keys to the car in her possession.

"If you want to leave I'm sure the bartender can call you a cab. Or try to pull Wanda away from her new dance partner and ask her to give you a ride home," Morgan said. She waved over the bar-back and started to stack the empty glasses. It was the first time in hours the young woman was able to make her way to their table. Morgan helped the girl remove the empty glasses.

"No, I'll stay." Bailey slumped onto a stool and leaned onto the now empty table. There was no way she was leaving without Shayla.

From the time she left for Europe after high

school, she tried to harden her heart against the feelings she had for her best friend. She had not asked her sister for information on Shayla for ten years. Not until the moment her discharge papers were in her hands did she even mention her friend's name. She shot off an email to her sister asking about Shayla, and was over the moon to hear that her friend had been single. She headed home relived Shayla wasn't in the arms of another woman. Now, tonight, she had the displeasure of having to live her biggest nightmare during her waking hours. The dagger to her heart she ran from years ago started to twist. Every sway of their hips or suggestive touch moved the knife more, and yet she was unable to turn away.

Two agonizing songs later Shayla exited the dance floor with her new dance partner in tow. Before they had time to sit down, the two youngest women in their party returned too.

"Hey guys, I want to introduce you to Dana. Dana, this is Morgan and her older sister Bailey, Sandy and Mac." Before Shayla finished her introductions, Wanda emerged from the dance floor alone. "And this is Wanda."

The introduction stung Bailey. Shayla's words reminded her that she was no longer number one in her friend's life.

"Nice to meet everybody, but we've met before, right?" Dana asked Sandy.

"Yeah, I think we were at the same party a few weeks ago," Sandy replied.

"Oh yeah, that's right. We should hang out sometime," Dana said.

"Sounds great," Sandy mumbled.

Wanda fanned herself and smiled at the new

woman.

Bailey lifted her beer to her parched lips. A lone drop slipped from the bottle before she realized Sandy had finished it. She slammed the glass to the table. “It’s getting kind of late. Don’t you think we should head out? You have to work in the morning and so do these two,” Bailey said to Shayla as she motioned to the younger women in their group.

Shayla’s smile disappeared. Bailey hated herself for causing the shift but she wanted the nightmare of an evening to be over.

“I guess you’re right. It was nice to meet you and thank you for the dance,” Shayla said to Dana. Her smile reappeared.

“Wait, here’s my card. Give me a call sometime.” Dana pulled a thick card from a beat up leather wallet before handing it to Shayla. Bailey didn’t miss the way she ran her fingers across Shayla’s palm as she passed her the card. She instantly recognized the move. It was similar to the moves she watched men on base use on women.

“I will.” Shayla slid the card into her back pocket.

Wanda continued to fan herself and smiled at the younger women. Her smile faltered when she got to Bailey.

She attempted to ignore Wanda’s perfectly arched eyebrow. Without a word, Bailey turned and made a quick retreat for the icy night air. She left the women to say their goodbyes. As she leaned against the building, tears stung the back of her eyes. For the past few months, she had been lucky. Tonight, drunk, it hurt worse than she had ever imagined. She leaned over and grasped her knees, pleading with the tears to stay where they were. The door to the club burst open as the rest of her small group poured out of the bar, shattering the quiet night. After a few calming breaths, she stood and made her way to the loud group, silently trailing after them.

"Oh my God, this is the best birthday ever. It's like right out of a book." Shayla danced with an invisible partner in the chill night air. She waltzed her way to the car. "How many days should I wait before I call?"

"At least three," Mac said.

Bailey wanted to say 'never' but held her tongue.

"Well ladies, it's been fun, but here's where I take my leave." Wanda stopped next to her car. She hugged the women before unlocking her door with the press of a button.

"Are you sure you're ok to drive?" Bailey asked. Wanda hadn't spent much time in their presence tonight and Bailey didn't know how much she had drank.

"Yes. I'm perfectly fine. I only had one glass of wine when we arrived and stuck to water after that. I'm sure I'm fine by now," she replied and slipped behind the wheel.

"Drive safe," Morgan shouted as she herded the small group to her car further down the block.

"She's so handsome. Don't you think so, Bailey?" Shayla asked as she threaded her arm through Morgan's, resting her head on her shoulder. Bailey wished it was her shoulder that her friend leaned on. She didn't know how, but she had to repair the friction she had caused with Shayla.

Bailey didn't respond and hoped Shayla wouldn't press for an answer. She didn't want to encourage her friend but she had never lied to her and didn't want to have to start now.

Morgan unlocked the doors before they reached the car and they all piled in. Bailey slumped against the back door, thankful Mac and Sandy leaned against each other and left her alone. She closed her eyes and prayed for sleep. She didn't want to have to listen to Shayla prattle on about the number she had acquired all the way back to town. She had to endure a few minutes of Morgan and Shayla's conversation from the front seats before she finally slipped into a peaceful slumber.

Morgan woke her when they arrived at the bookstore. The three older women helped their two young intoxicated friends up the steel staircase. They had decided it was best to let the girls sleep it off in the apartment.

Bailey was thankful Morgan remained silent on the drive home. She tried to fall back to sleep but the cold night air had slapped her in the face and woke her up. Her dreams from the drive from the club had been more like memories from earlier that evening and she wasn't in a hurry to get back to them. She knew her night was far from over.

Chapter Three

Hours later, dressed in nothing but boxers and a sports bra, Bailey shuffled into the kitchen to one of her favorite smells. The aromatic brew drew her to the cupboard. With her favorite cup in hand, she poured her first cup of coffee. She couldn't stop the moan that passed her lips after her first sip.

The house stood quiet, allowing Bailey a few moments of silence to ruminate on the previous evening. It was like a living nightmare. Only this time, when the night ended, she didn't wake up. Now she had to face the day knowing she had witnessed one of her greatest fears.

A smile appeared when she heard the clack of nails tapping on the linoleum floor. Her bad mood evaporated as she smiled at the comforting sound. She felt rough fur brush her legs before she saw her latest love, and bent down to wrap her arms around Buddy.

"There's my big guy. How was your morning?" Bailey was rewarded with a few sloppy licks from her little cairn terrier. Her fingers ran through coarse black fur. It was the only time she was ok with someone who was unable to control their licker.

"He's good. Already ate his kibble, marked a few more spots, did his rounds. Always vigilant, that one, constantly on the lookout for those scary squirrels you keep telling him about," Morgan said as she entered the kitchen in search of another morning jolt. "You might want to go and clean up any piles he may have left because it's supposed to snow. I don't think you want to be mucking through that when it melts. It's good to have you around now to help with yard duty."

"I'll do it later," Bailey replied and continued to lavish love on the little pooch. He fell on his side, baring his round belly and wagging his tail. Her fingers didn't rest until every inch of her furry little man had been scratched.

"He's so spoiled. You slept in late. It's a good thing I heard him scratching on your door or you wouldn't have had such a pleasant morning." Morgan bent to join in the scratch fest.

He was just as spoiled today as he was the first time Bailey brought him home a few years ago after her grandfather passed. She had been hesitant when she went to the pound looking for a puppy. Relief flooded her when she set the little guy in her grandmother's lap. Eyes full of sorrow brightened when Buddy reached up and gave the sad woman the first of many licks.

"Helping Sandy and Mac up to Shayla's apartment pretty much woke me up. I couldn't get to sleep when we got home. I think the last time I looked at the clock it was almost seven." Bailey finished with a jaw-popping yawn.

"Yeah, I had a hard time falling asleep, too, but I wasn't up nearly that late." Morgan rested next to her sister leaning against the counter.

"Are you ok?" Morgan asked and looked into the light brown liquid swirling in her cup.

"I'm fine, why do you ask?"

"Because, you didn't look or act too fine last

night." Morgan bumped Bailey's shoulder.

Bailey hoped her sister would leave it at that and allow her a few moments to figure out what she wanted to tell her. She had never told anybody about her feelings for Shayla. The weight of the secret had become a heavy burden over the years. No matter how much time had passed, the crush had snowballed into love. The feeling had frozen her heart to anybody else. It wouldn't thaw no matter how hard she tried.

Bailey sat at the same wood kitchen table her grandparents had bought in the seventies. The conversation she needed to have with her sister would take a while. She signaled her to take a seat. Buddy didn't need to be prompted as he took up his normal place resting his head on Bailey's feet. Morgan joined Bailey at the table after she topped off her coffee.

Silent moments passed as Bailey attempted to put what she was feeling into words. While she lay awake the previous night, she had realized that she was in a place in her life where she had nothing to lose, so she decided to tell her sister everything. But she hadn't thought about how to tell her sister how the rejection of her one true love had shaped her life.

"I'm in love with Shayla," Bailey said. She had never said the words aloud. Not even to herself in private. Yet, she realized they felt good rolling off her tongue. To get them in the open, to have another person share in her burden.

The words hung in the air. Bailey expected some sort of reaction from her younger sister. Her silence forced Bailey to squirm under Morgan's gaze. Unable to continue meeting her younger sister's quiet, Bailey played with the edges of her coffee mug.

"Is that why you ran away and joined the Navy?

Because you're afraid to tell your friend how you feel about her?" Morgan finally asked.

"Yes and no."

"Explain please," Morgan said and took a few sips of her coffee.

Bailey hated her sister's calmness. She acquired the trait while Bailey had been away. How she came upon it after years of dealing with grade school kids Bailey would never know.

Bailey sighed. She thought back to the day that changed the course of her life. She had never put it to words but once she opened her mouth, the words just flowed. "I don't know how much you remember about my senior year, but for me it's something I can't forget. At that time, I thought I had my future planned. Shayla and I were to go to state, and I hoped we would be going as a couple. I had even gone out and spent a whole paycheck on a necklace for her. I was so nervous to tell her how I felt. My hands shook and sweated like a river. It was the last day of school and I waited for her to get her locker cleaned. When she finally got in the car, my heart felt like it was going to pound out of my chest. It felt like I had just finished running a track meet. I gathered up every ounce of courage I had and gave her the necklace. When I placed it on her neck, I finally told her I loved her." More silent moments passed as Bailey relived the moment she had spent years trying to forget.

"And?" Morgan asked when Bailey didn't continue.

"And what? I just told you. I told her I loved her."

"That's not the whole story, did she turn you down? Did she slap you? Did she say she didn't love you?" Morgan asked as she ran her finger around the rim of her own coffee cup.

"No," Bailey said. Her fingers gripped her cooling mug.

"Then were you afraid to ruin your friendship by being with her?"

"No," Bailey said.

"OK, did you try dating while you were in Europe and it didn't work?" Bailey could hear frustration making its way into her sister's voice.

"No," Bailey said, irritated the short version didn't deter her sister from the whole story.

"Then what, because I'm truly at a loss as to what's going on in that heart and head of yours," Morgan said, her patience finally cracking.

"Fine, what hurt was when she said she loved me too, but like a sister. She put me in the family category. It's worse than being in the friend category. I mean people can date friends, but nobody wants to date their sister. No offense," Bailey said, once again reliving the hurt her seventeen-year-old self had felt.

"None taken. I understand, but did you tell her you love her or that you were in love with her?"

"I don't know. What's the difference? All I know is it was hard enough saying that," Bailey admitted.

"Well, saying you love someone is like telling your mother or father you love them, or saying you love peanut butter. But telling someone you're in love with them is telling that person you don't want to spend another second without them."

"I don't think even back then she would've known the difference." Bailey slumped back into her chair.

"You're not giving her enough credit. Since she's opened that bookstore, she's had a book club every month, and I've been to every one of them. I've even dragged you to a few, and do you know what most of the stories we read are about?"

"Yeah," Bailey said and leaned onto the table to grasp her drink. She wished her sister would just get to the point.

"And what kind of stories have we been reading?" Morgan asked and leaned on the table, mirroring Bailey.

"Lesbian."

"So dense," Morgan told her coffee before she took another sip. "Specifically."

"Romance." Bailey huffed and stood to pour out her cold cup of coffee before she refilled it with fresh java.

"Very good. Now this one you know the answer to. What is her all-time favorite book?" Morgan asked. Her fingers continued to skate around the rim of her mug.

"Romeo and Juliet. She reads it twice a year almost religiously," Bailey answered. "I didn't realize that I'd be having a test this morning." Bailey rubbed the back of her neck as she reclaimed her seat.

"It's not a test, but do you see where I'm going with this?"

"Uh...."

"Damn, for someone so smart," she again said under her breath, but just loud enough for Bailey to hear. Morgan tapped her mug until Bailey met her eyes. "Look. I know she's your best friend, or was your best friend. I'm sure you know her better than I do. But what I do know is that she wants what she finds in those books. She's looking for love, emotion, kisses, passion, everything. She wants to be swept off her feet, to fall so deeply in love that she doesn't know which way is up, and would rather drown in it than find the surface."

"Then there's nothing I can do." Bailey's head fell back and stared at the ceiling as tears stung her eyes.

"Haven't you been listening to me?" Morgan asked.

"Yes. You said she wants a fairy tale romance," Bailey mumbled. She looked into frustrated blue eyes that matched her own.

"That's not exactly how I would put it. She doesn't need someone to rush in and save her from evil, or pick her up on a white horse and ride off into the sunset. She wants someone to love her, bring her flowers, and make her feel like she's the only person in her lover's eyes. You could be that person. Tell her how you feel. You need to make her feel the love you have for her. It's not too late."

"I can't. I couldn't stand it if she turned me down again. It damn near killed me the first time I said something. I'm sorry but I can't chance it," Bailey said and held up her hands.

"Then you'll just have to deal with the lot that you've been dealt. If you don't ask for new cards, how can you expect to be a player in the game? But if the hand you're holding didn't win you anything but a wounded heart, why not ante-up and try again? Get back in the game."

"Have you been staying up late watching the poker championship again?" Bailey asked, a weak attempt to dodge the question.

Bailey stood and made her way to the ancient lime green fridge. A few silent moments passed as she kept her head in the fridge like an ostrich with its head in the sand. Bailey finally made her way back to the table with an apple in hand. Bailey had a habit of changing topics when things got a little tough. But if she knew anything about her sister, she knew it would be only a short reprieve. The past few years had been rough on both of them. With Morgan beating cancer, she had faced hardships Bailey couldn't even comprehend, and since then she hadn't backed away from any fight.

"No, but I was wondering what we were going to do on our girl's night coming up."

"I hope it isn't poker. I remember what you said about the last time you guys tried playing poker on your sleepover." Bailey let out a sigh when her sister didn't pick up the previous conversation.

"Wanda does love her gambling. I just can't believe she was knocked out after just five hands, but I can't fault a woman for taking chances, and since it will be here you won't be able to talk your way out of coming to this one," Morgan stated and shuffled back to the pot. Her sister nodded when she held it up.

"I haven't been avoiding them. I just thought I wouldn't be welcome. I mean I'm the newest to the group," Bailey said.

"If you weren't welcome you wouldn't have been invited and you've missed two. I think that's why they decided to have it here."

"I think since it's going to be here we should be able to decide the activities."

"It's called taking chances. But I'm sure Connie and Dion will pick something tame. Oh, and I forgot to tell you, Friday I made a doctor's appointment. I thought it was time since I can't seem to get rid of this cold. And your fussing is getting to me. You've been really moody lately. Hopefully this will make both of us feel better," Morgan said and refilled her coffee cup.

"You're the only family I've got. I can't help but worry. You've only been in remission three years. I want to make sure you're fine."

"I'm sure I'm fine," Morgan said, retaking her vacated seat.

"Bailey." Morgan reached for her sister's hand. "We still have things we need to talk about."

"I know, but this morning has already been a little intense. I just need some time to myself," Bailey said and pulled her hand away. "And I have to get to my writing. I have a deadline. It doesn't write itself."

Bailey left her sister sitting in the kitchen as she walked down the hall. The house had barely changed since her youth. There were a few new coats of paint on the walls and her grandparents were no longer there, but it was basically the same home that she and her sister had moved into when she was thirteen. She passed the closed door of her grandparent's bedroom. The silence from inside the room was deafening, and a constant reminder of what she had lost when she ran away. Touching the solid oak door, she paused for a moment before she hurried down the hall, rushed through the living room, and trotted up the stairs to her bedroom. The conversation with Morgan continued to race through her thoughts and she hoped a few hours writing code would expunge it from her mind. The room that had not changed in fifteen years had become her sanctuary.

Chapter Four

Bailey could always immerse herself in writing a new program. The mystery of making something out of nothing had always intrigued her, but after having to rewrite line after line, she found herself frustrated instead of inspired.

She rolled her neck, listening to the snaps, crackles, and pops before she pushed herself away from the desk. Unable to concentrate on work, she decided to check on Mac and Sandy and see how they were doing after their hard night of drinking and dancing.

Her old comfortable Navy sweatshirt was pulled over her head as she jogged down the stairs. Bailey called down the hall to her sister, who was still moving around the kitchen.

"Hey Morgan, I'm heading to the bakery. Do you want anything while I'm out?" Bailey asked.

"Yeah, a dozen bagels would be nice if they have any left. They're easy to fix in the morning, and help settle my stomach." Morgan stepped into the hallway, wiping her hands on a dishtowel.

"Ok, a dozen bagels, any particular type?"

"I would love some cranberry ones if they have them, or blueberry. Actually, why don't you surprise me?"

"I'll do what I can," Bailey said before she grabbed her keys on her way out. Buddy raced down the hall, destination, front door.

"Whoa, there little guy. I'm only going out for a few minutes. I'll be back soon. I promise to take you with me next time." Bailey almost broke her resolve as she looked into sad eyes.

"Don't give me those puppy dog eyes. I promise I'll come back. Then I'll take you on a walk around the block. That's if I can beat the snow."

A wagging of his tail was his only response. Suddenly he ran back into the house. Bailey knew he was searching for the other person in the house that gave into his puppy dog eyes and was a lot closer to the bacon flavored treats.

The frigid air bit into Bailey's skin as she hurried to her old truck. She had to use the key to unlock the door and prayed it wasn't frozen again. Not for the first time she could appreciate the convenience of a newer vehicle with their auto locks, but she would never give up the '56 Chevy pickup. She had spent many hours in her youth helping her grandfather restore the antique. There was something solid and comforting about the old clunker. She appreciated knowing if it broke down, she could fix it with her own hands. One major downside was the multiple calls she would have to make to the local junk yards. The truck sputtered a few times before finally turning over.

As she put the truck in reverse and saw the trees gently swaying in the breeze, she once again enjoyed the feeling of being home. During her ten years in the Navy, she had been given the opportunity to see most of the world. Every two years or so she had a new address, but it wasn't until she stepped back on Oregon soil did she feel totally complete. There was something about the lush emerald trees, thick green grass, and constant feeling of moisture in the air that felt like home. The cold wind whistled through the broken seals of the car, alerting Bailey that winter had officially arrived. As she drove down the street, there was a crispness in the air that never seemed to leave. She loved that feeling. It made her long for the day that she would be able to walk through her front door into a toasty home and cuddle up with the one she loved. The meteorologists had forecasted snow, but it had yet to make an appearance.

People flowed onto the busy streets in a frantic race to beat the oncoming weather. Oregon drivers excelled in driving in the rain but add a few white flake to the mix and they forgot how to navigate the streets. If there was a hint of snow on the roads, the city shut down.

She made a mental note to remember to stop by the hardware store to pick up a few bags of sand to put in the back of the truck. The weight would help give it some more traction.

Bailey quickly found a spot in front of the bookstore. Easily she maneuvered the truck between two cars parked precariously close to the lines, difficult for some without power steering, but years of practice and strong forearms made the task simple. Once again, she thanked her grandpa for his patience when teaching her to parallel park. The bakery was hopping. Not unusual for midday. She peeked in to see Dion and Connie helping harried customers trying to stock up on fresh pastries and bread before the storm set in. A miserable looking Mac cleaned a vacated table.

A few steps to the left and Bailey looked into a large glass window and observed the woman she still considered her best friend. Shayla sat on a stool behind the register. Her nose was stuck in a book as customers flitted through the multiple shelves. Bailey couldn't help but be drawn to the woman. She watched as Shayla brushed a lock of stray hair behind her ear; it must have come free from the loose braid that held the rest of her dark silky strands captive. In a classic move, she used her middle finger to push her glasses back up her straight nose, before resuming its previous position under the book. Gentle hands cradled the book. It wasn't until a customer walked up to the counter that Shayla's attention was pulled away from her reading. Bailey realized she was staring and stole a couple glances around to see if anybody had caught her. It only took a few steps before she found her hand on the glass door and pushed it open.

The clear sound of the bell rang out as she entered the warm building. She looked up and a bright smile from Shayla welcomed her. There was no hesitation when she replied in kind. Shayla continued to help her customer. While waiting for Shayla to finish, Bailey browsed the new additions. A few seconds later her fingers started to tingle as blood rushed back to warm the icicles on her hands.

"I'll be with you in a minute," Shayla said. "Just let me finish up here."

"Don't worry. I'm not in a rush." Bailey continued to browse the shelves even though she knew she wouldn't buy anything. She had never been big on reading and with work and the current book club reading, a new book was not in her plans. She stood aside as the older woman took her purchases and her child's hand before heading out into the blustery day. A gust of wind assaulted Bailey before she made her way to the counter.

"Man, it's freezing out there. At least you don't

have to worry about the weather when you make your way home." Bailey wrapped her arms around herself.

"True, it's one of the perks of owning your own building. But those metal stairs can get pretty slippery."

"How has business been today?" Bailey asked and leaned on the counter.

"It's been extremely slow, even for a Sunday. I think the weather's kept people away," Shayla said and placed her hand over the cover of the book she was reading. Her fingers stroked the glossy cover and Bailey wished she was that book at the moment.

"Well, you wouldn't know it from the traffic on the streets. Usually people wait for it to start coming down before they get all anxious about getting indoors," Bailey said, not knowing why they were talking about things each other already knew. She was frustrated that she still couldn't open up to Shayla. She was almost thirty and she still felt like a teenager. On the drive over, she had decided to take her sister's advice and test the waters, but still the words froze in her brain and would not make their way to her lips.

"You won't believe who called me," Shayla said, barely able to contain her smile.

"If you tell me I'll believe you. I always believe you," Bailey stated.

"Dana."

"Dana? How? She gave you her number. Did you call her already?" Bailey asked. The resolve to confess her feelings evaporated with the mention of Dana.

"No, silly. I woke up and came straight to work, but last night I told her where I work. When she called this afternoon, she said she wanted to talk and didn't think she could wait for my call. So she looked up the number and called me."

"Oh." Bailey didn't know what else to say. She wasn't about to say it was great or anything else that she didn't really feel. The only thing she felt now was a bitter cold that slipped into her heart and it wasn't from the weather.

"Yeah. I'm so excited; we made a date for later in the week." Shayla nearly burst when the words passed her lips. Bailey watched her bounce on her stool. Bailey was reminded of a little girl who just got the world's best birthday present. There was a glow surrounding the normally reserved woman.

"Wow, that's soon." Seeing Shayla's reaction, Bailey knew there was no way she would be confessing her emotions to the excited woman anytime soon. "So what do you know about this woman?" Bailey asked, turning away from the counter. She made her way back to the new releases and picked one up. Numb fingers flipped it onto the back but she couldn't read the words through the tears in her eyes.

"Well, we didn't have much time to talk. I only know a little. She's twenty-five, works at a movie rental place, she's getting ready to go back to college, and she's strong."

"Strong? How do you know that?" Bailey asked. A sniffle escaped and she swiped at her runny nose and brushed away her tears.

"Well, it's how we met actually. It was like right out of a book. I was trying to get to the bar when I tripped on a stray foot, and just before I hit the ground, she was there. She kept me from taking a face plant into the floor. It was like it was meant to happen. That we were meant to meet last night." A dreaminess had descended upon the book lover as she retold the story.

Bailey set the book back down and returned to the counter. She couldn't help but regret every action she had made from the last day of high school. She felt her hand tighten into a fist, the nails biting into her palm and shoved them into her pockets. She was the one who longed to make Shayla sound dreamy. This is what she had walked away from when she was younger. The anguish that coursed through her body was worse than she had ever imagined. She felt as cold as if she was standing on the other side of the window in nothing but her birthday suit. Her heart hurt, and her mouth opened but quickly closed as the bell sounded announcing a new customer. Bailey didn't know if she was relieved or annoyed to find Dion with a carafe of coffee, a tray of pastries, and three mugs.

"I saw you pass the window earlier and thought I would bring something over to warm you up. We're getting ready to close early. We had some extra inventory so I decided to share," Dion stated and poured each woman a steaming cup.

Bailey wrapped her hands around the heavy stoneware, trying to warm her thawing digits.

"So, did Sandy and Mac make it to work on time?" Bailey asked before she took her first sip. Heat infused her numb body. A moan escaped her lips as the tasty brew passed her lips. Dion smiled over her own mug. Bailey noticed a healthy glow on Shayla's rosy cheeks as she took another sip of the hot liquid.

"I don't know. I tried to wake them before I came down here, but don't know how successful that was," Shayla said before taking a sip from her own cup. "I stopped off and gave Dion the key to the apartment. Did you have to use it?"

A small smile played at the corners of the older

woman's face. "I didn't get to use it, but let's just say Connie does have a wicked side to her. Both women showed up a little after noon not looking forward to working their scheduled shift."

The three women laughed at the younger women's predicament. Bailey knew how they felt. More times than she could count she had showed up to work on the ship smelling as if she had crawled out of a dirty ashtray, her head pounding, and her mouth feeling like it had grown a bushel of cotton.

"Hey, before I forget. I need a dozen bagels for Morgan. She wants either cranberry or blueberry." Bailey remembered her sister's request.

"No problem, just pop on over when you're done here and pick them up. I'll even toss in a few plain if you want?"

"That would be great," Bailey said and snagged an apple turnover off the tray. She sank her teeth into the flakiest pastry she had ever had, and during her travels she had sampled her fair share of treats. "Man, if you weren't married, I would snatch you in a heartbeat. Especially if you baked like this every day."

Shayla nodded enthusiastically as she munched on her own cherry tart.

"Thanks for the compliment, but I'm married to the most wonderful woman." Dion blushed before she loaded the empty tray with the carafe and empty cups. "And how do you think I got her? Don't take too long. We'll be closing soon," she reminded Bailey before heading back to the bakery.

"Well, I just might close up too. I should go upstairs and get some cleaning done," Shayla grumbled.

"Yeah, I had better get back to work. I haven't

been able to get past this one piece of code that's been bothering me," Bailey complained.

"I don't know how you can sit all day and just write computer programs. That would bore me to tears."

"It didn't take me long to discover I love to write. To me it's like figuring out a puzzle, and when everything comes together there's such a feeling of accomplishment," Bailey explained. "Well, I'd better get going or I'm not going to get Morgan her bagels. I'll call you later this week."

"Ok. Bye." Shayla waved.

Before Bailey passed the large glass window, she glanced back at the woman she loved. Shayla was helping a customer. With one last glance at the shop owner, she made her way next door.

"Hey," Bailey hollered to Sandy as she walked to the counter. She knew it wasn't necessary to yell but she took a little glee in watching the younger woman flinch.

A low grunt and nod was her reward. Bailey took pity on the young woman as she had a bag of baked goodies thrust into her hand.

"How much?" Bailey asked in a much softer tone as she reached into her back pocket to retrieve her wallet. She was rewarded with a small smile.

"Don't worry about it. We were just going to toss them," Dion yelled to her from an empty table.

Bailey watched Sandy flinch again. The pain she saw on her face made her regret her earlier action. It didn't take much to realize that Dion and Connie had probably tortured the two women the greater part of the day.

Silently, Sandy set a full travel cup in her

direction, nodding to her laughing boss.

Bailey walked up to Dion as she filled a saltshaker.

"Thanks, but that's really not necessary. I can pay," Bailey insisted, once again pulling out her wallet.

"Put that away, your money's no good here, really. We would've just sent them home with the girls if you weren't taking them." Dion flung a damp rag over her shoulder as she stood.

"Well then, thank you," Bailey said before taking a seat and a sip of her cup of coffee. "This is really good. I needed it. I think you should take it easy on the girls. They look in rough shape."

"Yeah, I know. Connie stopped a while ago, but I think she got her good licks in at the apartment. I think they've learned their lesson."

"I'm sure they did."

The bell rang and they turned to see Wanda sweep in and head straight for the counter.

"I'm surprised she's here. She called this morning and said she had a great time and was sore this morning. Apparently her yoga class doesn't compared to dancing for hours," Dion whispered and sat down. She wiped down the table they were occupying although it already sparkled. "So tell me what's going on with Shayla."

"Didn't Sandy or Mac say anything?"

Dion simply shook her head and waited for Bailey to continue. "She has a date with some woman named Dana this week. I don't know much about her. We really didn't get into it."

"Good for her, but that's not what she's talking about," Wanda stated, using her momentum to push her sister further into the booth. Dion grunted and shifted over. "She's talking about you and Shayla."

"What is going on with you people? This is the second time someone asked me that today. There's nothing going on between us," Bailey explained, her hand gripping the paper cup.

"But you want something, right?" Wanda asked, searching for something in her large purse.

"Wanda," Dion admonished.

"What? I'm too old to beat around the bush. I'm lucky I can even find the bush, and don't tell me you don't see it. Please, it's written all over her face. You should've seen her last night when Shayla brought over that goddess. And let me just tell you if I wasn't straight I would pounce on that." Wanda pulled a bottle of sweetener from purse and doctored her coffee.

Bailey had admired the way Wanda didn't pull any punches or mince words, but today on the receiving end, she could have done without it. Worse than that, was how easily she had been read the previous night. She would have to continue working on masking her emotions when around Shayla.

"Look. I don't know what you think you saw last night. Maybe I was just having a bad night, or maybe I was gassy, I don't know what you saw, but I can tell you there's nothing going on between Shayla and me. We've been best friends since forever. That's all there has been or ever will be." It hurt to say the words, but after seeing Shayla's reaction when talking about Dana, she hated it more that they were probably the truth.

"But you haven't said you didn't want her." Again Wanda hit her square in the chest with her words.

"Wanda," Dion shouted. Bailey and Wanda

jumped when Dion's hand hit the table.

"What? She said what they had, or rather didn't have but she didn't say anything about what she wanted."

Bailey couldn't argue with her logic. The only thing she could do was lie to the two women that had quickly become more than just friends. She had started to think of Connie, Wanda, and Dion as her family. She hated to lie, but if she didn't she would leave her heart exposed and it already felt raw. "I don't want anything but friendship from Shayla."

"Ok," Dion said and gave her older sister a look that stopped the words her perfectly painted mouth was about to utter. "But that's not all I wanted to talk to you about. We'll leave that subject alone. I've also noticed how Morgan hasn't been feeling well. Is everything ok?"

Bailey's shoulders relaxed. She didn't realize she had become so tense. "As far as we know. You know how it is since she works in a giant petri dish. She works with kids, and schools are just a full of germs. She probably caught something she can't shake. She's made an appointment with her doctor so hopefully he can give her something to get rid of it."

"Well, I was just worried because she's only been in remission for a few years," stated Dion. Bailey could see concern in stormy grey eyes.

"Don't worry. I'm sure it's nothing." Bailey didn't know if she was saying it for Dion's benefit, or her own.

"You know, before your grandmother passed I promised to look after you girls. I don't plan on breaking my word." Dion tapped the table.

"I appreciate that. I really do." And Bailey did.

Bailey's grandparents had been her whole world, her safety net. When her mother continually moved strange men into the home, Bailey realized she couldn't protect herself and her sister. Before she entered her teen years she begged her grandparents to let them live with them. At the age of thirteen, her grandparents finally became their legal guardians. Soon after, her mother left town with her last boyfriend, who had been the worst of the lot. When her grandpa had passed two years ago, it had been an easy decision not to reenlist. She still had two years remaining on her contract but when those expired, she returned home to start a new life. She was glad she was discharged when she was. A month after she returned home her grandmother passed. The loss was still tangible in their small group as it had only been a few months since her passing. Now the only people she had were her sister and her closest friends.

"Well good. Hopefully she'll have some news for us when we arrive for the sleep over," Wanda added.

"I hope so, too. So, any ideas about what we're going to do?" Bailey asked, still leery of what the older women would come up with.

"Connie has some ideas, but she swore me to secrecy. She wants it to be a surprise." Dion smiled over the rim of her mug.

Everybody in their small group had been on the receiving end of Connie's wicked sense of humor except Bailey and she was sure this weekend was going to be her turn.

"When are these going to stop? I thought we were just doing them to keep the girls in high spirits?" Wanda asked.

"Well, if you don't like them you don't have to

go," Dion said.

"Are you kidding? I find them so much fun. It's like being a kid again. I would do anything to feel young again, but Connie's ideas scare me," Wanda said, patting her raven hair, which only kept its color from her bi-monthly visits to the hairdresser.

"Well, I should be going. I have some writing to do and a deadline that I won't make unless I get to it. Thank you again for the bagels." Bailey hefted the bag of bread as she slid out of the booth.

"You're welcome, honey. Tell your sister we said hi," Dion said, before Bailey rushed head long into the biting wind.

Shayla shut the door on the last customer. Her hand paused on the closed switch as she watched her best friend slide into her old truck. The flush from earlier returned when she thought of the moan Bailey released when she took her first sip of coffee. It had sounded so sexual to Shayla. It had been hard not to imagine she was the one making her friend groan. She hoped nobody saw her reaction. The erotica she had been reading at the time might have had something to do with her response.

It took a few moments to gather up the cash from the register and place it in the safe. The cold biting winds stole away her breath when she opened the door. Icy fingers trembled as she finally turned the lock. On her way to the apartment, she waved at the five women huddled around a table at the bakery. Dion waved her in, but she shook her head, wanting to get upstairs and start in on her new book. She would have taken it to work but didn't think it would be fair to read a book that wasn't even out yet in front of paying customers.

Slowly she made her way up the slick stairs and was welcomed into the warm embrace of her apartment. Shayla looked at her space and realized the only thing missing in her life was a partner.

It had been a surprise when Dana had called earlier. Quite unexpected. When she agreed to a date, she felt a twinge of excitement. She had a steady relationship through college but was so busy with school there was really no sparks. Even after she had sex for the first time, she thought she would feel something, but nothing came of it. Until last night, Bailey had been the only person who had ever stirred something in her. She didn't know if it was the plethora of drinks she consumed, or just the way it happened, but something about their meeting felt magical. Then to get the call this morning, it felt more and more right. If things were not going anywhere with Bailey, and if she felt a bit of a spark with Dana, then maybe her fairytale story was finally being written. She had thought chapter one had started years ago in high school. It had taken her all summer to get up the courage to tell her friend how she really felt, but when Bailey didn't return, she had closed that book.

After a quick bite of soup and a sandwich, she slipped into bed. Six was early, even for her, but as she snuggled under the covers, she looked over to the picture of her and Bailey. The same picture had been with her through high school, college, and every year since. Just looking at the picture, she felt the stirring of butterflies in her stomach that had long been dormant. Frustrated, she rolled over, picked up

Allura's book, and once again felt the inscription. Even though all her books were basically the same, there was something about them that deeply touched her. The longing in each word was something she knew herself. She couldn't wait to dive in. Turning to page one, she started to read.

Chapter Five

Bailey sat at her computer. The cursor continued to taunt her while her fingers hovered motionless above the keys. Silent moments ticked by while her deadline loomed closer. From the moment Morgan told her the doctor called and said she would have to go in for the results, her creative juices dried up like Death Valley. Rarely did a doctor ask someone to come in for good news. When Morgan asked her to go to the appointment with her Bailey couldn't refuse. The blank white screen reminded her how much work she had to do.

Along with the deadline, her job was also adding pressure to apply for a new management position that came available. Bailey was just starting to enjoy the comforts of working from home. If she took on a management position, it would require she not only get dressed in the morning but actually wear proper work attire. She had only been at the company for a few months but the suggestion by her manager to apply told her she must have been doing something right.

The cherry on top of her wonderful week was the fact that tonight was the highly anticipated night of Shayla's date with Dana. Not too high on Bailey's list, but their other friends couldn't wait to hear all the dirty little details. It annoyed her that every time she had gone into the bakery the past week she had to listen to the women prattle on. Just hearing Dana's name in the same sentence as Shayla's was eating her alive. No matter how much she wanted Shayla to be happy and have her happily ever after, Bailey couldn't shake the fact that something didn't feel right. The thing Bailey just couldn't understand was why would someone as stunning as Dana be at the club picking up women. An alluring woman like that should already be in a serious relationship. Something about the person made the hairs on her neck stand up, and she couldn't figure out why.

"Are you ready?" Morgan asked and pulled Bailey from her thoughts.

"Yeah. I don't seem to be getting much done. Just let me toss Buddy a few kibble so he isn't sad when we leave. He hasn't been himself lately. He seems a bit down." Bailey passed her sister, making her way to the kitchen. Buddy was at her heels every step of the way. He sat at his bowl and waited patiently for his food. As soon as the food left the scoop, his snout followed it into the bowl but came back without taking a bite.

"You might want to cut back on his food intake. He seems to be getting a bit thick around the middle," Morgan said and put on her coat.

"It's winter, he needs insulation." Bailey gave him a few pats before she took the coat Morgan thrust in her direction. "I don't know what's wrong. He won't eat."

"You know he doesn't like to eat alone. Plus he doesn't need any insulation, he's barely out the door doing his business before he rushes back inside to plant himself on one of the vents," Morgan said.

"Ready?"

"Not really," Morgan replied.

Bailey caught a shadow of fear in her sister's eyes but it was gone as quick as it arrived.

"Well, ready or not here we go." Bailey smiled at her sister. She prayed her sister couldn't tell it was forced. Even though her own insides wouldn't calm down, she had to do what she could to let her sister know she would be there for her.

Bailey drove to the hospital. Silence permeated the air. They pulled into the new parking structure and soon Bailey sat in the waiting room and flipped through a year old People magazine. With each agonizing second that passed, Bailey's nervousness washed away. Surely if something was truly wrong, they would already be sitting in the doctor's office.

Over twenty minutes passed before they were led to the doctor's office for more waiting. Bailey regretted not holding on to the magazine. A few more minutes of silence stretched out. Unable to take the quiet anymore, Bailey started talking. "So what do you think of Dana?"

"I don't know. We only met that one time, but Shayla told me she seems nice. They've talked on the phone a few times."

"I didn't know that." Bailey wanted to scratch out her brain. She didn't know why she asked about Dana. Of all the topics she had to choose from, she chose the one that she didn't want to know anything about.

"I know. Shayla says you still haven't been around." Bailey ignored the annoyed tone in her sister's voice.

"I've just been busy with work. Plus I have that deadline, and I'm nowhere near finished. I've hit a brick wall," Bailey said with a huff and slumped into her chair.

"You've hit rough spots before. This one will pass too," Morgan said.

"So what did she say about Dana?" Bailey asked. She figured she was in for a penny in for a pound. Now that the subject was already up, she might as well find out as much as she could. If Dana was going to be her competition then she had better start stocking her arsenal of information now. With each day that passed since she had been home, regret for staying away so long grew. The wall between them was so large that if she stood any chance with Shayla she needed to make a move, and do it soon, before it was too late.

"Not much really. Why?"

"I don't know. I guess I just don't have a good feeling about her, that's all," Bailey said and picked at a piece of lint on her jeans.

Morgan turned to look at her sister. "Seriously? Why is that? Because she's young, beautiful, and into Shayla, and actually had the nerve to ask her out?"

Each word was like a slap. Bailey leaned forward and played with the cup of pens on the doctor's desk. She couldn't look her sister in the eyes. "No, that's not why. I just think something's wrong. I mean what's a beautiful woman like that doing at the club and not already taken?"

"Why are you still single? Do you think I didn't see all those women coming up to you and asking you to dance Saturday night? But you turned every one away. Why was that?" Morgan tapped her chin with her index finger.

"I just didn't want to dance. I wanted to focus on Shayla. It was her birthday after all," Bailey said. Even as the words passed her lips, she knew her excuses didn't hold water.

"Right. You just don't like the idea of Shayla seeing someone else. At least Shayla's going on a date with someone who is willing to ask her. You can't possibly expect her to stay single. She's a bright beautiful woman, and I think it's extremely selfish of you to be upset because she has finally found someone and is happy," Morgan said. They were sisters but it seemed that in this case blood was not thicker than water. Morgan was supposed to be on her side, but her words clearly put her on the other side of the fence.

Bailey knew her sister was right. Even though Morgan was speaking the truth, a rebuttal had formed on Bailey's lips, but the words stayed frozen by the knock on the door. Nothing could've been worse than the dressing down her sister would have surely given her if the topic had continued, even if the harsh words were warranted.

"Hello ladies," Dr. Harrison said as he took his place behind the cluttered gunmetal grey desk. He didn't meet their eyes as he opened the thick file in his hands.

"Hello Doctor. This is my sister, Bailey," Morgan said. Bailey nodded.

"Nice to meet you, Bailey, and thank you for taking time out of your day to come down here. I know you're on Christmas break, Morgan, so I'll try and make this as fast as possible. I'm sorry to have to pull you away from your break."

"Thank you," Morgan said. "I appreciate that."

Bailey wasn't comfortable with the way he kept his gaze locked on the papers laid out on the messy desk. She squirmed in her seat until her sister grabbed her hand, giving it a squeeze. The gesture made her feel worse. The reason she was there was to support Morgan and she was failing. Her instinct to run started to kick in and it took everything in her to continue to sit in the hard plastic chair and wait for the doctor to continue.

"I'm sorry to say this and there's no gentle way to put it. We need to do more tests, but we believe the cancer has returned," he stated, finally making eye contact with the women.

Bailey felt sucker punched. She couldn't catch a breath. Her brain screamed at the doctor 'It can't be cancer. She's in remission. Everything had been fine on her last checkup. How could it be cancer?' but the words froze on her lips.

"Are you sure?" Bailey finally forced out. Tears threatened to fall. She tried to hold them back. To be strong for her sister who sat like a silent pillar beside her. The only thing that indicated that she had any fear was the death grip she had on Bailey's hand. Bailey was sure she felt a few of the smaller bones in her left hand crack under the pressure.

"Before we go any further, let me explain what's going on. There is a marker, CA 15.3, in the blood that is elevated when cancer is present. When we tested Morgan's blood, we found her levels to be a little high. We still need to do more tests, but we wanted to prepare you."

"How can that be? How can you miss something like that? I would think you would be more diligent if they're in remission." Bailey couldn't believe what she was hearing. She wanted to crawl over the desk and smack the man seated in front of her. The only thing that held her glued to her seat was the death grip her sister still had on her hand. It kept her rooted when her initial reaction would have been to run for the door, but her sister needed her.

"I'm sorry." He didn't even attempt to make excuses for their poor care. Bailey's anger flared and she couldn't help the words that burst from her mouth.

"Don't tell me you're sorry. This is bullshit. I would think you would be more diligent. This is fucking ridiculous. This is totally unacceptable," Bailey sputtered, rage overcoming her fear. She scooted closer to the edge of her chair to get in his face but the words on the tip of her tongue did not come.

"Please, Miss Hutsell. Again it may not be anything. We have a few more tests to run to know where we stand," the doctor said.

Bailey knew if someone could beat cancer on pure will and determination it was her sister. Last time the chemo and radiation had been hard, but she didn't let it get her down. She continued to work through the whole treatment. She hadn't been there to help through it, but she did what little she could over the phone. No matter how much it tried to get Morgan down, she stood tall and kept moving forward. This time would be different. She would be there for all the bad times as well as the good. She would support her sister every step of the way. Through the fury that clouded her mind, she had failed to notice Morgan had released her hand and sat silently in her own chair.

Dr. Harrison held up his hands, a meager attempt to deflect Bailey's anger. "Please remember. We have to do more tests, but there's something else we have to talk about." The doctor folded his hands over the papers. He looked directly at Morgan with her arms folded over her stomach. "You know, don't you?"

Morgan's only response was a slight nod of her

head as she started to rub her stomach.

"What?" Bailey asked, confused by the silent conversation that had just transpired. "WHAT?!"

"I'm pregnant," Morgan whispered.

"WHAT?" Bailey asked.

"I'm pregnant." Morgan's voice had regained a little more strength.

"I heard you the first time, but how?" The new development knocked all the air out of her sails as she turned to look at her sister. Bailey slumped back into her chair.

"I don't think I need to explain the birds and bees to you," Morgan replied. "Plus, you know I hate it when you make me repeat myself unnecessarily."

"Fuck, Morgan, don't joke with me now. This is your life we're talking about." Bailey turned her attention to the doctor. Hopefully he would give her a straight answer. "What are our options now? I'm assuming this was the other thing that needed to be discussed."

"Well, it is a huge hurdle, but we do have options. But right now, we don't have to do anything but schedule more tests and make sure your sister's pregnancy is going ok. But if the cancer has returned, there are options. The most obvious would be to terminate the pregnancy."

"No. That's not an option," Morgan said, her hands still covering her belly.

"But Morgan, this is your life we are talking about. You can always try and get pregnant again," Bailey said and turned to her sister.

"Aborting this baby is not an option." Morgan's hands started to rub her stomach.

"Well then, that leaves us two other options.

We can have surgery to remove the infected tissue, possibly taking the whole breast. Or we can wait till the second or third trimester and administer a low dosage of chemo, then after the baby is born we can add radiation depending on how advanced the cancer has become. After that we could make any other adjustments that would be needed," Dr. Harrison said, flipping through papers before finally closing the thick manila folder.

None of the options seemed strong enough for Bailey. But ultimately, she could only wait to hear if the cancer had returned and if it did, her sister would be the one with the last word. All she knew was she would support her sister with whatever she would have to face in the coming weeks. The only thing Bailey could do now was wait.

"So we need to set up an appointment as soon as possible. Once we get those results back we can talk some more," Dr. Harrison said.

"Thank you, Doctor." Morgan stood on shaky legs and exited the room.

Bailey wiped at her wet eyes and quickly scrambled after Morgan. She had tried to fight back her tears but a few had escaped. She paused at the door and watched Morgan talk to the receptionist and leave the office.

"Here." Bailey handed Morgan her keys when she caught up to her on the way to the parking lot. "I think I'm going to walk home. I need to think."

"But it's freezing out and the forecasters are predicting snow again. It's at least ten miles to home." Morgan shoved the keys back.

"I'll be fine. I just need some time to think and running helps me do that. I haven't run since I've been back. Plus it seems like you've had more time to come to terms with this." Bailey again thrust the keys to her sister's hand. It was hard to keep the venom from her voice. She felt blindsided and betrayed by her little sister and now she didn't try to stop the tears that ran down her cheeks.

"Bailey, don't cry, please."

"I'm sorry. It's just a lot. I don't know how you are so calm," Bailey said and took another swipe at her tears.

"Right now I don't know anything but that I have a person growing in me, and right now that's what I'm focusing on. And you should too," Morgan said. She grasped Bailey's hands in hers.

"I'll try but just give me some time. I'll try and focus on the positive but I can't help…."

"Stop. Let's not talk about the other until we know for sure. I have an appointment for tomorrow so we should know something soon. I want to know just as much as you but until then I'm going to focus on the good news," Morgan said.

"Ok, I'll try, but I still want to be alone for a little while." Bailey found it hard to focus on the little one growing in her sister if it meant that she would lose her in the process. But she was getting ahead of herself. She needed to clear her head and a run would help with that.

"Please promise me that you'll call if you need a ride." Morgan pulled Bailey into a tight hug. "I love you."

Bailey clutched her sister as if it was the last time she would ever hold her. "I love you too."

Morgan slid behind the wheel of her car. She waved as she exited the parking garage before she turned down the street.

Bailey made sure her sister was out of sight before her knees hit the hard pavement. She wailed and cursed a god who had taken her grandparents, who now attempted to reach down to take her sister from her too. Two years separated her grandparents passing and now her sister's life was on the line. Sometimes life was unfair. Cold air lashed at her as she attempted to stand on shaky legs. She wasn't sure she would be able to run ten miles but she would only know if she started. With every step she took, she resolved to be with her sister every stage of the way no matter what. Soon Bailey was running from the news she just heard. Her feet pounded the frozen pavement and yet she was unable to outrun the fear that had taken ahold of her heart.

Chapter Six

Bailey didn't know where her feet were taking her. She had set for home but soon she found herself half frozen and in front of Shayla's bookstore. The sun had set behind the mountains long ago and the florescent lights from inside the shop blinded Bailey. It didn't take her but a moment to realize the young body bent over the counter was not Shayla's. She pulled her coat tight around her frigid body and made her way to the back of the store. The bakery lights were also dark when she passed the store. Legs that felt weighted down by lead trudged up the stairs leading to Shayla's one bedroom apartment. She had never been inside Shayla's home but knew where it was.

It wasn't until frozen knuckles met the metal door and pain raced up her arm that she realized her hands were numb. Bailey's body trembled as the cold attacked her while she stood on the metal entryway. Frigid seconds passed before the door opened. The smile that greeted her was quickly extinguished as Shayla reached for her.

"Hey, what's wrong?" Shayla asked.

"I've just been out walking. Do you have time to talk?" Bailey stood frozen on the porch, waiting for an invitation to enter.

"Of course. Please come in but do you mind if I continue getting ready for my date?" Shayla said and moved aside.

"Oh shit, I forgot about that. Sorry, I didn't mean to bother you. It's ok. I can just talk to you later. Bye." Bailey turned and raced down the icy steps.

"Wait," Shayla shouted as Bailey hurried to leave.

Bailey ignored the shout but slowed as she turned the corner and leaned against the frigid brick building. She heard the chirp of her cell phone. Numb fingers fumbled in her pocket. The display illuminated Shayla's name. She slid it back into her coat and let it roll to voicemail. Bailey didn't feel right dumping on Shayla right before her date. Ten years ago, she would have had no problem turning to Shayla. The chasm that had been built between them had left Bailey with no place to turn. Knowing she couldn't continue to run from the bad news, Bailey started the long trek home.

Frozen fingers grasped at the cold door handle. Bailey sighed as the knob turned. On her walk, she hadn't even thought of the fact she didn't have her house keys. As she entered the house, she was engulfed in warmth, but didn't shed her coat. She found her sister sitting on the couch with Buddy lying across her lap, thoroughly enjoying his tummy rub, ignorant to the dark cloud that hung above the sisters. She stumbled to the steps and plopped down on the bottom stair to kick off her shoes.

"Where have you been? I was starting to get worried," Morgan said, her eyes never leaving the pooch perched on her lap.

"I told you. I needed some time."

"Shayla called a while ago. She mentioned you stopped by and didn't look too good. After you left she was so upset she asked me if she should cancel her date and come over."

"Fuck. What did you tell her?" Bailey asked. She hadn't thought Shayla would have called the house. A groan escaped as she flexed her icy toes and fingers, trying to get the blood flowing back into the frozen digits.

"I told her you were having a bad day, and to go on her date. I also said you would call her in the morning," Morgan said. Her fingers continued their ministrations through the coarse fur. She looked at Bailey. "Don't make me out to be a liar."

Bailey finally shed her thick down coat as her body started to warm up. She moved to the hall closet and hung up the bulky jacket before she plopped down next to her sister. Bailey's fingers started to burn as the blood began to flow, but the needle prick pain didn't keep her from scratching under Buddy's chin. The small dog closed his eyes and his tail moved a mile a minute.

"What should I say when I talk to her tomorrow?" Her head fell back on the couch. Her eyes lingered on the popcorn ceiling.

"I don't know, but I would appreciate it if you didn't mention anything about my doctor's appointment."

"Why not? She's your friend. It feels like she's more your friend now than mine. More than that she's like family," Bailey said. Tears sprung to her eyes by the truth in the words. Her emotions were so raw that she was hanging on by a thread, and even that was quickly unraveling.

"Because I don't want to ruin the get together," Morgan said, her voice distant.

Bailey sprung forward and her elbows landed on

her knees. Her hands clenched into fists and her body shook. "Who the fuck cares about the get together? This is your life we're dealing with. These women are our friends and they need to know," Bailey said, finally unable to control her temper.

Buddy jumped off the couch and scrambled out of the room.

"Please calm down," Morgan said. Her empty hands started to play with the hem of her skirt.

"Calm down? How the fuck am I supposed to calm down?" Bailey sprung from the couch like a rocket and started to pace the small room.

"Try taking a few deep breaths," Morgan suggested.

"Stop doing that." Bailey tore her hat off her head and slapped it against her jean-clad thigh.

"Doing what?"

"That. You're just so fucking calm about this whole thing," Bailey said.

"What do you want me to do? Until I get the results back from the other test the only thing I have to focus on is the baby growing inside me." Morgan shrugged her shoulders and leaned back into the couch. Her hands rested on her stomach.

She couldn't comprehend how her sister was so calm. She would have been ranting and raving and cursing everything under the sun. But her younger sister just sat on the couch as if it was just another day.

"I don't know, but you're just too calm. This is a huge deal."

"I know. You should've seen me last time. I was just like you. But this isn't my first rodeo. I've already been through this once. Plus what will getting all crazy and worked up do? I'm sure when my hormones start acting up I'll be more than bat shit crazy enough for you. Plus with the good news I received the prospect of the bad has been a bit diminished until I know all the facts."

Since Bailey arrived home months earlier, everything seemed to go downhill and now with this, it seemed like it was never going to get better. Unable to help herself, she flung herself into her sister's lap and allowed herself to cry. She cried for the loss of her grandparents, the girl that she loved, and possibly her only sister. "Why, why did this have to happen?"

Bailey felt strong arms wrap around her. For the first time in a long time, she felt protected and safe. She could not remember the last time she felt this way.

When she heard her sister reply, it was barely above a whisper. "There was always the possibility of it reoccurring. Remission doesn't mean cured."

"I know, but I've only been home less than six months and I just got you back. You're all I have," Bailey said as the tears continued to fall.

"Bailey, the reason I'm so calm about this is I've had longer to come to terms with what's going on with my body. I've always known there was a possibility of this coming back. I've been able to prepare myself for the possibility of bad news. Every time I've step into the doctor's office I primed myself for the c word," Morgan said, her hands never stopping as she rubbed tiny circles on Bailey's back.

Bailey calmed at the touch. The tears had dried up but she continued to take comfort in her sister's embrace. "But you're so young. You have your whole life ahead of you."

"Don't think I'm giving up." Morgan pulled Bailey out of her lap and looked at her with a fierceness

Bailey had never seen. "I'm not giving up. I'll fight with everything I have, but I have to give this life growing inside me a chance too. I'll do everything I can for both of us to make it."

Bailey could only nod. A lump had formed in her throat. It took a few seconds before she could speak. "Then will you promise me you'll start treatment?"

"I can't promise that right now because we don't even know if the cancer is back, but I will promise that if it has returned I will listen to everything that will help me and this baby. I'll weigh my options and then make a decision."

Bailey nodded. "That's acceptable and I promise not to tell anybody anything until after the sleep over. I won't ruin that for you or anybody else. But once it's done, I think we should tell them as soon as we find out the results. I wasn't here to help you last time and they were. Plus they might be hurt if we wait too long. Just know that I'll be here for you every step of the way."

"I understand and I didn't expect you to wait long before telling people. I appreciate your support. Be prepared, because there will be good days, bad days, and worse days, and when those happen I'll need for you to be there. And please, whatever I say or do don't take it too personal."

"I can't say I won't take it personal or that it won't hurt. But I promise to try not to retaliate. I don't really know how I'll react because unlike you this is the first time I'll be here to go through this with you. You're the only family I have left. Can I ask you something?" Bailey stood to shed her sweater and tossed it onto an empty chair before she started to pace the room again. Even after walking more than ten miles to get home she had too much pent up energy. Emotionally she was drained but her body was tense and she didn't know how to relieve the stress.

"Of course, you can ask me anything," Morgan said, her eyes tracking her sister as she paced the small living room.

"How long have you known about being pregnant? You seemed to have some previous knowledge before we even went into the doctor's office," Bailey asked.

"A few weeks give or take. I'd missed my past few periods. I'm usually really regular. Last time the cancer had thrown it off so when I missed my periods I started to think the worst," Morgan said.

"So you really did have time to prepare for this news."

"Yes and no. When I started getting sick every morning and my breasts started getting really tender, I knew something was different. Three weeks ago, I took a pregnancy test and it came back positive. That's why I made the appointment. I was prepared to hear the news that I was pregnant but I was just as shocked as you were when he brought up the cancer."

Bailey stopped and faced the window. The first of many fat white flakes floated to the frozen ground and memories of years past floated through her brain. She thought of the years her and her sister would sit at the window, watching the snow blanket the front yard, praying for a school cancelation the next day. Her sister's voice pulled her from her memories.

"I promise if the cancer does return I'll fight, but who knows if it will come back. There are no guarantees in life. I realized that during the first fight. You have to take what you're given and roll with the punches. When you get knocked down all you can do is get back up. Right now I've been given a gift and I plan on protecting that, even if it means my life."

"But..." Bailey started but saw Morgan hold up her hand in the reflection of the window and stalled any other words she was about to utter.

"No, you know me. There are a few things I've wanted in life and a child is one of them. The first time I went through this I was scared. I've been through it and came out on the other side. I'm not scared anymore. Now I have something to look forward to. Death is not something I fear right now. I'm thinking more about life, specifically the one inside me. Hell, even if I abort this baby my life is not guaranteed, but if I can come out of this alive and with a baby, then every second of my life will have meaning."

Bailey understood what her sister was saying. Finally, Bailey looked into Morgan's reflection in the window. She found eyes filled with fire and determination.

"So who's the father?" Bailey asked and turned from the winter storm that raged outside. She had been curious since Morgan didn't have a boyfriend that she knew of.

"I don't know," Morgan said.

"How can you not know?" Bailey asked.

"All I was given was a number."

"What the hell are you talking about?" Bailey flung her hands in the air.

"Geez, Bailey." Morgan looked away. "I was artificially inseminated."

"What?"

"I had started trying before Grandma passed and it wasn't taking so I stopped. I had promised myself after I was cancer free for three years that I would try and get pregnant. I went to the last appointment after Grandma passed. I didn't think it would take since the others didn't but who knew. I was supposed to go to my last follow up appointment the week of her funeral but I had canceled it and didn't reschedule. I figured it had failed like all the previous attempts."

"You never told me, why didn't you tell me?" Bailey asked.

"Because I know you. You would have tried to talk me out of it. I told Gran and swore her to secrecy. I knew it would be hard to keep it from you and we worked together to keep you in the dark."

"So how far are you?" Bailey asked.

"I would say around ten weeks. That would have been around the time I had my last session."

Bailey watched as Morgan's hands rubbed her flat stomach. Even though the baby was probably no bigger than a bean, and Morgan couldn't feel it, she was still protective. There were no words Bailey could utter about being betrayed by the two women she loved more than anything. The deception stung but she knew she had to get over it. She knew the love for her sister would heal any wound she had now.

Morgan yawned before saying, "I'm sorry. Even though I was prepared for this news, it seems to have taken a lot out of me. I think I'm going to go to bed."

"But you haven't had dinner. You need to keep up your strength," Bailey said.

"I'm fine, Bailey, really. Now that I know what's going on with my body, I know what I can do to help it, and right now my body is telling me it needs rest."

Bailey walked over and helped her sister to her feet.

"Get used to that because in a few months you

don't know how many times a day you'll be pulling me out of this couch," Morgan said as she headed for the stairs.

"I don't mind. I'll do anything I can to help," Bailey said.

"I know and I love you for it, too. I suggest you get as much sleep as you can now, because once he or she is born sleep will be in short supply." Morgan smiled and patted the sweater covering her belly.

"Ok, well, I'm still going to make some dinner and I'll leave some in a container in the fridge in case you get hungry during the night. And if you need anything, you come to me. Even if it's someone to talk to, or if you just need a shoulder if this gets too much, you come to me," Bailey said. Her voice left no doubt that she wanted to be the person Morgan turned to.

"Thank you, Bailey. And the same thing applies if you need anything. The next few months will be difficult for both of us. I'm sure more than once I'll be taking you up on that offer. Good night," Morgan said before she trudged up upstairs.

"Good night," Bailey said and watched her feet disappear.

Exhausted, Bailey flung herself back into the couch and smiled when Buddy scrambled into her lap. She had not heard him reenter the room. Whenever someone was on the couch, he made it his job that no lap should ever get cold. Bailey ran her fingers through his short curly hair and thought about what she would need to do in the coming months to help her sister. The first thing she would have to do is clean out her grandparent's old bedroom on the first floor. It was something they had put off the past few months. They had closed the door the day after her grandmother passed away and only opened it once to get her Sunday dress to bury her in. Neither wanted the task of cleaning out the room. Now with Morgan in the condition she was, it would be impossible for her to continue to climb the stairs every day. The added weight increased the possibility of her falling down the stairs. It was a scary thought. It was best just to change their environment.

The easiest thing to do would be to wait until after the slumber party and ask Mac and Sandy to help. Bailey knew it would only take an offer of a few beers and a couple slices of pizza to get the two younger women to help with the tedious chore.

She would also have to try to cut back at work. All the writing she was doing would have to slow down. The possibility for applying for the management position would also have to be shelved, at least until next year. There was no way she could take on more responsibilities at home and work. Not if she planned to have any semblance of a social life. If she wanted to start rebuilding a relationship with Shayla, something would have to give. Bailey knew there would not be much free time coming up on her schedule. She would have to take on a lot more responsibility around the house. Her days of sleeping in were going to be few and far between. Responsibility had been a priority in the Navy and now she was going to have to grow up and show how much she learned.

One more scratch on behind Buddy's ear brought a smile to her face as both his tail and leg shook. She gently pushed him off before heading to the kitchen.

"Come on, Buddy, let's go into the kitchen and see what kind of mess we can make. If you're extra good there might even be a hamburger patty with your name on it." Bailey laughed as his tail wagged so hard his butt flailed from side to side and he scurried to the kitchen. It felt good to laugh. Alone in the silent living room, she made herself a promise that no matter what it took, she would try and make her sister laugh daily for at least the next six months, and hopefully years to come.

Chapter Seven

Shayla picked up the phone for the fifth time. Her fingers hovered over the redial button. When she couldn't reach Bailey, she called her sister. Morgan insisted everything was ok and not to worry, but she couldn't help but remember the haunted look on Bailey's face. Puffy eyes and unshed tears made her rethink going on her date. In all the years she had known the woman, she had only see her cry twice and that was from a distance at her grandparent's funerals.

Resolved there was nothing else she could do, she returned once again to her bedroom. If Bailey did need someone to talk to she would have turned around. When the distraught woman continued to walk away, Shayla realized how much distance really stood between her and her former best friend. She had tried to push Bailey from her mind and focused on the date that loomed closer. A bit of excitement clawed its way into her chest and with a smile back on her face she returned to the chore of picking out an outfit.

Life had not turned out the way Shayla had hoped. The last time she had been on an actual date was her freshman year of college. It could hardly be considered a date. Her and her roommate wanted to spend the evening celebrating making it through their first finals. After a nice dinner, the two girls ended up at a frat party and wandered back to the dorm sloppy drunk. Before the night was out, they had shed their clothes and fell into her twin bed. That spontaneous night was the springboard for a two-year relationship.

Clad in only white cotton briefs and a matching bra, she stood before her outdated wardrobe. She couldn't remember the last time she had been shopping for new clothes. As the minutes ticked by, the discarded clothes on the bed continued to grow.

Finally she found a little black dress she had worn to celebrate her father making partner at the largest law firm in Portland.

She shimmied into the velvety outfit. The material hugged her body like a second skin. The dress was almost too snug in some places. As she examined herself in the full-length mirror, she realized the junk food she had been living on recently had made her slim hips disappear. The few extra pounds on her stomach she could've done without, but she understood she had to take the good with the bad.

The chunky watch on her wrist showed the evening had gotten away from her. Now she only had enough time to put in her contacts and add a little mascara. She raced to the bathroom and pulled out two new contacts. After two attempts on one eye and three on the other, she finally was able to see. Red puffy eyes were not the first impression she wanted to give and dug through her drawer for a bottle of eye drops. A few more minutes passed before her eyes dried so she could apply a quick application of mascara. As she finished the final swipe at her eyes, she heard a knock at the door.

Bare feet padded across the hardwood floor. Shayla slowed as she approached the entryway. With her hand on the knob, she took one long breath before she opened the door. The woman standing before her caused all the fluids in her body to head south. Dana was even more beautiful then she had remembered. Tight black slacks displayed long toned legs and the blue polo enhanced her ocean blue eyes. The cherry on the top was the heavy black leather jacket casually tossed over her shoulder.

"Wow, you look amazing," Dana said and snapped Shayla out of her stupor.

"Oh, I'm sorry, I'm being rude. Won't you please come in?" Shayla moved aside, allowing the younger woman to enter her apartment.

"And you look very nice too," Shayla said. Her eyes were glued to the way the trousers hugged Dana's round ass. Ashamed of the way she was staring at the woman, Shayla shook her head, trying to get herself back in the moment.

"You have a beautiful place here," Dana said and turned to her hostess. "How did you luck into such a great apartment?"

Shayla missed the question as she continued to appreciate her guest's attire. She couldn't help but enjoy the way Dana's shirt displayed a nice rack and bulging muscles. There was no way she got her curves from junk food. Only hours in a gym could produce the body she was admiring.

It took a moment for Dana's words to penetrate the spell her body had woven around the bookstore owner.

Cold air whipped in from the open door and snapped Shayla out of her stupor. "What? Oh, I'm sorry. No. I actually own the whole building plus the parking lot in the back," Shayla said as she closed the door.

"Can I offer you something to drink?" Shayla suddenly remembered her manners. It had been a very long time since she had anybody in her apartment.

"A beer would be nice," Dana said.

"Oh, I'm sorry, I don't have one, but I do have wine." Shayla made her way to the fridge.

"That's ok. I'll pass. Thank you. If you're ready, we can head out and probably beat the dinner crowd," Dana said and made her way back to the front door.

"Sure, let me just grab my jacket and put my shoes on," Shayla said and hurried back to her bedroom. She slipped into the nicest pair of black flats she owned and grabbed a long wool coat. It wasn't the best accessory for the dress but it was either that or her down jacket.

She exited the room and took a few seconds to enjoy the view as Dana bent over and browsed her personal library. At least they would have something to talk about at dinner. It was only a few minutes into the date and Shayla didn't know how it could get any better. She cleared her throat. "I'm ready when you are."

"Your chariot awaits," Dana said and directed them to the door. "Well, more like a Subaru wagon."

Dana assisted Shayla down the slick metal stairs. She didn't release her hand as they made their way to the silver car.

"It's actually my parents'. I was in an accident a few months back and totaled my car. I'm still waiting on the insurance check so I can get a new one," Dana said, holding the door open for Shayla.

"That's awful. I hope everybody's all right," Shayla said and settled into the leather seat.

"Yeah, everybody was fine. The other driver side

swiped me." Dana slid in and buckled up.

"Well, I'm glad nobody was hurt. An accident like that could do some serious damage," Shayla said, running her hands along her dress.

"I hope you like Italian. I know this little restaurant. It's just a little hole in the wall but they have the best food."

"I love Italian. It's one of my favorite. I'm half-Italian and my grandma used to make the best marinara. You can't beat authentic," Shayla said. Her fingers moved from her dress to the buttons on her jacket as Dana pulled onto the street. She picked at a long string hanging from one of the buttons.

"Good. I'm looking forward to getting to know you better, but I know I already like what I see." Dana took her eyes off the road.

Shayla watched the younger woman scan her from head to toe. She enjoyed the attention and blushed as Dana's eyes hovered over her cleavage before returning to the road. She turned to look out her own window into the dark night. Her fingers moved from her buttons to back to the hem of her dress.

The next few moments the two women silently listened to the music that filled the car as they continued down the highway. After a few turns Dana pulled into a small parking lot and cut the engine. "Here we are, Giovanni's. It's small. Some would even call it a dive but I think it has the best food."

Shayla didn't mind the outside appearance. The building was a little run down and could use a new coat of paint. But she knew looks were just that, looks. What mattered was on the inside. Shayla had learned that a cover of a book did not mean the content was going to be any good.

"I've never been here before but I've heard about it. Everything I've heard has been really good."

Dana smiled before exiting the vehicle. She jogged around the car and held the door open for Shayla. So far, her date was turning better then Shayla could have hoped for. The night was still young and Shayla tried to keep her mind open. She had read so many romance novels and her favorite scenes continued to run through her head. Hopefully she would have a real one to add to her collection.

"Thank you." Shayla took the extended hand. The only thing missing was the tingling she had always read about. Pushing the thought to the side, she climbed out of the car. Again Dana didn't release her hand as she closed the door. She pulled Shayla close as they made their way to the entrance. Dana held the door open and gently ushered Shayla into the cozy building with a gentle hand to her lower back.

The outside of the tiny restaurant may have been off putting, but the inside was anything but. Rich dark wood and exposed brick were a welcome sight. Tables were cozy and covered with a simple white tablecloth. A single candle sat in the middle of the table, adding to the ambiance. Though the inside was dark, romance seemed to flicker around the room.

"Ah Dana, welcome back," the heavyset hostess said in a thick Italian accent.

"Hi Sophia. Do you have a table?" Dana asked and helped Shayla remove her coat.

"Of course. Please come this way," Sophia said and led the two women to a table nestled in a dark corner in the back.

"Thank you." Dana pulled out Shayla's seat,

earning the young woman another point on Shayla's romance scale.

"Here are your menus and Tammy will be your server. Is there anything I can get you to drink?" Sophia asked.

"I would like a beer and Shayla will have a glass of white wine please," Dana said, taking her own seat.

"Ok, and please enjoy your meal."

"I hope you don't mind that I ordered you a glass of wine?" Dana said before she moved her menu to the side and leaned on the table.

"It's fine, thank you, this place is lovely. However did you find it?" Shayla asked and picked up her menu. Everything looked delicious. She quickly realized making a decision might be harder than she thought. At most Italian restaurants they had roughly the same thing, but this menu held items on it she had only heard of in her grandmother's kitchen.

"My parents used to bring me here when I was younger before we moved to Gresham. I don't get out this way very often, but when I do I make it a point to stop by," Dana said. Her menu still lay on the table untouched.

"I would suggest the lasagna but the carbonara is also very good. If you like white sauces that is," Dana suggested.

"It all looks wonderful." Shayla's eyes never left the menu.

"Here are your drinks. I'm Tammy, I'll be your server the evening. Have you decided, or do you need a few more minutes?" A young waitress said and set their drinks on the table before she removed a pad and pencil from her apron.

Shayla didn't miss the wink the server gave her

date.

Dana turned to Shayla and smiled. "Are you ready?"

Tammy's face soured as she turned towards Shayla.

"Yes, I'll have the carbonara. Thank you." Shayla thrust her menu at Tammy.

"And I'll have the lasagna, please. I think we would also like to start with an order of bread sticks with Alfredo sauce. Thank you," Dana said.

Shayla's smile disappeared as she watched Tammy's fingers slide over Dana's when she retrieved the menu. It was reminiscent of the way Dana had handed her the card that still sat on her nightstand. She hoped Dana didn't get the same thrill she had those few days earlier when the move was used on her.

"I'll be right back with your appetizer," Tammy said. With a flick of her long blond hair, she turned and disappeared into the kitchen.

"Don't mind her," Dana said and reached across the table to grab one of Shayla's hands. "She's just jealous that I'm here with the best looking woman in the place."

"Do you think we should request to be moved to another table?" Shayla asked. Even though Tammy's actions bothered her, she couldn't help but smile as Dana's thumb caressed the top of her hand.

"No. I'm sure we'll be fine. I'm sure she will get the hint and stop after a while."

"Have you been through this type of thing before?"

"A few times. They usually get a clue after a while and stop, but enough about that. Let's talk about you," Dana said, using her empty hand to take a long pull from her beer.

"What would you like to know?" Shayla took the first sip of her wine. It was a little too sweet for her liking.

"Hmm, let's start with the basics. Ok. I know where you work. Why did you decide to work there?" Dana asked.

"I actually own the bookstore. I only have part time help, so I'm usually there from open to close. It's open six days a week so it takes up a lot of my time," Shayla said and opened her napkin and placed it on her lap.

"So I gather you love books then?" Dana asked and took another large drink from her beer.

"I do. I've loved to read since I was a kid. I'm an only child and both of my parents had a tendency to bring their work home so I spent most of my time reading. I actually went to school to become a librarian, but quickly realized I would much prefer to own my own bookstore. So my sophomore year I switched to business management, and here I am."

"I can't imagine it would be profitable with all these large bookstores around. It must be hard to keep a business like that running."

"It's been a challenge. I'm lucky I have other investments that take care of most of my living expenses. I've thought about maybe adding more shelf space to add a section for used books. New books can be expensive. I thought if people were given the options of doing trade-in business, it might draw more customers. I love to read and I don't know where I would be without books. During these times, I've been trying to think of things to keep the customers coming through my doors. Reading is something done out of love, and during economic downturns like we're in now, it's usually one of the things that's cut since it is not a necessity," Shayla said. She realized she was rambling and possibly boring her date. "So do you like to read?"

"Nope. I probably haven't picked up a book since my last class a few years ago. Actually I can't ever remember reading a book that wasn't assigned in school," Dana said and picked at the label of her sweating beer bottle.

"Oh, I assumed you liked reading since you were looking at my books." Shayla shrugged.

"I was just wondering if there were any titles I recognized. Out of all of your books, I only recognized Romeo and Juliet. I think it was assigned reading in the eighth grade. It was way over my head then. The whole old English writing and having to look at the bottom of the page to find out what was being said was just too much. I think I only got through a quarter of the book."

"It's actually a play. It's one of the all-time classic romances," Shayla said. Shayla didn't fault the young woman. Shakespeare was hard to read. She could give Dana this one pass. The date was still better then she had hoped for.

"Yeah, I never could get into that mushy stuff. I like things with a little more action or horror thrown in. If Steven King had been on the required reading list, I may have actually finished a book. I love his movies."

Shayla didn't like horror, but as a business owner, she understood people gravitated to certain genres. It was one of the main reasons for creating book clubs. She enjoyed reading an assortment of books and loved to see individuals introduced to something different. She couldn't count the number of women who had joined her groups with one preference, but discovered they had interests in multiple genres.

"So what do you do for fun?" Shayla asked when their breadsticks and Alfredo was placed on the table.

Tammy didn't hang around to flirt with Dana as she scurried off to take the order from a new table.

Dana grabbed a breadstick and broke it in half before she slid it through the creamy white sauce. "I enjoy watching sports, playing video games, going out to the movies, and just hanging with friends. How about you?" Dana said and popped the appetizer in her mouth. A little of the sauce dripped down her chin and she swiped at it with her thumb before sticking it between her lips. A loud pop sounded when she removed her digit.

"I enjoy reading, listening to music, and spending time with friends. I don't even own a television set." Shayla moved a piece of bread to her plate and broke it up into small pieces before dabbing it into the sauce.

"No way, how can that be? Everybody owns a television. I think we have four or five in our house," Dana said and tossed another drenched breadstick in her mouth.

"I don't know. Even when I was a kid, I never really watched TV. I read a lot. When I'm reading it's like I'm watching a movie. I get more invested in characters and I don't have to wait weeks or even months to know what happens, unless I'm reading a series. Reading to me is more instant gratification."

"Oh man, I don't think I could live without my electronics. I'm usually on my computer playing games with my friends or on my Xbox. My cell is always with me and I'm usually texting someone." The moment the words left her lips a loud trill interrupted their conversation. She pulled the small phone from her pocket and checked the brightly lit screen.

"Is everything ok?" Shayla asked. She watched Dana's fingers blaze across the screen.

"Yeah, it's just a friend verifying plans for this weekend," Dana said and set the cell on the table. "See what I mean?"

"I do. That's why I don't have one."

"You mean you don't have a television and a cell phone? How do you do it? I don't think I could function without them."

"I've never owned a cell phone and have done just fine. I mean, there are times when I just want to be alone with no distractions. I can take my phone off the hook. Plus I find cell phones too intrusive."

"That can be true, but what if there was an emergency?" Dana asked. Her eyes continued to glance at the device sitting on the table.

"I think I could be resourceful enough to be able to find my way out of an emergency. My parents never had one when they were my age and they did just fine. I don't know, I just find that cell phones have taken away a lot of, if not most, human interaction. The same with computers and televisions. I don't even have a personal computer. I have the one for work and that's it. A friend recently bought me an iPad but I used it once. Actually, I don't even think I've turned it on since she gave it to me. But I'll admit that I have thought about getting a cell phone. I figured I could get one that just makes calls. I don't need all the other bells and whistles."

"It's almost like you're still living in the dark

ages. I think with all the advances we have made, they have been invented to make our life easier." Again Dana took another drink from her beer, finishing the first bottle.

"I can see how it has made some things easier, but it has also taken away a lot of human interaction. Take consumers for instance. You mentioned earlier about having a hard time against large bookstores, but in actuality my biggest competition comes from online retailers. People don't even have to leave their house and can buy a book at discounted prices. Why would someone take the time to get in their car and drive to my shop? Now, people don't even have to leave their house to go grocery shopping. They just click away on their computers and the next day their food shows up on their door step." Shayla continued to nibble at the buttery bread on her plate.

"Right, that's my point. It's convenient," Dana said and held up her empty bottle to Tammy as she rushed past.

"Convenient true, but now what are people doing with their time? Are they spending it with their families? No, they choose to sit in front of the TV or the computer and waste their life with another electronic device. I've had customers complain that they have to text their family when it's dinnertime, then they take their plates into the living room and eat while watching TV. That's no way to live. I mean, who wants to have to call their partner or child that's just in another room? It's ridiculous. And we complain about what's going on with society but we do nothing to stop it. Every day the newest device is released and people rush to be first in line to purchase it all the while complaining that they have lost contact with their family."

"I understand. I've been guilty of many of those things myself."

Tammy returned with the beer. Another waiter who placed their meals on the table followed her. Shayla looked at the portion and knew she wouldn't have to worry about what she would be eating for lunch the next day.

"Thank you," she said to Tammy.

The plate was hot and she decided to let her food cool and continued with their conversation. "I mean, couples now have to plan dates. Life has lost its spontaneity. Humanity is almost dead. Computers and convenience have taken over. It's one of the reasons I've fought it. Working at my little store keeps me grounded. I like interacting with people. I may disappear into a book every once in a while but I haven't disappeared from society. Think of it this way. You say our computers and phones have made life easier but for what? What have we done with the time we have saved ourselves? Nothing, we even waste the gift that has been given us." The topic had started to depress Shayla. It was time for a change. "So what were you going to school for?"

"I didn't know what I wanted to do. I was just going for my associates in general studies. I figured it would give me time to think about what I really wanted to do," Dana said between bites.

"So since some time has passed, do you know what you want to go back for?"

"I was thinking about game design. I mean, they get to think up all these cool games and play all day. That sounds like the perfect job to me," Dana said and cut off a large wedge of lasagna.

Shayla chewed her pasta slowly. She could understand where she was coming from. She couldn't fault Dana for wanting to make a career out of something she loved. Even if it seemed more like playing than work. She swallowed her bite before replying, "Well, that's true. You know what they say. A job is something you have to do and a career is something you love to do."

"Exactly, but I don't know if that will happen. It sounds nice and all, but right now I need to find a job so I can save up to go back to school."

"I thought you were working? What about grants and a school loan?"

"I was working at a video store, but the hours weren't steady," Dana said. "But I have a few applications out. I expect to hear something back soon."

"Well, that's promising," Shayla said and set down her fork. More than half of her food remained on the plate. "Wow, the portions here are larger than I thought."

"I know, it's one of the reasons I love this place," Dana said and looked at her own empty dish. "I should have stopped earlier but it was just too good. How about we go for a walk and work some of this off?" Dana said and leaned back, patting her flat stomach.

Dana held up her hand when Tammy breezed by. Soon Shayla had her lunch stuffed into a carry out box and they were back in the car speeding towards downtown Portland.

"I know this isn't in the direction of your place but I thought we could go for a stroll along the water. I don't know many places in Hillsboro that have water or walking trails," Dana said.

"That's fine. It's nice actually. I don't get into the city much."

"I'm glad you were there last weekend," Dana said and reached over to grab Shayla's hand.

"Me too. I was celebrating my birthday."

"Oh, well, happy belated birthday. How old are you if you don't mind my asking?"

"Twenty-nine. Just one more year till I'm over the hill." Shayla enjoyed the feeling of her fingers intertwined with Dana's.

Dana looked at Shayla. Another smile played across her lips and displayed perfect white teeth. "You're nowhere close to a hill."

"Thank you," Shayla said and bowed her head to look at their hands. She hoped her blush was not visible.

The rest of the drive passed in comfortable silence. Dana finally parked under a bridge and turned off the engine. Shayla shivered as she exited the car. The wind from the flowing river whipped freezing air around her body. Dana slid her arm around Shayla, drawing her close. "If it gets too cold, let me know."

"I will," Shayla said. Even though the air was cold, the strong chivalrous arm wrapped around her warmed her body. The date had not been without its hiccups but she still hoped there would be another one in their future. Even though they didn't have a lot in common, just being near Dana excited her more than anything she had felt in a long time. The evening was something she could have read about in any of the books that lined her bookshelf.

They walked in silence along the paved route next to the Willamette River. Periodically a drunk pedestrian stumbling out of one of the many bars that lined Front Street shattered the silence. Naked branches danced in the breeze while leaves crunched under their feet. Their breath would briefly appear before their faces before the frigid winter wind tore it away. Shayla tried to fight the biting cold but failed miserably when another shiver ran through her body. A strong arm pulled her close. Shayla had not seen another person on their path for a while, and enjoyed the solitude. Thirty minutes into the stroll, she noticed another woman heading their way. She felt the arm holding her tighten. Soon she found herself directed off the path into frozen grass that shattered with every step.

"Is everything ok?" Shayla asked, curious why they left the comfort of the concrete path.

"Yeah, everything's fine, I just wanted to get us away from the wind and water. I thought it might be warmer by the street," Dana said and pulled Shayla through the grass.

The serene night they previously enjoyed by the water disappeared. Along the street, they choked on fumes from the traffic and the quiet was gone as the bass reverberating through brick walls assaulted them. They only continued the walk for a few more minutes before Shayla finally spoke up.

"Do you mind if we turn around? It's getting late and I still have to work early tomorrow," Shayla said and tried to keep her teeth from chattering. The trip back to the car was made in a hasty speed walk. Soon they were inside the car with the heater on full blast, trying to warm numb limbs.

"Maybe a night time stroll during the dead of winter wasn't a good idea," Dana said as she ran her hands up Shayla's arms.

"No, it was beautiful. If I had dressed differently maybe we would still be walking," Shayla said, relieved her teeth had stopped chattering.

"I think you look sexy in what you're wearing," Dana said.

Shayla smiled and knew she could get used to looking into Dana's sweet baby blues.

"Well, I should be getting you home."

Shayla wanted to stay longer and enjoy more of the evening, but she really did have to open the store. Normally her part time help would open the store on the weekends but Ivy had requested the morning off to attend basketball camp.

"Yeah, I do have to get up early and open the store, but I had a great time."

The only reply Shayla received was another smile from Dana. The added bonus came when Dana took her hand. Again she held it the whole drive home. Sooner than she would have liked, Dana was pulling into the parking lot.

"I had a wonderful time," Shayla said and shifted to look at Dana.

"I did too. I hope we can do it again."

"That would be nice."

With Dana's right hand still holding Shayla's captive, Dana turned to face the bookstore owner.

"So beautiful," Dana whispered.

Before Shayla could pull away, Dana leaned in and softly pressed her lips to Shayla's. Only a few seconds passed, but Shayla lost herself in the kiss before she pulled away.

"Thank you again for a lovely evening," Shayla said. Reluctantly she extracted her hand and exited the car. She hurried up the steps and turned on the top stair to wave at Dana, who continued to sit in the idling car. She unlocked the door and rushed inside, shutting out the cold. Her heart pounded. She never thought there would be another perfect night like the one she just had. No story she had ever read had truly prepared her for the butterflies that had taken flight in her stomach, and she couldn't wait to feel them again. In the dark apartment, she shuffled to the bedroom and shed her clothes from the evening.

Her fingers felt under her pillow for her nightgown. The soft fabric floated around her and she realized that for the past few hours Bailey had not even entered her thoughts. Maybe she was well and truly over her old flame, and now she could work on getting their friendship back on track. Before she extinguished the light, she reminded herself to call Bailey and take the steps needed to move forward.

Chapter Eight

Bailey had wanted to go with Morgan when she went for her follow up but Morgan had told her it wasn't necessary. All they would be doing was more tests and it wasn't necessary that she be there.

Secrets were not something Bailey was very good at keeping so to make things easier she had avoided the bakery. Bailey had returned Shayla's call the next day but just blamed her sudden appearance on a bad day. Before they could really get into a conversation, she had cut the call short. She knew Shayla was not happy with her answer but Bailey knew she would have to face the firing squad soon enough. The days leading up to the sleep over had dragged and now only a few hours remained until the ladies would start making an appearance.

The plan was for them to start arriving around six. Unlucky for Bailey, Shayla was the first to knock on their door. Prompt as always. Bailey was in her room when she heard Morgan welcome the shop owner. She continued to hide out in her sanctuary until Morgan asked for her help in the kitchen.

Bailey walked into the room and stopped when Shayla turned to face her. Bailey couldn't take her eyes off her former best friend. The tan sweater she wore hugged her curves. Curves she had not seen until now because Shayla's normal wardrobe had consisted of loose clothing and dresses that hung on her frame. The woman standing before her was a much more grown up and filled out than the girl she remembered in high school.

"Sorry, I know you are working but I needed to know if you've seen Grandma's platter. You rearranged everything and now I can't find anything," Morgan said and slammed another cupboard door shut. She stood in with a huff and folded her arms.

"Uh yeah, let me look. Hi Shayla," Bailey said and brushed past Shayla. Morgan had been in a sour mood the past few days. It seemed every little thing set her sister off. Bailey hoped that once the other women arrived, her attitude would change, since they had been on one of the longest rollercoasters Bailey had ever seen. In the past few days, she had seen her sister cry and then yell while grading papers. She was at a loss of what to do. She was sure her hormones wouldn't be out of whack this early in her pregnancy, but she wouldn't question anything and just do whatever was asked of her.

"Hello," Shayla said and leaned against the counter.

"Ok, I'm going to finish getting ready. I still have to make the beds," Morgan said and exited the kitchen. Her smile at Shayla told Bailey she had already jumped another track.

Bailey bent and rummaged through the cupboards, looking for the serving dish. She knew where it was but banged pots and pans around, hoping the noise would deter Shayla from trying to have a conversation.

"Hey, is everything ok?" Shayla asked and softly laid a hand on Bailey's shoulder.

The touch sent a spark through Bailey and she flinched and slammed her head against the cabinet.

"Fuck," Bailey said and rubbed the back of her head. She emerged from the cabinet and sat on her haunches.

"Oh, I'm sorry, I didn't mean to scare you," Shayla said and felt where Bailey had banged her head. Bailey jerked away from the touch even though her body wanted to revel in the way the strong fingers had moved through her hair.

"It's ok. I was just startled," Bailey said and moved to the cabinet where Shayla had been standing. She bent down and pulled out the serving tray. "Found it."

Bailey started to leave the kitchen but found herself trapped. Shayla stood in the doorway with her hands on her hips, blocking any escape. In all the years Bailey had known Shayla, she had never known her to be so forceful. She kind of liked it.

"Excuse me," Bailey said and still attempted to get around the woman.

"I'm sorry but you didn't answer my question. Are you ok?" Shayla asked and dropped her arms to her side.

"Yeah. It's just a little bump. No big deal. I'm fine." Bailey leaned against the counter and tried to avoid Shayla's penetrating stare. It wasn't Shayla's fault Bailey was a coward. Why should she have to pay; if she wanted to talk, the least Bailey could do was try.

"Not about that, but I'm glad you're ok. I mean the other day when you stopped by my apartment."

Bailey had known what she meant. "Oh yeah. I was just having a bad day and needed someone to talk to. It was just one of those days." Bailey tried to brush it off, still kicking herself for the stupid detour she had made on her way home from the hospital. She had expected the question, but what she didn't anticipate the tears that appeared in her eyes. She thought she had dried out when she cried herself to sleep. She wiped at the moisture on her cheeks and couldn't ignore the impatient throat-clearing coming from the doorway.

"You know you can always talk to me. I miss that," Shayla said and slipped out of the way and back into the kitchen.

"I miss that too," Bailey admitted.

"Bailey, I think it's about time we talk," Shayla said and made her way to the table and sat down.

Bailey stayed where she was.

"I was worried about you. You seemed a little distressed that night."

Clearing her throat, Bailey attempted to put on a brave face. "Yeah, I just had a bad day at work and thought I could talk to you about it. I had forgotten about your date, sorry." Knowing that wouldn't stop her friend, she gritted her teeth before asking the one question she knew could derail Shayla's current train of thought. "How was your date?"

Bailey detested the joy that appeared on her friend's face. She hated that another person had put a gleam in Shayla's eyes.

"Oh my gosh, it was so fantastic. I don't think a first date could've gone any better." The dreaminess in her voice twisted the knife in Bailey's heart that had been lodged there ten years ago. The thing she had run from was finally happening. She didn't know how she was still on her feet as she listened to her friend.

"What did you do?" Bailey asked through gritted teeth. She didn't even know how she was able to choke out the words. She couldn't stand watching Shayla beam. She turned back to the cabinet. Her knuckles turned white as she gripped the counter and hung her head. The subject matter made her want to vomit but she couldn't allow Shayla to go back to the previous topic. She didn't know what was tearing her up more, watching the woman she loved fall for someone else or just the thought of possibly losing her sister. If things didn't change, there was a big possibility Bailey would end up alone. The thought knocked all the energy out of her and she slumped against the counter, waiting to be tortured with details.

She was saved from hearing the gory insight to their date by another knock at the door.

"Oh hey, hold that thought. I have to go get this." Bailey was out the door before Shayla could even form a reply.

Dion and Connie were inside the door and started to shed their coats before she even reached the hall.

"Hey, well it's about time. Just drop your stuff at the door and I'll take it to the room. When everybody gets here, I'll give out the sleeping arrangements. Now tell me what we're doing tonight," Bailey said and hugged the women. Normally she wasn't a touchy feely person, but needed the comfort the two women unknowingly gave.

Connie bent and held up a large tote. "We're making personal pizzas."

"Yeah, I love pizza," Morgan said from behind Bailey. Bailey hadn't heard her come downstairs. Odd, as Morgan normally sounded like a herd of elephants when she descended from upstairs.

"It sounds great. I hope we have enough room

in the kitchen for everybody," Bailey said and took the heavy tote Connie held out. Bailey grunted under the surprise weight.

"And I brought the beer." Wanda lifted the two cases as she waltzed through the still open door.

"Great, the good stuff." Sandy divested the cases from Wanda as she breezed in right behind the old woman.

Mac closed the door and silently followed Sandy into the back.

"What, did you all caravan or something?" Morgan asked, bringing up the rear. Buddy followed close at their heels.

After giving out the room arrangements and depositing bags, Bailey finally made her way into the bustling kitchen. She was relieved when Connie and Dion didn't have an issue sleeping in their grandparent's old room. As she changed the sheets, it had stirred feelings of regret in Bailey. But she pushed them aside, knowing she needed to focus on the future and her sister, and not wallow in past mistakes. She hadn't been there for her grandparents at the end of their lives but she would be there for her sister for the rest of hers. Instead of running away from life, she decided to look forward and take it one step at a time. Her running days were in the past.

The room erupted into multiple conversations. Laughter could be heard throughout the small abode. As the night progressed, Bailey made sure to keep a safe distance from Shayla. Bailey watched her sister leaning against the counter with a decaffeinated tea in hand. Tears popped into her eyes as she realized she may not have many more experiences like this.

"Hey you, get your little butt over here and roll

out your dough. I'm not doing everything for you," Connie said and avoided a pile of flying flour Mac tossed Sandy's way. It wasn't long until most of the women had a light layer of powder dusting them; even Wanda's jet-black hair looked more salt than pepper.

"That's a good look on you, Wanda. You should let your hair go natural," Sandy said to the older woman and attempted to dislodge the powder from her own multi colored locks.

"Not on your life. No thirty-five year old woman would ever have salt and pepper hair," Wanda scoffed before she rolled out the ball of dough in front of her.

"Yeah, but you're not thirty-five, you're si..." Dion suddenly found her mouth filled with pepperoni.

"Thank you, Connie. That will teach you to tell a lady's age," Wanda said.

"Lady? What lady?" Dion asked around pepperoni, unable to dodge a face full of white powder.

"Ok ladies, maybe this wasn't such a good idea," Connie said and gently wiped flour from her partner's face.

"I'm having a great time," Bailey said, concentrating on her own pizza. It felt good to laugh. For the past few days, she hadn't been able to think of anything but her sister and the fight ahead. But since the women had arrived, she hadn't thought about the battle they faced. Bailey decided tomorrow she could continue to worry. Tonight she was going to enjoy her friends' company.

"Me too," Morgan said as she worked on her own masterpiece.

Twenty minutes later, everybody sat in the dining room with their personal pizza and beer, except Morgan who stayed with tea.

Bailey realized Buddy had positioned himself between Connie and Dion and was helping himself to scraps the two women were sliding off the table. She was about to scold them for feeding him bread, but it was a night to splurge and she allowed him his treats too.

After the pizza had been consumed, they cleared the table and it didn't surprise Bailey when Connie said they had been test subjects to see if personal pizzas would be a good addition to their lunch menu. The room erupted with a resounding yes. Conversations started between the three business owners about the customers that fresh pizzas could draw. Bailey knew there was a greater possibility for her showing up for lunch with the draw of pizza.

The clock was heading towards eleven when the women found themselves in the living room, comfy, cozy, and ready to play games. They had settled into all the available chairs with a few forced to find a seat on the hardwood floors. With too many bodies to choose from, Buddy had to take turns making sure each woman had enough time to rub his belly before moving on to the next open lap.

"Ok ladies, what are we doing now?" Bailey asked and turned to Connie since she appeared to be the brains behind the operation.

"Well, I thought we could play truth or dare," Connie said.

The air filled with groans and a few cheers from the women around the room.

"Come on, we're not in high school anymore," Sandy said, falling back into her chair. "Let's play quarters or beer pong."

Bailey could understand her reluctance. Sandy

and Mac had probably been the only two who had played the game in the last decade. Secretly, she was filled with excitement and fear of what the game could reveal. Silently she sat with her fingers crossed and waited for Connie's decision.

"When you can start to handle your liquor then we can play drinking games again. Last time you were the first to pass out, and I don't want to have to carry your ass to bed again," Wanda said. The other women laughed at the young woman's expense. Carry had been an overstatement. Wanda had dragged the younger woman more than carried. Sandy had been lucky there were no steps at Wanda's house or she would have probably ended up with a concussion to go along with her bruised ego.

"I'm ok with truth or dare," Morgan said. "I mean, I haven't played since junior high. And I think it would be fun to get the dirt on some of you women. But I don't know how long I'm going to be able to stay up. I'm a bit tired." She rubbed her hands as she looked at the women seated in the living room.

"That's the good thing about the game. It can be as short or as long as we want. I'm sorry dinner took longer than we had thought," Connie said.

"Dinner was wonderful. I'm just sorry I'm a bit of a party pooper," Morgan replied.

"Nonsense. It's settled then." Connie clapped her hands. "Ok, here are the rules. Once you're asked a question or a dare then you get to pick the next person, but nobody can be picked more than once on any given round. Second, if you pick truth and you don't want to answer you can then opt to for a dare. Third, if you do choose a dare there's no nudity, and lastly if you are given a dare and another person is involved they have to consent, and if they don't then that's that."

"Sounds fair to me," Bailey said, ready to get the game started. She rubbed her hands at the thought of the questions she could ask the innocent bookstore owner who currently was tickling Buddy's tummy.

The other women nodded in agreement.

"Fine, I'll start," Wanda said before anybody else said anything. With a glint in her eye, she turned to her sister. "Dion, Truth or dare?"

Dion replied quickly. "Truth."

"Did you break mother's china when you were thirteen?" Wanda asked.

Dion's head snapped back. "What the heck kind of question is that?"

"One I want an answer to," Wanda said and folded her arms under her ample breasts.

"Fine. Yes. Yes I did," Dion said and matched her sister's stance.

"Why, you little brat. I got grounded for a month because of that. I was supposed to go to the spring formal with Ben. I had to miss it because of something you did," Wanda said, bitterness dripping from her voice like venom.

"It's in the past. Time to move on. Shayla, truth or dare?" Dion asked the shop owner

Shayla continued to run her fingers through Buddy's hair as she made her decision. "Uh, truth."

"What kind of woman are you attracted to?" Dion asked. Almost everybody's eyes were trained on Shayla, waiting for her response, but Bailey didn't miss the wink Dion threw in her direction. Bailey blushed and turned to the woman about to answer.

"Well, I like women who are more tweeners, not

too butch and not too fem. Someone down the middle. I want a woman that's just as comfortable in a pair of jeans as she is in a skirt. A woman who is kind and gentle, but will also take charge when she needs to. She has to be romantic, but can appreciate it if I bring her flowers. What I really want is someone who looks good in a suit. I find a femme in suits just as much a turn on as a butch."

Bailey hadn't been expecting such an in-depth answer but hung on every word. She would have to thank Dion at a later date for asking it. Even though the wink already told her it was more than likely asked for her benefit.

"Morgan, truth or dare?" Shayla turned to the young teacher.

"Truth." Morgan said and scooted back into her chair while she rubbed her hands on her flannel-clad knee.

"Have you ever kissed a girl? And I don't mean like you would kiss your sister," Shayla asked.

"Yes." Morgan blushed. She buried her face in her hands as the room erupted in cheers and high fives. Questions started being tossed at the younger Hutsell sister. Eventually the questions ended and her face emerged from her hands, red enough to be mistaken for a tomato. "I answered the question, and remember I did attend college." She didn't pause before continuing the game. "Now, Sandy, truth or dare?"

"Might as well go with the group and say truth." Sandy sat back into her chair.

"Who was your first kiss?" Morgan asked.

Bailey watched Sandy's eyes glance at Mac before answering.

"Mac. Connie, truth or dare?" She asked quick enough to cut off any additional questions.

"Truth, of course," Connie said.

"Have you ever been with a man?" Sandy asked.

"No. I have not. I'm a gold star lesbian. We're a dying breed," Connie said and leaned into Dion to give her a small peck. Kind eyes turned to Bailey. "Bailey, truth or dare?"

Bailey paused and weighed her choices. Knowing what the woman already knew about her, she didn't like either option. Connie was crafty and Bailey knew the question she was probably dying to ask. She feared even more what she would have to do if she took a dare.

"Truth." Bailey knew if she didn't want to answer she could try her luck at a dare.

"Who was your first love?" Connie asked, innocence saturating her voice.

Bailey felt her stomach drop. Sweat dotted her forehead. She would never answer that question while the person sat less than ten feet away.

"Dare," Bailey quickly amended.

"Fine. You have to kiss Shayla. And not just a peck on the cheek either," Connie said. The satisfied look she sent to her wife informed Bailey she had been set up from the get go.

Bailey eyed Connie and knew it would never be a good idea to play chess with the older woman. She had played right into their hands.

She was out of options and turned to Shayla. "Do you consent?"

Her only response was silence.

Bailey realized Shayla had not been paying attention. "Shayla, do you want to do this dare with me?"

"What?" Shayla asked with her fingers still scratching the fur ball lounging on her lap.

"Bailey took a dare and I dared her to kiss you. Is that ok?" Connie asked.

Bailey's breathing stopped as she waited for her answer. Never before had she been so torn. She desired the feel of Shayla's lips pressed against hers, but she hoped if it was ever to happen it wouldn't be with an audience.

Shayla paused. The room was so quiet you could hear a pin drop. Then she shrugged. "Sure."

Bailey wanted to run. The one person who could have ended her misery had just sealed her fate. Slowly she crawled on her knees to where Shayla sat on the couch next to Dion. She placed her hand on her friend's knees, leaned in, and gave her friend a chaste peck on the lips. In just those few moments her lips were pressed to Shayla's, it sent a tingle down her spine. She attempted to retreat to her previous position before she was stopped.

"Wait. Stop right there missy. That's not a kiss. If you need for me to show you how to kiss someone properly, I'll be more than happy to demonstrate with my partner. You have to kiss her for at least ten seconds for it to count," Connie amended.

"You didn't say that," Bailey whined. She sat back on her hunches and picked at her cuticles.

"It was implied. Now get back over here and do it right," Connie said.

Shayla pushed Buddy off her lap. Before Bailey fully reached the couch, she slid to the floor.

Slowly Bailey made her way to her friend. With each millimeter that she moved, she felt as if she was being sent before a firing squad.

"Are you ready?" Shayla asked after Bailey had finally stopped in front of her.

Bailey could only nod in response. Any and all words had frozen on her lips.

"It's only ten seconds. I'm sure you'll live," Shayla kidded but Bailey saw something in her eyes, something she had never seen before, something she couldn't place.

Bailey planned to count to ten when their lips met, but once she felt Shayla's lips against hers, soft and yielding, all thoughts fled her mind. Bailey melted into Shayla's velvety kiss. She felt a pull from her core that exploded and made her whole body tingle. Everything around her dissolved into nothingness. The only thing she knew was the soft lips that gently moved against hers. She almost fainted when she felt the tip of Shayla's tongue brush her lips. She didn't know when it happened but she found herself caressing Shayla's cheek. When they finally parted, she felt as if a rug had been pulled out from under her as reality came crashing back. She couldn't hear anything over the pounding of her heart. Her initial response was to lean back in for another kiss but Shayla had already moved to take back her spot on the couch. Slowly she crawled back to her seat to wait for the game to resume even though all she wanted to do was go to bed and dream about the kiss she had just had, but she couldn't let everybody in the room know how it had affected her. Bailey opened her mouth to pick her next victim but was interrupted.

"I'm sorry to cut the night short but I'm really not feeling well. My stomach's a bit upset," Morgan said. Her hands gently rubbed her stomach.

"Are you all right, dear? You haven't been feeling well for some time. You said earlier you had a doctor's appointment. How did that go? Did he give you something?" Connie asked. She reached over and rubbed the younger woman's back. Worry was etched on her motherly face.

Bailey tried to grasp onto the feelings she had just experienced, but they fell through her fingers like sand with the reminder of her sister's health.

"Oh, they ran some tests and took some blood but they don't know anything yet." The lie fell from Morgan's lips. "They think it might just be a cold. There's a nasty flu going around now. They instructed me to drink lots of fluids and get lots of sleep." Morgan pushed herself out of the chair.

Bailey popped out of her seat like a shot to get the living room ready for the four women who didn't have a room to sleep in.

"But Mac didn't get a turn," Shayla said as she gathered up some blankets in her arms.

"That's perfectly fine with me. I didn't think you guys would be so ruthless. I'm good with keeping my secrets just a little longer," Mac said. Her arms tried to contain two bulky sleeping bags.

"Well, it's getting late, so I guess we had all better be turning in," Dion said and pulled Connie to her feet. "Let's get out of here so these young folk can get their beds made up."

"I'm glad you don't have to work tomorrow." Bailey tossed some bedding onto the spot that the two women just vacated.

"It was the right thing to do. The bakery tends to slow down during the winter. Plus it gives everybody some time off to recoup from the holiday rush. When spring comes we'll be back to seven days a week," Dion said as she headed towards the hall.

"I know I'm thankful for the break. I wish it would've started earlier last week but oh well," Sandy said as she unfurled her sleeping bag.

"You ladies sleep tight," Wanda said and trailed Morgan upstairs. "And thank you for letting me have your room for the night, Bailey. I don't think this old body could take sleeping on the floor."

"It's no problem. You have a good night," Bailey said before she helped Shayla lay a sheet on the sofa. They moved the love seat against the wall and turned the coffee table upside down before placing it on the loveseat to make room for Sandy and Mac's sleeping bags. Bailey rolled out her own sleeping bag in front of the couch and prepared to crawl inside.

"I can sleep on the floor," Shayla offered.

"No, I wouldn't be a proper hostess if I had you sleep on the floor. It's really ok. I'm fine. It's just like camping except less rocks," Bailey said. She laid back with her head nestled in her hands.

Shayla lay down and rolled to the edge of the couch. Bailey shifted her view and saw something fall from Shayla's night shirt. "Is this what I think it is?"

"Yep, I told you when you gave it to me I would never take it off and I haven't. Well maybe when I have to dress up, but I go right back home and put it on." Shayla grabbed the necklace Bailey had given her the last day of high school. "It's one of the most important things to me. Good night." Shayla rolled over and snuggled into the couch.

"Good night," Bailey whispered.

Bailey lay on her back. Unable to sleep, she watched light dance across the ceiling when cars passed by. Her body hummed with residual feelings of the kiss. There were no words she could use to describe it. Her mind filled with cotton when she thought of how Shayla's lips felt against hers. Her eyes became misty from the pure joy she had felt in those few seconds. She listened for the familiar soft snores from Shayla. Unfortunately, all she heard was the sound of dueling chainsaws from Sandy and Mac. She didn't know which one was louder. With a sigh, she rolled over and burrowed into her pillow. Bailey finally found sleep while dreaming about the lips that hovered above her.

Chapter Nine

Shayla stood at the counter, double-checking her invoice to make sure she had everything correct before faxing the requests for the new books. She glanced outside to rest her tired eyes. Her exhausted senses caught a glimpse of a woman dressed in a suit as she hurried past the large window. Quickly she rushed to the window to see the woman disappear into the bakery next door.

"Hey Ivy, I'm going next door to get a coffee. Is there anything I can get you while I'm over there?" Shayla asked. Her eyes never left the door, hoping the woman wouldn't leave. She loved to see women in suits and by the quick view she had, this one was edible. Even though she had another date with Dana coming up, there was no reason she couldn't window shop. It was only their second date and she didn't even know if it was going anywhere. Not to mention the kiss from Saturday night that she couldn't get out of her head. Her perfect date and Saturday's kiss had her normally dormant hormones raging in high gear. She was torn in two different directions. Hopefully heading north was her prospects with Dana and getting back on the road was her relationship with Bailey. Years ago, she would have gone down that road in a second but now she wasn't so sure if she had enough left in the tank to even try.

"Nope. I'm good. Do you want me to fax off

those invoices?"

"Yeah, that would be great. I won't be long," Shayla said before she escaped through the door and hurried to the bakery.

Taking a few seconds, Shayla stood outside the bakery and watched the woman through the door as she leaned against the counter. Such a simple stance, but even that drew Shayla in. The woman had removed her jacket and flung it over her shoulder before tossing her head back laughing at something Connie said. Even through a thick pane of glass, Shayla could feel the confidence ooze off the woman. Shayla couldn't help but stare at the way the pink stripped shirt was tucked into black slacks that hugged her hips and accentuated a pert ass. The suspenders were a bit of overkill, but gave her a quirkiness that was endearing. The short shag haircut gave her a 90's Meg Ryan quality she found adorable. Now if she looked as good from the front as she did from the back maybe she would have someone else to try her recently acquired flirting skills on.

Who was she kidding? She would never make a move. It had frustrated her to no end that she read about love almost every day of her life, yet she was afraid to go after what she wanted. Her life was finally starting to turn into the story she had always desired; now all she had to do was wait for her happy ending.

It wasn't until her body started to shiver from the cold that she realized she had left the store in such haste she had forgotten her coat. She opened the door and was soon engulfed in warmth and a fragrance that only the bakery could fill her with. The heat was infused with a cinnamon and coffee combination she had come to love. Her glasses steamed up and she had to remove them to clear the condensation. When she placed them back on her face, she couldn't believe who was staring back at her.

"What happened to you?" Shayla asked. A different type of warmth spread through her veins and the butterflies in her stomach took flight.

"Why, you don't like it?" Bailey ran her fingers through her short locks.

"No! I mean you uh…you look very nice." Shayla wanted to say something else, but didn't know how her friend would take it if she said she was beyond hot. She was lucky she had been able to capture the words before they burst from her mouth.

Bailey's wardrobe change had surprised her, but her reaction startled her more. But if the kiss they shared a few days earlier was any indication, the feelings she had felt in high school had not disappeared as she had previously hoped. The moment Bailey's lips touched hers she hadn't wanted it to end. When she pulled away and found Bailey with her eyes still closed, she had been tempted to go in for another kiss until she heard the other women in the room. It took everything in her at that moment to return to her seat.

"Why the change?" Shayla forced her feet to take her to the counter. She couldn't keep from staring at her friend. When she looked up into the shorn locks, she wanted to run her fingers through them just to see if they were as soft as they appeared.

"Well, when I went for my drive on Sunday, I ended up at the mall and decided to get some new clothes. It's been years since I was shopping and now that I'm home, I thought a little change would be good. What do you think?" Bailey asked and shook her curls.

Shayla happily accepted the invitation to inspect

the tresses. She took a few strands between her fingers and gently tugged. She wanted to continue to run her fingers through the soft locks but was afraid of how her body, and friend would react. "I think it really suits you. It looks fun and free and very easy to take care of."

Bailey's face lit up at the compliment and Shayla couldn't help but return the smile. "I'm glad you like it, but I think I'll miss my long hair. It wasn't even this short when I had to cut it for boot camp. But then again I could never braid my own hair like you can," Bailey said and tugged on Shayla's thick braid.

"I'm assuming you came over for coffee?" Dion said. The banter was shattered and Shayla turned away from her friend. A tiny smile played at the corner of the older woman's lips and Shayla wondered what it was about, possibly something Bailey had told her before she arrived.

"I'm sorry, yes, that would be lovely." When Dion left, Shayla turned to look at Bailey. She couldn't get enough of her friend.

Dion left for only a moment and quickly returned with a large cardboard cup. "Did Ivy want anything?" Dion asked. Again she forced Shayla to look away from Bailey.

"No, but I was thinking since she's been a huge help with inventory I need two cookies to go. She sure can't get enough of your sweets."

"Sure. I think she's one of our most loyal customers," Dion said and went to the glass case.

"So when do you interview for the position?" Dion asked Bailey.

"What position?" Shayla asked and turned to her friend.

"Oh, some management position that just came open at my job. But I don't know if I'm even going to apply. I went into the office and talked to my boss about what would be needed of me if I took the position. Right now I don't think I'm in the right state of mind to take on more responsibility," Bailey said.

"Oh, I think you would be surprised at what you could handle," Shayla said.

"Yeah, well, it's something I'll really have to think about. It won't be an easy decision. And that's even if I'm offered the position." Bailey took a sip of her coffee and moaned with appreciation. "This is really good."

"Well, I would hire you," Shayla said and couldn't stop the blush when she heard the sound coming from her friend.

"Thanks, if I need a second job I know where to go." Bailey lifted her cup and smiled.

"Hey Shayla, when's your next date with Dana?" Mac asked as she emerged from the back with two fresh pots of coffee.

"Oh, we have a date tomorrow night. I can't wait. I think the plan is a movie, then coffee. I can't wait to just sit and get to know her better. I mean, I would have passed on the movie but it's what she wants to do," Shayla said. She felt a little out of sorts. For the past few days, Dana had been the top thing that captivated her mind, but not once since she stepped foot into the bakery had Dana been a thought. She felt a bit guilty. Yes, it was only a second date but that was more dates then she had ever been on with anybody. She didn't know where the whole thing was going, but from where she stood, it was heading in the right direction.

"I've seen Dana around. You're lucky you caught her on a good night. By what I've seen of her, she normally has a flock of women surrounding her. Plus she isn't that bad on the eyes," Mac said while she straightened the display case.

"I agree. She's extremely sexy. Plus really courteous. She opens the car door for me, and holds the door open. I'm really looking forward to getting to know her better. So far I've no complaints," Shayla said, every word adding to her guilt.

"Hey Shayla, I actually came down to ask if you could come over to dinner sometime this week?" Bailey pulled Shayla away from her conversation with Mac.

"Sure. How about Thursday night? I can be over around eight," Shayla said.

"Eight. Thursday. Perfect. Well, ladies, I hate to leave but I need to get home. I'll talk to you later and see you in a few days," Bailey said. She was out the door to a symphony of goodbyes.

"Wow, she really looks hot with that new haircut and wardrobe," Mac said as she leaned against the display. Her hands played with a dishtowel that smelled of bleach.

"Yeah, she does," Shayla agreed, but then again she had always thought Bailey was attractive. Her friend had never tried to stand out and the new wardrobe was totally opposite of anything she had ever worn. It seemed to her that Bailey had always dressed to hide her beauty. Now that she was actually concerned with her looks, Shayla couldn't help but take notice. A little over a week ago, she had fallen into the arms of someone whom she thought was the perfect woman, but seeing her stunningly beautiful friend walk out the door, she now wasn't sure. For years, Shayla had always held on to the certainty that Bailey had been the other side to her coin, but when Dana entered her life, she dropped that belief. It took years of Bailey's absence for her to give up and move on. Now that she had come back into her life, she wasn't so sure she really wanted to give up on her. But she had to at least give Dana a chance.

Chapter Ten

It had only been a day since Bailey had surprised the gang at the bakery with her transformation. Her stomach had still not settled from having to listen to Shayla go on about Dana. She would rather drive cross-country with a hemorrhoid flare-up then have to listen to another word about Dana. The time on her computer had only moved five minutes. Her sister had called her on her way home from the doctor's. She would have gone with her but she had a meeting she couldn't get out of. Plus she was going to the doctor's in two days for Morgan's first check-up. She tapped the keys, trying to get the code onto the screen but she was too worked up. The minutes ticked away as she waited for the front door to open and the frustration of Shayla and Dana had stopped all of her creative juices. Her boss had started calling for daily updates but she had nothing to show for it. He had threatened to make her go into the office if she didn't have anything by the end of the week. And that was only two days away.

She heard the front door and she bolted from her room with Buddy on her heels. Morgan didn't bother to remove her heavy coat or scarf when she closed the door. She leaned heavily on the door. From the top of the stairs, Bailey knew the news was not good. Her feet thundered down the stairs as she hurried to get to her sister. Strong arms pulled Morgan away from the door into a tight embrace. No words were needed as Morgan broke down in her arms. Minutes ticked by while the sisters held on to each other. When Morgan's tears dried, she pulled away and shed her coat and scarf. Bailey took them from her and hung them in the hall closet before she followed Morgan into the living room.

"I don't even need to ask, but what did the doctor say?" Bailey asked and took her sister's shaking hand in hers.

"It's back." Morgan's voice cracked on the two words.

"What are our options?" Bailey asked. She hoped that her words let her sister know she would be there for anything.

"It's in the early stages. That's a good thing. The obvious option was to abort the baby and attack it, but I worked too hard to get pregnant and I'm not giving up the baby. The second option is to remove the infected tissue and have small doses of chemo. I'm sure there are other options out there and I'll discuss them with my oncologist next week." Morgan's head fell back and tears again slid down her face into her hair.

"Well, I think the best odds would be to abort and attack. You can always get pregnant some other time," Bailey said. She reached over and pulled her sister into her lap. Tender fingers played with her hair. It was something she had always done when they were younger and her sister had nightmares. Now that the boogie man was ravaging her sister's body, she didn't know how she could help, but right now she would do everything in her power to support her.

"I told him and I'm going to tell you it's not an

option. I think the most aggressive thing I'm willing to do is have a mastectomy. I did some research while waiting for the results and it says that aborting the baby doesn't improve the chances of me surviving this. The only thing it will allow is radiation and I'm willing to wait. The doctor said I have a few days to decide. So I'm going to take every minute and then make my choice. I don't want to do anything too hasty," Morgan said. Her hands rested on her stomach.

Bailey respected her sister's decision and would be there for her no matter what she chose. "Well, I bought take out and it's in the oven. Do you think you are ready for dinner?" Bailey asked as her hands stalled in her sister's hair.

"I'm not really hungry right now." Morgan nudged Bailey with her shoulder. Bailey continued to run her fingers through her hair.

"I understand but you have to keep up your strength. At least a few bites then you're free to do whatever you want."

"Fine. The news had worn me out anyway. I think I'm going to turn in early," Morgan said and pushed herself off the couch. "Thanks for being here for me."

"Always."

Bailey shoved the casserole in the oven and slammed the door. After a few swigs of her now warm beer, she wandered into the living room. She found Morgan with her feet up, grading papers and lazily running her fingers through Buddy's shaggy hair. A smile appeared on her face. The week had been hard on both of them, but it seemed like Morgan was back to her normal self. It surprised Bailey that Morgan could bounce back quicker than a rubber band.

"Hey, can I get you something to drink, maybe a hot tea? I could even help you grade those papers you know," Bailey offered and leaned against the hall wall.

Morgan let the papers fall to her lap. Bailey watched her sister's head fall back on the couch. The long sigh that followed made her cringe.

"Will you stop? I'm perfectly fine to grade these papers. If I want something to drink, I'll get it. I'm fine, just like I've told you the last hundred times you've come out and asked me," Morgan said, her feet hitting the hardwood floor. Buddy jumped off the couch and scurried around the couch before disappearing down the hall.

Bailey ran her fingers through her short hair, a new habit she had picked up in the last few days. "I'm sorry. I just want to help."

Morgan softened her tone. "I know you're trying, and if I want or need anything I'll ask. I promise. I'm not an invalid," Morgan said. Her eyes focused on the ceiling as if it contained all the answers to the mysteries of the world. It hadn't been the first time she had snapped at her sister since they had found out about the cancer.

"It's just after the appointment when I heard that little heart beat it hit me how real this is. I realized the only way I could help that little person inside you was to help you," Bailey said, her hands returning to her hair.

"I know." Morgan laid a hand over her mid-section. There was no visible bulge yet but a comforting hand circled her stomach. "I'm just frustrated. It's not your fault. I guess I've realized I probably won't be able to finish the school year. I hate that I have to tell my kids I won't be able to continue being their teacher. It's taken me this long to get them to trust me and now I have to hand them off. I also called and verified my appointment with the oncologist to go over all treatment options."

"Do you want me to go with you to that appointment too?" Bailey pushed off the wall and sat next to her sister.

"No, I think I'll be ok. I know we talked about the few options but I'll have to make a decision then. I have to think about what's best for me and this little bean here. Plus you have to finish your writing. It won't write itself. As you've always said."

"I know, but you're more important." Bailey wrapped her arm around Morgan.

"But your job depends on it. I know your boss has been breathing down your neck. You have to have something to show him by tomorrow. And I'm not going anywhere. Now, how is dinner coming?" Morgan asked and pulled herself out of her sister's embrace.

Before Bailey could respond, there was a knock at the door. Buddy shot like a rocket from his hiding place in an attempt to beat Bailey to the door.

"Someday, little man, I'll be standing here when someone knocks and you'll finally have to concede." Bailey could have sworn she heard Buddy scoff at her before heading back to the warm lap that he had vacated earlier.

Shayla stood on the stoop. Her body continued

to shiver as the cold night air assaulted her. The coat she wore did nothing to protect her from the frigid elements. Only seconds had passed as she walked from the car to the house, but she already missed the warmth of her heated Honda. A gush of hot air engulfed her when the front door was opened.

"Come in," Bailey said and stepped aside.

Shayla hurried in, and couldn't help but stare at Bailey. The short hair had totally transformed her and she couldn't get over how different her friend looked. Shayla again felt a pull to run her fingers through the short curls.

"Here, let me take your coat," Bailey said and relieved Shayla of her heavy down jacket.

"Wow, it's getting really cold. I think it's even too cold to snow. It feels like my toes have turned into popsicles just from the short walk from my car." Shayla stomped her feet on the carpet.

"Dinner should be ready shortly but can I get you some coffee or maybe a hot tea to help warm you up?" Bailey asked as she hung up her coat.

"Tea would be lovely. Decaf if you have it. I've been having problems sleeping lately and I'm trying to cut out caffeine after five." Shayla didn't add that she hadn't been sleeping well because of the erotic dreams she had been having. They would start out with her and Dana on a date that ended back at her apartment. Once she had finally shed all of Dana's clothes and looked into blue eyes, they turned out to be Bailey's. Even in her dreams when Bailey's lips touched hers she felt a flutter in her stomach that Dana had yet to be able to create. When she would wake up, she would be more confused and frustrated than ever. When those nights happened, she would pick up a book and wait for dawn to arrive. She had yet to sleep through the night since Monday.

"Good idea," Bailey shouted from down the hall as she hung up Shayla's coat. "I'll be back with your tea in a few minutes."

Shayla sat on the couch beside Buddy and joined Morgan in giving him love. "Is everything all right with Bailey?"

"Oh, don't worry about her. She has a few things she needs to work through. But how about you? I heard you had date number two last night. Was it as good as the last one? Why don't you tell me about it while we set the table?" Morgan asked. She set her papers aside to stand up. Buddy shot off the couch and disappeared down the hall, probably in search of a few treats.

The plates and silverware were already on the table. They began to set out the dishes before Shayla started her story. "It was wonderful. I couldn't have thought of anything better. She showed up with a bouquet of flowers; they were simple but thoughtful. We then went to a movie. It wasn't what I would've chosen. But I got to spend the whole two hours snuggled into her arms and that made up for her poor choice. We held hands through the whole movie. Then we ended the night at a small coffee shop and just talked. We talked for hours about anything and everything. It was nice just getting to know her." Shayla set down last dish. She pulled out a chair to get comfortable before continuing her story.

Bailey had put the teakettle on before she checked dinner. She couldn't help but overhear the conversation taking place in the next room. Disgusted by the topic and losing her appetite, she whistled for Buddy before opening the back door. With a beer in hand, she followed him into the cold night with the wish that the freezing temperature would wake her from the nightmare she was currently living.

During her time in the Navy, she had lived in five different ports, and not one felt like home. Every place felt empty. The only time in the past ten years that she had felt whole was when she was with Shayla. The more she listened to her prattle on about her new girlfriend, the more Bailey felt like a stranger in her own home. Buddy ran up to her and put his wet nose against her cold hand. She reached out and ran her numb fingers through his thick coat, smiling down as his tail moved a mile a minute.

"Hey, dinner's ready," Morgan said as she popped her head out the door, allowing Buddy to scurry into the warm embrace of the house.

"I'll be in there in a minute," Bailey said.

"Ok. I'll put everything on the table."

"No, just wait. I'll get it," Bailey barked.

"Bailey," Morgan warned.

"Please, just humor me," Bailey pleaded and turned to look at her sister.

Morgan simply nodded and left her alone. In two gulps, she finished her beer. On cold limbs, she trudged back into the warm house. The kettle screeched and she retrieved two mugs from the cupboard and placed the tea bags in the cups before filling them with steaming water. She entered the dining room to find Morgan and Shayla still at the table talking about books. Now she could handle this subject. She attempted to add what she could about the new book they were reading for the book club. Both Morgan and Shayla had already finished the book and Bailey was barely half way through it. She allowed them to continue their conversation and went to get the meal. A large salad was placed on the table along with three types of salad dressings, and the gooey casserole. Bailey had followed the instructions Morgan had given her and hoped it was at least edible.

"Well, dig in. I hope it's ok," Bailey said and dished herself a large helping of salad, just to be on the safe side.

"I'm sure it's fine," Morgan said. She took two large scoops of the cheesy chicken bake.

Bailey took her own large scoop. Relief washed over her when she found the casserole tasted better than it looked.

"It all looks wonderful." Shayla placed a large helping of salad and pasta on her own plate.

Morgan and Bailey had agreed earlier not to tell Shayla until after the meal. Morgan was able to keep the meal light by regaling their guest with stories about the cute things her students had done the previous week. The women laughed and joked until Bailey took the last dish into the kitchen to soak. She put on another pot of water to boil for more tea. She wanted to go back into the living room and spend more time with Shayla but needed a few minutes to prepare herself for what she was about to tell her friend. Her sister was so much stronger than she was. She admired her strength and courage. It puzzled her where she had acquired that trait. It surely did not run in their family. If the past was any clue, they were full of women who did nothing but run from their troubles. The whistle pierced her thoughts and brought her back to reality.

Again she filled the cups with fresh tea bags and grabbed another cold beer for herself before making her way back to the living room.

Morgan sat in the loveseat across from Shayla. The conversation between the two women went on like a tennis match. Bailey waited patiently before she could jump in. Morgan paused to take a sip of her cooling tea and she knew it was now or never.

"Shayla. I want to thank you for coming over tonight and I'm sorry to say it wasn't just to experience my culinary skills, or lack thereof. We have something we need to tell you," Bailey said. She looked at her sister, silently pleading for Morgan to take over.

Shayla looked at one sister then the other. Quiet minutes passed before Morgan took a deep breath and finally started.

"I'm pregnant," she said.

Not the bit of news Bailey had expected first, but she understood why she started with the good first. It was probably better to butter Shayla up before they had to tell her the bad.

Bailey jumped as Shayla squealed and lunged for Morgan. She squeezed her tight.

"Oh my god. I'm so excited for you." Shayla looked at Bailey. "Is this why you stopped by my apartment the other day? Why didn't you tell me then? This is so exciting."

It hurt Bailey to know that in a moment a few words would shatter this happy moment. "I didn't tell you because that's only part of the news. There's more."

Shayla turned again to Morgan. "What? What's wrong? Is it the baby?" She asked and placed her hands on Morgan's belly.

If Bailey had not already been head over heels in love with Shayla, she would have been at that moment. That one little action of trying to protect her sister's baby made her want Shayla all the more. It also let Bailey know that if she was forced to raise this baby then she would have someone close willing to help her. There was no doubt in her mind she would be able to lean on Shayla for support. Even if it meant she had to accept her new girlfriend.

"No, the baby's fine," Morgan said.

"As far as we know," Bailey added.

"Then what? What's wrong?" Shayla asked.

Bailey watched her sister take a few deep breaths. She would have jumped in and said something, but she let her continue since she would have to get used to saying the words. She would have to tell many more people and Bailey couldn't be there for her every time she would have to utter the words.

"The cancer returned." Morgan finally got it out. One simple sentence. Three little words but together they had a mammoth meaning.

"No," Shayla said before looked to Bailey. The tears that hung in Bailey's eyes confirmed Morgan's words.

"How did this happen? You were in remission. Your last checkup came back clean. How is this possible?" Shayla asked, her hands never leaving Morgan's stomach.

"They missed something. It happens," Morgan said.

Bailey watched as a calmness returned to her sister and again admired her strength. The only signal Morgan gave of her predicament was the constant rubbing of her belly.

"No. No, dammit, they should be more diligent, that's why you go back as often as you do, so this doesn't happen." Shayla stood and started to pace the room. "This can't be. They must be wrong."

"They did more than one test," Morgan said, her eyes following Shayla.

"I can't believe this. It's not right. It's not fair." Shayla walked the room. Two pairs of eyes watched her every step, allowing her time to come to terms with the news. "This is bullshit! We've been through this. It's not fair we have to go through this again."

Bailey watched the woman she loved talk out her frustrations. She had appreciated the fact that Shayla had stepped into her shoes and helped her family the first time. She had helped both Morgan and her grandmother when neither were able to help themselves. She had taken Morgan to her radiation appointments, waited with her before taking her home, and made sure she was ok. Sometimes she even stayed the night when Morgan was going through a difficult spell. Bailey knew it had cost her money since she had to hire a second part time worker to cover her lost shifts. Bailey felt worse the more Shayla paced. It dawned on her that she had never thanked her for all she had done.

A few minutes later, Shayla sat down and took Morgan's hands in hers.

"What's the plan? What are we going to do to beat this? What about the baby? Is the baby ok?" Shayla asked.

Again Bailey felt lower then slime. When she found out about the cancer, her first thought was to abort the baby. Shayla's initial reaction was to protect them both. Bailey knew Shayla was a good person, but she had never known how wonderful she truly was until that moment.

"Well, as of now, nothing," Morgan said.

"Nothing?"

"Yes, nothing. I have another appointment with my oncologist this week and we'll go over all our options then. As of right now, I know radiation is out of the question. It messes too much with my system, plus I can't do that pregnant. There's the option of trying to take out the infected area and maybe a low dosage of chemo to halt the growth, but until I know how it will affect my unborn child, I'm choosing to do nothing. It's only a stage one so I have a little time to decide," Morgan said calmly while her hands continued to play on her flat stomach.

The only sign of Bailey's frustration was her constantly bouncing knee. Bailey sat silently as her sister talked about her future. But she had been doing a little research of her own. All of the options were viable, but she knew that if they did not attack the cancer with force then her sister's chances of success dwindled. She spent the bulk of her days on the computer, and after she heard about the cancer coming back, a major portion of that time was spent doing research, even going as far as looking into homeopathic options.

"It's your body and I'll agree with anything you decide. I might not like what you choose either, but I won't fight you. I'll be here for you any way I can," Shayla said. She turned and pinned Bailey with eyes also holding back unshed tears. "And if you need anything, please let me know."

Bailey wanted to go to her friend and hug her, and hold her tight, and tell her everything would be ok.

But she didn't trust herself touching her. Her dreams and the kiss they had shared still consumed her in a way she didn't like, and she didn't think touching would have helped the situation. She knew if she took Shayla in her arms, she would never want to let her go.

"Thank you, that means a lot. Can I get you more tea?" Bailey asked, sure their tea had gone cold. She had to do something to escape the room. Her emotions were too close to spilling over and she didn't want to break down in front of the two women in the room. She knew she would spend another long night silently crying into her pillow. She had to at least appear strong even though she was dying inside.

Shayla shook her head. Wild hairs escaped from her braid. "No, thank you. I should be heading home. We all have to get up early for work tomorrow and we need to get some rest."

Bailey retrieved Shayla's coat from the closet and allowed the two women on the couch to finish their hug. She waited for Shayla at the door. Before she could open it, she found herself pulled into a tight embrace.

"It will be ok. I promise we'll get through this," Shayla whispered in Bailey's, ear causing the woman to shiver.

Bailey wanted to melt into the embrace but reluctantly pulled away.

Shayla slipped into her coat and gave a quick wave before she disappeared into the unfriendly night. One last honk of the car and Shayla was gone.

"That was hard." Bailey leaned against the door to watch the red lights fade into the darkness.

"It was. I hate to do this but do you think you could tell the ladies at the bakery and Wanda? I know

I'm going to have to tell a lot more people, but I would appreciate if you told them for me. I know Shayla won't tell anybody and you've become just as close to them as I have."

"Of course," Bailey said. Tomorrow she would probably be able to get them all together at once and tell them, but her sister would have a harder time telling her co-workers. Even that will be a cakewalk compared to when she would have to face the bright smiling faces of her third grade class and tell them that she will have to leave and may not return.

"I think I'm going to go write a bit," Bailey said, frustrated that she still needed to get the assignment done. In the coming months, she would have little precious time of her own as she took on more responsibilities at the house.

"Ok. I'm going to take Shayla's advice and get some sleep. I don't know how much longer my energy is going to last and I don't want to crash and burn. I might as well start taking care of myself now," Morgan said and made her way to the stairs.

"Good night. Oh and maybe tomorrow, we can talk about our dietary changes. I know there are certain things you can't eat or drink while pregnant so we'll have to make some modifications around here." Bailey sat back in the lounge chair before dragging out her laptop. A few silent moments passed before she continued her latest project. The stark white screen and blinking cursor continued to taunt her and as her fingers hovered over the keys. She knew something was going to have to give. Her life was getting too hectic and it was going to get worse before it got better. Soon she would have to start letting things go.

Chapter Eleven

A week later Bailey entered the bakery dressed in her old jeans and tee. Work had kept her busy and she hadn't been able to get to the café as soon as she would have liked.

"Hey, haven't seen you in a while." Dion waved from behind the counter. "Where have you been?"

"It's been a busy week. I haven't been hiding or anything, I had a pressing assignment I needed to finish. I kept putting it off and it just got out of control. I had to buckle down and get it done," Bailey said. A coffee was waiting at the counter when she reached it. "Thanks. I needed this. I can't seem to make a decent cup at home. It's like drinking sludge. So how's Connie doing?"

"Oh same ol' same ol. Not much changes around here. And I wasn't accusing you of hiding. I was just wondering what you had been up to," Dion said.

"Sorry, just a bit touchy lately." Bailey gulped the pleasant brew, trying to gather her strength to tell her friends about the turmoil that had become her life. She knew she had offended one of her friends but her nerves were getting to her. Everyday Morgan continued to pester her about telling their friends. When she had to reply in the negative, it felt like she was letting her sister down. This morning she woke realizing she couldn't take the disappointment in her sister's eyes one more day.

"Hey, has Wanda been in today?" Bailey asked. She hoped that she would be able to tell everybody at once. Wanda tended to only go into the bakery one time a day and if she missed her then her hopes of a one and done would be shot.

"Nope, but I suspect she'll be in any minute," Dion said as her restless hands continued play with the pastry rack. Bailey watched the older woman straighten the pastries a few minutes after she had just rearranged them. There was another piece of business she needed to take care of before she left the building.

"Hey, do you mind if I borrow Sandy for a few minutes? I need to talk to her about something," Bailey asked. She was tired of hearing how wonderful Dana was. It had been a few weeks since she asked Sandy to get the dirt on the supposedly wonderful woman. She had yet to get an update and was curious if Sandy had found out anything. She was truly torn at what she wanted to hear from her little spy. The only thing she hoped was that in the end her friend would not get hurt.

"Sure. SANDY!" Dion hollered. Bailey laughed, knowing she didn't have to shout. The bakery wasn't large by any stretch, but it got the job done. Seconds later Sandy emerged from the back. White powder streaked her flush cheeks.

"You bellowed?" Sandy asked, hunched over, dragging her foot.

Both Dion and Bailey couldn't help but laugh.

"Yeah, this customer would like to talk to you," she said.

"How can I help?" Sandy asked and rubbed her nose. When her hand moved from her face, Bailey smirked at the flour it had left behind.

"I was wondering if you have a few minutes so we can talk a bit," Bailey asked. She reached up and, using her thumb, removed the evidence of Sandy's work.

Sandy looked to her boss. Dion nodded her head before she made her way to the back of the store to give the women some privacy.

Even though the store was empty, Bailey made her way to the booth at the front of the store away from any ears that might be eavesdropping from the back.

"So have you heard anything about Dana? It's been a few weeks. I figured it's been a while. Well, enough time to actually get some new information," Bailey asked before the younger woman was even seated in the booth.

"Well, I haven't been to any parties or the club a lot lately. I haven't actually seen her since that night, but I've been able to ask a few mutual friends about her. I had to lie a bit. I said I was interested in asking her out. They must have bought it. Most of the people I talked to say she's ok and pretty nice. She can't be all bad, they say she's a very giving person, at least to them. She picks up the tab a lot if she goes out. But I find it hard to believe when nobody can tell me what she does for a living. It seems she is continuously between jobs, but then again she does still live with her parents. One thing she does is she brags a lot about the women she's with. She likes to think she's a stud and can get anybody. And by the way her friends talk, she usually does. I tried to get more details but when I dug a bit deeper, they seemed to shut down. I know it's not much but I hope that helps," Sandy said. Her hands straightened the condiments on the table.

"It does. It's more than I knew a few minutes ago. Thanks," Bailey said, letting Sandy escape the table to get back to work.

Bailey hadn't seen Mac cleaning table next to them, but as soon as Sandy exited the booth, Mac filled it. "Hey."

"Hey, what's up?" Bailey asked, again taking a sip of her coffee.

"I couldn't help but overhear what Sandy had told you. She had told me what you asked of her that night at the club. I decided to do some snooping of my own because, like you, I think Dana is not what she appears. I mean, seriously, someone who looks and acts like her should already have a girlfriend. I think you might be interested in what I found out though," Mac said, leaning across the table.

"Why do you think I think that?" Bailey asked and mirrored Mac's position.

"Because, you wouldn't have asked Sandy to find out more about her if you didn't have questions about her."

Bailey couldn't dispute her logic and didn't. The truth was a little more in-depth than that but she allowed the young woman to believe what she wanted. Her only response was a simple nod.

"Let's just say I wouldn't trust anything those people told Sandy. They're going to blow smoke up her ass. They'll say anything to put Dana in a good light. I mean, why would they say anything against her, she's their friend. I went to the people who could tell me the real story, her exes. Well, I didn't go searching for her exes. I just happened to stumble into one."

"What'd you find out?" Bailey said, impressed by the woman seated across from her. The more she hung out with the two young women of the group, the more she realized they were more than they appeared to be. Bailey realized Mac was an extremely intelligent woman and not just a flighty young girl as she initially thought. And Sandy may appear gruff and intimidating on the outside but on the inside, she was extremely kind and giving.

"I don't know the woman or her story, but I was in the bathroom at the club and I overheard two women talking about Dana. So I asked what was up with her. They were more than willing to tell me what she was really like. Believe me, it wasn't pretty. I think they thought I was interested in her, because the first thing they told me was to stay away. They said she's a lazy slob who lives at home not because she wants to but because she has to. She can't seem to keep a job. And if she does get with someone, and they don't watch out, she will mooch off them till she sucks them dry. They basically called her a parasite. One woman said she heard the same thing from a few of her other exes and didn't believe it until it happened to her. The worst thing that the lady said was if there is nothing she can gain from the women, she's a fuck'm and chuck'm type of gal. It seems she's willing to say and do anything she can to get into someone's bed. Dana seems to think that it's her sexual prowess that keeps the ladies. But her ex said she was actually a lousy lay and worse kisser. They had been drawn in by her looks and chivalrous ways too. Basically they said she was toxic."

Bailey's initial reaction was to bolt next door and tell Shayla everything Mac said. It took all she had to remain in her seat. This news was something that could sway Shayla away from Dana. Excitement coursed through her but she didn't want to jump to any conclusions. It was only fair to give Sandy some time to find out anything else. Initially she wanted to believe the woman from the bathroom, but she didn't know if the horrible things were because the woman was a jilted ex and wanted revenge. She didn't want to unwillingly hurt her best friend and possibly ruin something that had the potential to be her real life Romeo and Juliet. Hopefully minus the death. Plus she didn't want to hurt a friendship that she had just started to rebuild with her friend. Their bond was still on shaky ground. It had taken a long time to get back to where they were because her cowardly actions. It had been a knee jerk reaction back then to run and she didn't want to jump too soon now either.

"Thank you, Mac. That helps," Bailey said.

"Glad I can be of some assistance. I just want Shayla to be happy. I want her to find her true love and not someone who's going to wine and dine her then leave. She deserves her storybook ending. We all do," Mac said. Her eyes spoke to her own hidden secrets as she glanced at Sandy. Bailey knew eyes could tell secrets that mouths kept quiet. Hopefully she could get this younger woman to speak up and confide in her.

"You need to start reading something other than romances," Bailey joked, trying to ease into the conversation.

"Why? I believe we all have someone out there for us." Mac again looked at Sandy before continuing. "I just want to be able to see someone happy, like Dion and Connie."

"I do too," Bailey said. "Look, if you ever need someone to talk to, you know just a friendly ear. I'm here for you."

Mac looked away and nodded. "Thank you. I'll keep that in mind. I should get back to work," she said before she hurried into the back of the store.

Bailey leaned back into the booth. Her mind raced with the information the two women had told her. It was hard to weigh the news. One had nothing but good and the other side nothing but bad and neither came close to the other. With her warm coffee in hand, she mulled over her options and decided it was best to wait a little bit more before going to Shayla. She already had a lot on her plate and hoped that the relationship would fizzle out before she had to use any of the information.

It wasn't long before Wanda finally made her appearance and headed straight for the one person in the room who didn't work there.

"Where the hell have you been? And why haven't you been answering your phone?" Wanda asked and slid into the seat Mac had recently vacated.

Bailey tried to melt into the seat, afraid of the irate woman. "What are you talking about?"

"You haven't been around, and I've been trying to call and your phone goes directly to voicemail." A blood red manicured nail punctuated each word on the wooden table.

"Well, you haven't left a message or I would've called back." Bailey defended her decision to turn off her phone.

"I don't like leaving messages, it's too impersonal. Plus you would've seen the call come through as a missed call. You still could've called back." Wanda had a head of steam and Bailey needed to head her off.

"Well, I'm here now. Did you want something?" Bailey asked.

Wanda tilted her head. "What the hell did you do to your beautiful hair? When Dion said you cut it I didn't think she meant butchered it."

"That's what you wanted to ask me?"

"No, but now that I have, answer the question."

"I thought it was time for a change," Bailey simply stated.

"Oh. I think it's kind of cute. In a shaggy unkept sort of way," Wanda said. "Hmm, I wonder what I would look like with shorter hair."

"Wanda, you've had the same haircut since forever. Just because I didn't know you back then, didn't mean I didn't know of you," Bailey said.

"True. Plus I'm not sure how it would look on me. But it would be easier to take care of."

"You know there are computer programs that allow you to upload a head shot and it can give you any hairstyle. It's like you get to try it on before you actually cut your hair," Bailey said and took a pull from her cooled coffee, thankful the older woman had calmed down. Even though it was cold, it still tasted better than anything she had made in the past week. "Now what did you need me for?"

"Nothing really. I just hate being ignored."

Bailey couldn't help but laugh. It felt good to laugh. It was something she had not done in a while. Envy surged through her as she watched the women behind the glass counter go on with their day, ignorant to the turmoil that she had been living. She dreaded what she had to do next, but knew she couldn't put it off any longer.

"Can I have a moment of your time? But I need

to get everybody else together first. I have something to tell everybody and I don't want to have to repeat myself."

"Fine, but can you get me a coffee while you're up there?" Wanda asked before she removed her coat, draping it over the back of her chair.

"Sure."

"Hey Dion, can I get a coffee for the drama queen? And can I get you and the others to join us at the table? I have something important I need to tell everybody," Bailey said. She grabbed the fresh cups of coffee the woman offered. She appreciated the way the older woman always had a fresh cup waiting for her when she approached the counter.

"Sure, you go ahead and have a seat and I'll round up the crew and the coffee," Dion said and shooed Bailey away with the flick of her wrist.

Bailey returned to the table but didn't take a seat. Now that the time was here, her nerves would not allow her to calm down. As the women took their seats, she continued to pace in front of the booth. She hated giving speeches. Even though the women were friends, she still had to deliver bad news. Maybe instead of coffee she should have taken a shot of liquor. Quicker than she had hoped the women were seated around the table. Five sets of eyes watched her pace the small space. The women sat patiently waiting for her to say what she needed to say.

Finally she stopped in front of the small group. Bailey closed her eyes and took three calming breaths. She couldn't ignore the concern in the looks she was receiving.

"I just want to start by asking you to please let me get through this before you ask any questions.

First, I want to apologize now for not being around the past few weeks. A lot has been going on that you've been in the dark about. As you know, Morgan hasn't been feeling well. A few weeks back we went to the doctor's and we got some good news and bad news." In a split moment, Bailey followed Morgan's lead and started with the happy news. "The good news is she knows why she hasn't been feeling well. She's pregnant." Bailey expected the smiling faces, and even a few cheers. She waited for the chatter to settle down before she continued.

"Like I said we were given good news and bad news. The bad news is the cancer returned. She's lucky because they caught it early and it's only stage one, but still the pregnancy throws a wrench into treatment." Bailey again expected chatter. This time she was prepared and held up her hand to quell the barrage of questions. She hoped that the rest of her practiced speech would preempt any concerns that the women had. "As of now Morgan knows radiation is out of the question. Radiation is harmful to the baby and she absolutely will not do anything that could harm her unborn child. We still have many options and she is weighing each one before she makes a decision. But she's agreed on a small dosage of chemo. She talked to the oncologist and he said as long as she is well into her second trimester, as she is, the placenta will protect the baby. Right now she is even contemplating having a mastectomy to remove the infected area. They will closely monitor her and the baby. Also she's decided to try and finish out the current school year but we're not sure if that's actually feasible. Her job already knows and they're going to do everything they can to support her."

Bailey stood on shaking legs, waiting for the questions that didn't come. Soon she found herself crying in Connie's comforting embrace. Dion, Wanda, Mac, and Sandy sat stunned at the table. Silent tears streaked down the younger women's cheeks.

Wanda was the first of the small group to speak. "When your grandmother was weak we all made a promise to take care of you girls. That's what we're going to do. Right ladies?"

With tears in their eyes, Dion and Connie nodded.

"Yes, so you tell us what you need and we'll make it happen," Wanda said. Her face was the picture of grim determination, as tears hung to her long lashes.

"Right now, all we need is your support. We're both still in shock. Morgan is so strong. I don't know where it comes from. I'm a total mess. I find myself breaking down at odd times during the day. I actually think this has hit me harder than her."

"Of course it's hit you hard, dear. You're going through this for the first time. Morgan's been through this before and come out on the other side just fine. She knows what to do. You'll be fine. All you need to know is that you need to be there for her. To champion her good days and pick her up when she's down. And when you're down we'll be there to pick you up." Connie again engulfed Bailey in her arms.

"I don't know how I can ever thank you enough," Bailey cried into Connie's soothing embrace.

"We don't need thanks. Just your being in our life is all we need. You don't realize how much happiness you bring us. We'll get through this. You'll see," Dion said, her own voice cracking.

Bailey was thankful for the support that

surrounded her and Morgan. They had a great team behind them. She knew with all the backing they had they would make it through this.

Chapter Twelve

Ten women browsed the stuffed shelves while patiently awaiting the start of January's book club. The bakery group and Wanda were the last to arrive. They hurried over as soon as the store closed, weighed down with pastries and carafes of coffee and tea. Bailey was relieved when the troop wandered through the door so she wouldn't have to continue to watch Shayla and Dana cuddle on the couch. The bookstore didn't have any unused space as Bailey unfolded the last chair and settled in. Pastries and coffee were balanced precariously on knees as the group of women waited for Shayla to start.

Bailey sat sandwiched between her sister who was comfortably encased in an overstuffed chair and Wanda who couldn't sit still on her own folding metal chair. As she sat between the two women, she was befuddled as to why two straight women would attend a book club that only read lesbian novels. They were the only non-lesbians seated in the store. Bailey knew Shayla had more than one book club and Morgan attended them all, as did Wanda. It would seem that they already had enough to read without adding a lesbian love story to the list.

"Ok, let's get started." Shayla's voice pulled Bailey from her thoughts. From her corner of the couch, she leaned into Dana, who was perched on the arm, and began. "Does anybody have any comments on the recent book?"

"I do. Why the hell do we have to keep reading romance novels? Can't we read something with a little more action to it?" Mac asked from her own hard chair. It was a price the women paid for being one of the last ones through the door. Well, Connie and Dion had soft chairs but the women had decided since they provided the refreshments they should be allowed some comfort.

"Something about this book specifically, and I promise the next book will have more action," Shayla said. Her hand ran over Dana's jean-clad knee.

Bailey couldn't take her eyes off the way Dana's hands lazily caressed Shayla's hair, or how Shayla leaned into the touch.

"Ok, I'll start. I have to say I enjoyed the way the author didn't follow a standard pattern that a lot of lesbian authors do. The main characters didn't meet and bam, instantaneous love. It was more like a slow burn. Then when they did finally come together, I could feel it. I could feel every emotion each woman felt. I mean, I have nothing against love at first sight," Shayla paused and looked at Dana.

Bailey couldn't continue to watch the two women. When she finally forced herself to look somewhere else, she noticed Amanda watching her from three seats down. A small smile appeared on the other woman's lips before she looked away. Bailey continued to watch the young woman but her eyes remained focused on her flaky pastry.

"I thought it was a good book," Connie said, "But I do have some issues with it. Nothing major but one issue I have with this book and a few we have read in the past. And I don't know if the author does it on purpose, but I hate forced drama and tension. It didn't feel right. I mean, Shannon thought she saw Stevie kiss another girl. Instead of talking to the woman she had been dating for six months, she runs away. I mean come on. Don't people talk? It's something relationships are built on. I just hate that. It's so contrived. It makes me want to throw away the book. I would've believed it more had they talked about it and even had a fight over it. There could've been more emotion in a heated argument then someone running away."

Bailey felt like Connie was speaking right to her. The ability to speak up had never been one of her strong suits. Especially when she was younger. Her mother, and what she had put her and her sister through, had taught her actions speak louder than words. She had learned to do anything to protect herself. That was what she thought she had done when she had deserted Shayla all those years ago.

"I agree," Sandy said. "Sometimes people don't talk. Who knows what would happen if they just opened their mouths. I didn't like that about the book and it frustrated me beyond belief, but the author more than made up with all the hot steamy sex."

A few women around the group nodded and fanned themselves with their books. A few even blushed.

For the next hour, Bailey listened as the women went on about how well paced the book was, how they could identify with the characters, and character development. After the first half hour, Bailey started to tune out the women. Her attention kept going back to the couch as Shayla continued to touch her new girlfriend. With every minute that passed, she just wanted to get up and excuse herself, but leaving had never helped her in the past. She chose to be an adult and stick it out. Finally the group broke up and started to put the store back to its original state. Some women followed Shayla to the front to get their books for the next few groups while others mingled around the small store.

"Hey," Bailey heard before she felt the hand on her arm.

"Oh hey, Amanda, how are you?" Bailey said to the young attractive woman at her side.

"I'm good. I'm sorry I missed November's book club. I didn't realize it would be so long until we had another," she said.

"Yeah. Shayla thought there was just too much going on with the holidays and everything. So how were your holidays?" Bailey asked and reached for a few chairs.

"Ok, but lonely. How about you?" Amanda said.

"They could've been better," Bailey said. Her eyes continued to volley from Shayla, her sister, and the woman standing in front of her.

"So uh... I was wondering. I know you're not seeing anybody, and I was wondering if you would like to go out sometime." Her eyes were unable to meet Bailey's when the words passed her lips. A slight blush emerged on her cheeks.

Bailey caught sight of Dana at the counter with Shayla playing with her hands. The simple gesture answered the question for her.

"Sure, that sounds great." Bailey couldn't help but smile as the small woman practically glowed at her response.

"Here, let me just give you my number and we can make plans," Bailey said and made her way to the counter to get a piece of paper and pen.

"Shayla, do you have something to write on back there I can use?" Bailey asked when she reached the counter.

"Sure. Here you go," Shayla said and took some paper from the register tape. "What are you doing?"

"I'm giving Amanda my number so she can call me so we can make plans for a date," Bailey said. Bailey didn't know why she mentioned the date. It just rolled off her tongue.

"That's wonderful. Hey we should go out on a double this week. How does that sound?" Dana said.

Bailey watched Shayla for some sort of reaction but none was forthcoming. Shayla didn't comment as she helped the next customer purchase her book for the next club. Secretly Bailey had hoped Shayla would be jealous of her upcoming date, but her friend remained silent.

A double date didn't sound great to Bailey at all. It sounded more like torture and she started to decline when Amanda beat her to the punch. "That sounds great. How about Thursday night?"

"Works for me," Dana said and looked to Shayla for her answer.

"That's fine with me," Shayla said. She didn't say anything else as she helped the next customer with her large stack of books.

Amanda and Dana turned to Bailey to await her response.

"I'm free Thursday." Reluctantly Bailey agreed. She didn't want to say it sounded great, because it didn't. It sounded like an awful night and now she wasn't looking forward to it. She would prefer taking a roll in broken glass and then take a nap in salt then have to spend another evening with Shayla and Dana locked at the hip. She knew this was an opportunity to use her words, but again they failed her. Rather than make a scene, she would go along with the group and hope for the best. Her resolve to move on had bitten her in the ass and now she would have to prepare for a very uncomfortable evening.

Bailey paid for her and her sister's books and excused herself to find Morgan. She had looked forward to this night. She had hoped to get Shayla alone for a few moments, but it hadn't gone the way she wanted. Now all she craved to do was get home and crawl into bed, and hopefully wake up in the morning to try her luck for a better day.

Chapter Thirteen

Bailey had always hated doctor's appointments, but when Morgan asked her to go, she knew she would never deny her sister anything. The chair in the examining room was uncomfortable. She drummed her fingers on her jean-clad knee that continued to bounce. The three-month-old magazines didn't interest her in the least.

"Stop. You're making me nervous," Morgan said, perched on top of the table wearing nothing but a paper dress.

"Sorry, just nervous," Bailey admitted. She had missed the first sonogram because of a work meeting and was thankful she could attend the appointment, but hospitals in any capacity made her nervous since she had yet to receive any good news at one.

Bailey listened to her sister's heels hit the metal table over and over. It raked her nerves and she could say something like her sister did to her, but she wasn't the one freezing on a noisy padded table. Bailey watched as another shiver passed through her sister and wished they could turn the heat up. She never knew why hospital rooms had to be set to the temperature of a meat locker since they were only given a paper dress that was slit from top to bottom. No matter how hard they tried, they couldn't get the dress to close and Bailey had even draped her coat over her sister's legs to try to give her a smidgen of warmth.

"Well, don't be. You're not the one sitting up here in a paper dress with a bladder that feels full enough to fill an Olympic size pool. I hope they get here soon or I'm not going to make it," Morgan said.

There was a knock at the door and soon a tech was rolling in an ultrasound machine. Bailey retrieved her coat and sat down again, still unable to stop her knee.

"Ok, if we could just get you to lie back on the table," the nurse instructed and assisted Morgan as she got as comfortable as the table would allow.

Bailey continued to sit on the chair and waited for the machine to whirl to life. The tech pressed a few buttons, turned a few knobs, flipped a switch, and finally pulled out what she referred to as a wand.

"If you want to come over here, we're about ready to start." She motioned to Bailey.

Slowly Bailey shuffled to her sister's side. The nurse uncovered Morgan's belly and Bailey couldn't believe her sister was five months pregnant. Her eating habits had hardly changed. Bailey had tried to keep their meals healthy by adding more vegetables. She couldn't believe the change in her sister's body. Her belly was now round. It looked like it could have been a few extra pounds of padding but Bailey knew it was the baby making its existence known.

"Sorry, this is going to be a little cold. What this does is acts as a conductor to allow us to get good view of your little baby there." The tech squirted a liberal amount of gel on the metal wand before placing it on Morgan's exposed belly.

"Wow, that is cold," Morgan said.

The tech didn't respond as she moved the wand around her stomach. Silence permeated the air as three sets of eyes focused on the screen. Bailey had no idea what she was looking at. All she saw were grey globs in shades of black and white.

"There you are." The tech smiled at one of the blobs.

Bailey watched the screen and couldn't see anything but kidneys, a spleen, and intestines float around in a gray haze. Nothing looked any different from a second ago until the tech moved the wand just slightly and used her finger to show them what she had seen.

"You have a very active baby," the tech said.

Things were moving so fast Bailey didn't know what she was looking at until it happened. There was no mistaking the body that had rolled onto the monitor and just as quickly roll away. She looked down at her sister, whose gaze was fixed on the screen. Bailey had already heard the heart beat but now she could see the proof this was real. Morgan was really pregnant. The life that grew inside her body had finally shown itself and was playing peek-a-boo with the tech. As Bailey watched the little person flip and flop over the screen, her first thought was they might have to get this little one into gymnastics, and quick.

"She's beautiful," Bailey said to her sister. Tears appeared in her eyes. She couldn't believe that just a few weeks ago she had asked her sister to forgo the life that she watched bouncing across the monitor. Even though she couldn't hold her or touch her yet, she knew she was already falling in love with the little bean in her sister.

"She?" Morgan asked and looked away from the monitor for the first time.

"I don't know why I said that. I guess I just feel

like it's a she," Bailey said.

"Well, if this little one would calm down for just a few seconds I might be able to get the sex for you," the tech said and continued to chase the rascal around its very cramped living quarters. "But by what I can see, everything looks to be right on target. Development looks good."

Bailey squeezed her sister's hand. It felt good to finally get some good news.

"All done here. You can get dressed and the doctor will be in to see you in a few minutes. I'll make a DVD and some pictures for you to take home. They should be ready soon and the doctor will bring them to you," the tech said as she turned off the machine and wiped the jelly off Morgan's stomach.

"Do you think I could go to the bathroom first?" Morgan asked.

"Sure. I see no problem with that," the tech said as she pushed the machine out of the room.

"I'll be right back," Morgan said. She grabbed her clothes on her sprint out the door.

Bailey sat alone in the room and reveled in what she just saw. She would never have believed it if she hadn't seen it with her own eyes. Amazing didn't even begin to cover how she felt about seeing the little head, arms, legs. In only a few more months, she would be able to hold the little bundle in her hands. She had never thought she wanted a family until she saw the little person on the screen. She could now understand how her sister would do anything to protect that baby. Even if it meant giving up her own life. Alone in the examining room waiting for her sister to return, and the doctor to arrive, Bailey knew she would do anything and everything in her power to keep both of those lives alive. That baby was her niece, and she would protect it with everything she had.

The door opened and Morgan entered, followed closely by a beautiful woman in a lab coat.

"Look who I found on my way back," Morgan said.

Bailey stood and allowed Morgan to take the one available seat in the room.

"Doctor, you remember my sister Bailey?"

"Yes, it's nice to see you again," the doctor said. Bailey took the outstretched hand.

"Nice to see you again too," Bailey said. It took a few seconds before she was able to take her hand back. Bailey returned the attractive woman's smile. The doctor's golden hair was pulled off her strong shoulders by a large clip. Dark eyes exuded a confidence that intimidated Bailey. She had to force herself to look away.

"So Morgan, how are we feeling? Do you still have the morning sickness?" Dr. Hill asked Morgan and took a seat on the stool to examine the chart.

"Not really. It got bad there for a while, but for the past few days, nothing," Morgan said.

Bailey had been relieved when her sister had been able to go a few days without getting sick. It had been taking a toll on her sister and making her days and nights miserable and it hurt Bailey that she couldn't do anything to help but offer a few plain saltine crackers.

"Well, that's good to hear. Any other concerns?"

"Nope. Everything's good. I've been taking my prenatal along with the chemo, and I seem to be doing fine. I might get a bit tired earlier but other than that I'm good," Morgan said.

"Good, good. Well, I would like to see you again in another two weeks to run a few more tests, but everything looks great. I took a quick look at the video and the baby looks healthy. Very good heart beat and extremely active. Here's the video and also some pictures so you can show off your first baby pictures. I know you have your surgery coming up soon to have your breast removed. Once that's done we will make an appointment a few days after that just to check up on the baby," Dr. Hill said.

"Thanks." Morgan said. She stood and slipped on her jacket.

"You can make a follow up appointment with the receptionist on the way out. I believe we're all done here," Dr. Hill said. She turned to Bailey and smiled again. "It was a pleasure to see you again."

"You too, Doc," Bailey said before Dr. Hill exited the room.

"Well, well, well," Morgan said to Bailey as they approached the reception desk.

"What, and let me see those." Bailey held her hand out for the pictures.

"Dr. Hill never smiles at me like that," Morgan said.

"Well, maybe it's because she knows she won't soon be between my legs," Bailey said. A smile spread across her face as she looked at the little one on the picture.

"I'm thinking it's more like she wants to get in-between your legs, and not in a 'let's see how far you're dilated' way." Morgan bumped her shoulder against Bailey's.

Bailey tried to ignore the comment but the more she thought about it, she realized she wasn't opposed to the idea. There were only two major flaws. The first being she had her double date with Amanda that evening. That would be easy to get past. But being in love with someone else might put a damper on anything she started with the good doctor.

Since her senior year, she had gone on only a few dates. Every time she went home alone because she never felt anything. She knew even before she went on tonight's date that she wouldn't have any feelings for Amanda. Guilt surged through her. The date shouldn't have even been made. When she said yes, she knew it was wrong. Since she had started making decisions for herself, it felt like every one had been about survival and protection. But now she wanted more, but the more she thought about it, a partner didn't seem to fit into her future.

As she flipped through the photos, she realized if she couldn't have Shayla, maybe there was another girl who could consume the bulk of her life. Become her primary focus. Only one other person had been able to induce the same intense feeling of love Shayla had, and she was looking at her first picture right now.

"What, no witty come back?" Morgan asked when she finished making her next appointment.

"Nope. You know it's not too late for me to cancel the date tonight if you want. I mean if you want company, or just someone to help you with your work. I can do that."

Bailey stopped when Morgan paused in the doorway.

"Look. I don't want to sound mean or ungrateful because I am grateful for everything you've done for me, but you need to stop thinking you need to put your life on hold for me. I'm fine," Morgan said, her fingers running over her baby bump. "Really, I promise if I ever need anything, anything at all, I'll ask. I just want you to continue to live your life. I appreciate everything you're doing. I know it will get tougher before it gets better and that's when I'll need you the most. But right now I'm doing fine and I know you want to help. I thank you for that, but please just go and enjoy yourself, because soon you're not going to be able to. I'm going to need you to be there to help me, and believe me you're going to get tired of rubbing these feet in a few months." Morgan said.

Bailey smiled. "I look forward to the foot rubs, but only when you get your corns removed. Those things are nasty," Bailey said. She bumped her sister's shoulder as they made their way to the truck.

"Hey, I'm on my feet most of the time."

"You're going to change that right?"

"I know my limitations, and no, I won't push myself. I know how to take it easy. And since you won't be home tonight to cook can we pick up some Chinese on the way home?"

"Sure. I'll get extra so I can have some for lunch tomorrow," Bailey said and unlocked the truck. Each time she slid the key into the lock, she grew tired of the menial task. She loved the truck and would never get rid of it, but the thought of purchasing a new car crept into her mind.

"Moo shu pork here I come," Morgan crowed.

Only a few touches left and Shayla would be ready for her double date. She couldn't believe it when Dana had invited them to Amanda and Bailey's date.

At the time she didn't want to hurt her girlfriend by declining, but as the days passed she started to regret not speaking up. She wanted her friend to find happiness. The same type she had found, but her emotions were becoming more conflicted since the kiss they had shared. Often times she had caught herself looking at Bailey's lips, thinking about how they had felt pressed against hers. Feelings she had tried to suppress from high school would rush back. Unfortunately she had yet to capture that feeling with Dana, but she was having fun trying. Dana wasn't a bad kisser, as kissers go, but something was missing. When Bailey had kissed her, she felt something that started at her toes, slowly crept up her body, and exploded in her head. She never wanted the kiss to stop. Where they were exactly in their friendship Shayla didn't know, but she knew that she was happy every time Bailey was in her presence. Sometimes it even felt like she remembered from years past.

Bare feet slipped into black loafers. Shayla stood before the full-length mirror and admired her handy work. Her hair remained in its thick braid, and to save time she kept on her black rimmed glasses. The white blouse showed plenty of cleavage, but not too much, just enough to temp her date. The black slacks were ironed with a crisp crease down the front. As she put the second diamond stud ear ring on, she heard the knock at the door and raced to answer it.

Shayla answered the door and allowed her eyes to take in the beauty that was on her stoop. Dana looked almost edible. So far, every time she stood on her front porch she looked good. Not for the first time Shayla questioned her stupidity for not taking their relationship on to the next level. The sexual tension was high between them but she was still reluctant to move forward. Every date had been almost perfect. Dana had been more than eager to move the relationship forward, but every time they moved towards her bedroom, Shayla put on the brakes. As the weeks passed, Dana had become more insistent. Perfection began to wash away and masks were removed. Their relationship has started to change. On more than one occasion, Dana had reached out to her and asked to borrow money. Shayla had been happy to lend her the money, even her car on a couple of occasions. But as days passed, Shayla fought to find the person she met at the bar.

Shayla stepped aside and let Dana enter. As the younger woman passed, Shayla couldn't help but stare at her ass. It was practically flawless. She enjoyed running her hands over it when they made out. She looked up; she could only shrug when she realized she was caught staring. No words were necessary as it wasn't the first time she had been caught watching her ass. Dana's body was one of the things that kept Shayla in the relationship. She had never thought of herself as shallow but when she was seen on Dana's arm, she couldn't help but enjoy the looks other women threw her way.

"I bought you something." Dana pulled Shayla to her and gave her a sweet kiss.

"Was that it?" Shayla asked. Her fingers toyed with the buttons on Dana's shirt.

"No, but I wouldn't mind another," Dana said and kissed her again. "That was nice too. I know you've been helping me out lately by letting me borrow your car. I wanted to say thank you. I've noticed the necklace you wear is kind of old so I bought you this,"

Dana said and pulled out a jeweler's box from the pocket on her leather jacket.

"Oh, you didn't need to do that," Shayla said as she removed the top off the box. Inside, sitting on a cloud of cotton, was a small gold chain with a gold book pendant. "It's beautiful, thank you."

"Here, let me help you put it on," Dana said.

Shayla paused. She rarely took off the necklace Bailey gave her, and now she was reluctant too. To not insult her new girlfriend, she turned and pulled her hair to the side. The pendant fell below her slim throat. It felt odd. The metal was slightly heavier than she was used to. "Thank you."

Dana handed her Bailey's necklace. Shayla went into her room and set it on her nightstand. When she turned to exit the room, she found Dana leaning against the door jam, effectively blocking her exit. "How about we call and cancel dinner tonight? We could just stay in and enjoy each other's company."

Shayla was about to respond but was saved by the knock at the door.

"Too late," Shayla said. Dana moved aside as Shayla squeezed by.

Shayla hurried to answer the door. When she swung open the door, her jaw dropped. Before her stood one of the most stunning couples she had seen. Amanda clung to Bailey's arm. The young woman wore a sensible dress that went just past her knee. The plunging neckline enticed eyes to her ample cleavage. Shayla tore her eyes away and gazed at her best friend. Bailey again tempted Shayla by wearing black slacks, a purple button up shirt with the top two buttons undone. The cherry on top was a black tie that hung loose around her neck. The leather coat obviously was for looks and did nothing to stop the cold as she stood shivering on her doorway. It took another shiver from the young woman before Shayla came to her senses.

Bailey gritted her teeth to keep them from chattering as she stood on the step waiting for her friend to invite them in. She couldn't stand the cold and realized she should have rethought her outfit for the night.

"Are you going to let us in?" Bailey asked after another shiver racked her body.

"Oh, I'm so sorry, yes, please come in and warm up." Shayla pulled the two women inside.

"It's colder than I thought it would be," Bailey said. She started to rub her arms until she noticed Amanda start to shiver and pulled the younger woman to her. She wrapped her arms around her slim frame in the hopes her body heat would help warm her up.

"Yeah, we have another chance of a storm tonight," Dana said. She stood behind Shayla and pulled her close.

Bailey narrowed her eyes at the possessive move. It grated every nerve she had to see Shayla touched by another woman. She had weeks to get used to the thought of Shayla with someone else and still the idea irked her. The frigid body pressed up against her distracted her for a second.

"It's nice to see you again, Dana," Amanda said as she leaned into Bailey. The popsicles she called arms stole the breath from Bailey's body. Bailey rubbed her arms in an attempt to warm them up.

"It's nice to see you again. So where do you ladies

think we should go?" Dana asked.

"Well, I was thinking just so we don't have to travel too far we could go to the Copper Kettle on the corner. It has great food. It's also close enough to walk," Bailey suggested.

"That sounds really good. I haven't been able to get over there in a while. It's a really relaxed atmosphere," Shayla said.

"Well, that sounds good to me. As long as they have a bar I'm in," Dana said.

"They do." Bailey rolled her eyes.

"Well then, let's get going before the weather forces us to call it a night," Amanda said.

Bailey and Dana helped their dates with their coats before assisting them down the icy steps. The restaurant was just a few blocks away and they chose to walk instead of drive. As they strolled down the street, they noticed the stillness in the night and an obvious lack of traffic. A few store windows were already dark as once again the city prepared for a storm. When they arrived at the restaurant, Bailey held opened the door and ushered the women inside to find it empty of everyone but the staff.

"Good evening," the hostess said.

If Bailey had to guess, she would say the young lady was still in high school. She smiled and thought back fondly on her high school job at the local Burger Barn that no longer existed. It was a constant reminder how their little town had evolved while she was away. Some things stayed the same, but not many.

"Hi," Shayla said. "Um… are you still open or were you considering closing early?"

"Oh no, we're open for at least another two hours. The storm isn't supposed to hit for a while and we saw no reason to close early. Now that you're here you're welcome to sit anywhere you like," the hostess said and reached for four menus.

Bailey led the way to a large corner booth. Amanda slid along the vinyl bench before she followed close behind.

"Your waitress is Tina and she'll be with you in a moment. Is there something I can get you to drink?"

"Sure, I would like coffee," Bailey said.

"That sounds good. I'll take one too but decaf for me," Shayla said.

"I would just like water with lemon," Amanda added.

"Scotch on the rocks, top shelf," Dana said.

"Tina will be back with those drinks and to take your orders shortly," the hostess said and left to fill their drink orders.

Amanda and Dana picked up their menu and started to look at their options. Shayla and Bailey left their menu untouched.

"So what's good here?" Dana asked.

"Everything, actually," Bailey replied. "I've probably had almost everything on the menu. If it hasn't changed. I used to come here with my sister and grandparents every Sunday."

"They have really big portions and everything is homemade and from scratch," Shayla added. "Oh and Bailey, it hasn't changed."

"The salads look good," Amanda said.

Three pairs of eyes turned to her.

"You can get a salad anywhere. Get something good. The open-face roast beef sandwich is the best. My grandfather got that every Sunday for almost a year," Bailey said and turned to her date. She leaned into the younger woman and pointed out her suggestions.

Their drinks arrived and their orders were placed for two open-faced roast beef sandwiches, a chicken fried steak dinner, and a Cuban sandwich with a side salad. They had tried to talk Amanda into the onion rings or fries but she was adamant about the salad.

They made small talk about the weather and the book that they were currently reading for the book club. Shayla and Amanda had the most input on that part of the conversation. Before their meals were set before them, Dana started her third glass of scotch.

On more than one occasion, Bailey had restrained herself from crossing the table and using her tie to capture Dana's roaming hands. Shayla had her own hands full swatting them away. Bailey could tell her playfulness left long ago, and now the normally stoic woman was as close to angry as she had ever seen.

Soon the conversation stalled as the women dug into their meals. Before the food had been consumed, two more scotches were brought to the table. Frustration marred Shayla's face when she pulled out her recently purchased cell.

"Is everything ok?" Bailey asked.

"Yeah, I just want to make sure Dana is safely on her way home. She borrowed my car today and in the state she's in I'm not going to let her drive it home. I'm not sure if the buses are still running so I'm going to call her a cab. I figure it should be here shortly after we get back to my apartment," Shayla said.

"Hey, I thought I could possibly stay with you," Dana said, leaning heavily into Shayla.

"I don't think that's a good idea. We don't know how long this storm will last and I don't want you stuck here," Shayla said. She continued to swat at her roaming hands.

A few minutes passed as they waited for the check. Before they received their change, Dana's chin rested on her chest.

"We may have to wait to help her out. I don't think she will be able to make it back to the apartment without us having to carry her," Bailey said, disgusted at the young woman's actions. She thought that maybe it was a good idea to check in with Mac and Sandy to see if they had found out anything else on the drunk woman.

"I'm sorry this happened," Shayla apologized and called the cab company back to change the pick-up.

"It's perfectly fine. I know I've ended up a little inebriated on a date a time or two," Amanda said.

Eventually Dana passed out and they laid her down on the bench. They continued their conversation as they waited for the taxi. They had to call back twice before they were finally able to pull her out into the cold night. Bailey and Shayla had left a generous tip for their waitress. They felt guilty as they had kept the restaurant open an hour past closing time. The cold air had slightly woken up Dana and made it easier for Bailey and Amanda to slip her into the cab while Shayla paid and gave the driver her address.

The three women slowly walked the two blocks blanketed in an eerie silence. All storefront lights had been extinguished and just the street lamps cast weak light onto the sidewalks. The concrete had become slick in the past few hours. Bailey walked between the women, trying to help them all stay on their feet. There were a few close calls and they were relieved when they made it back to the store without one incident.

"Thank you for your help tonight," Shayla said.

"No problem," Bailey replied.

"Well, I had better get home. I don't want to hit any black ice. I'm far more afraid of that then the snow right now," Amanda said.

"I'll walk you to your car," Bailey said before she turned to Shayla. "Good night."

"Good night," Shayla said. Carefully she made her way up the slick metal stairs.

Quietly the two remaining women made their way to the only cars in the parking lot.

"I had a wonderful time," Amanda said when they arrived at her car.

"I did too. I'm sorry about Dana," Bailey said. Her initial attempt at a first date was a huge failure. She had again felt no spark with the young woman. The whole time she sat next to a beautiful woman but wanted to spend it with the lady across the table who spent the evening fending off the aggressive paws of someone who did not deserve her. It would be easy to try to make something work with Amanda, and she was sure they could have good times, but she wanted someone that she had more than just a physical attraction. In her life, she had settled, but as she got older, she realized that there was more to life than just ok.

Bailey opened the door for Amanda and pulled back when Amanda leaned in for a kiss. She slipped and would have fallen had it not been for her hold on the door.

"I'm sorry," Amanda said and reached for Bailey.

"Don't be sorry, Amanda. I'm the one who's sorry," Bailey said, feeling like a heel, actually lower than that, shit on a heel was better than her. Slowly she got back to her feet.

"She is a lucky woman," Amanda said when Bailey was back on steady ground. She slipped into her car and searched for her keys in her messy purse.

"Who?"

"Shayla."

Bailey opened her mouth to deny it but Amanda beat her to the punch.

"Don't try and deny it either. I saw the way you were watching her. Not just tonight either, all those other times at the book club too," Amanda said.

Bailey didn't realize she was so easily read. It seemed everybody but Shayla could tell that she wanted to be with her.

"I was going to deny it, but I think it's time I realize that I can't help it," Bailey openly admitted. "If you saw how I felt about Shayla then why did you ask me out?"

"Simple. I saw how you felt about Shayla. I've been going to those book clubs for a while now. We continuously read about romance and seeing emotions in people's eyes. It wasn't until you joined and I saw how you would look at Shayla and it finally clicked. I wanted that. I hoped maybe if we went out a few times that you would look at me like that too."

"Then why did you invite them along?" Bailey asked.

"Actually, I didn't invite them. They invited themselves. I guess I didn't want to seem rude. Maybe if it had just been us, the evening would have ended differently, but I guess we'll never know." Amanda leaned in and kissed Bailey on the cheek. "Thank you for an interesting evening. I really did have a lovely time. One last piece of advice. Go for it. Dana's not right for her, but you are."

"Thank you. I'll keep that in mind. Drive safe, the roads are getting nasty," Bailey said and closed the door. As Amanda slowly drove away, fat heavy flakes started to float to earth. Bailey stood and watched the empty streets, thinking about the advice the younger woman had given her. She had never been good at taking advice. If she were to take Amanda's advice, she would run straight up the metal stairs and tell Shayla what she thought of Dana before she professed her undying love. It would be something someone in one of her books would have done. But this wasn't a book. It was life. Bailey turned towards her truck with the knowledge she would never climb those stairs. She slid into her cold truck and knew her life would not be resolved in less than a hundred and eighty pages. She had to live with the consequences of her actions. As she sat in her idling truck, she watched the roads turn from grey to white. She prayed the book of her life would end with 'and they lived happily ever after'.

Chapter Fourteen

With Amanda's parting words stuck in her head, Bailey made the decision to take a break from Shayla. It hurt too much to see her with someone else. The pain was more than she had ever imagined. Desire to put on her sneakers and sprint as far away from Shayla exploded in her chest as she drove the deserted roads. As quick as the yearning appeared, it vanished just as sudden. Morgan had not asked much of her, and she had made one promise. She wasn't about to break her word. Plus she had lost so much the last time she did something on instinct and she wasn't willing to miss anything else.

Instead, she decided to stay home and concentrate on work and Morgan. Chances were she would be taking leave when the baby came. Before that could happen, she needed to make sure all of her projects were complete. She was still new at the company and wanted to give a good impression. One kink in her plan had been her almost daily visits to the bakery. She had become dependent on their coffee, the occasional pastry, and her blossoming friendships.

Days then weeks passed and she was forced to drink the sludge she prepared. She didn't know if she would make it as the mud she was drinking was slowly eroding her stomach lining.

The women from the bakery quickly realized what game Bailey was playing and made their own visits to her. Bailey enjoyed their stopovers as it pulled her and Morgan from the monotony that had become their life.

Shayla had attempted a few calls but if Morgan didn't answer the phone to tell her Bailey was busy, the voicemail did. After one book club came and went, Bailey knew she was in trouble. Without a word, Morgan set down the stack of books, threw Bailey's at her, and headed to bed. Bailey knew she should have attended the meeting, but right before they were about to leave, she realized she couldn't stand to watch Shayla and Dana together. It nauseated her to no end, almost as bad as the coffee she had been forced to drink. Morgan left with a few choice words ringing in Bailey's ears.

Eventually the weeks turned into months. Days before the second book club arrived she hadn't even bothered to pick up the book. But with each passing day, her desire to see Shayla grew. Every time she stepped out her door, even if it was to go grocery shopping, she would look for the store owner. It wasn't until she brewed another pot of coffee the day before the meeting she had reached her boiling point. The dark bitter brew taunted her as it continued to drip. As soon as it finished, she poured out the whole pot and grabbed her keys. She needed some good coffee, and she needed it now. The thought that she would finally be able to see Shayla, even if it was just through the window, forced Bailey to press harder on the gas pedal, pushing the limits of her truck.

The street was busy but there were plenty of empty spaces in front of the bakery. Tempted by convenience, she knew she couldn't chance it and pulled around the corner. Winter had finally left and spring was in full bloom. The past month had been a wet one but now the sun shone brightly. Bailey left her jacket in the truck and enjoyed the sun as it warmed her face and exposed arms. She glanced in the bakery and found it busy like always. Before she entered the crowded shop, she propelled herself another few steps until she could peer into the large plate glass window. She stopped shy of the glass and found Shayla helping a customer. Bailey couldn't help but smile as she watched Shayla chat with the elderly woman. She allowed herself a few more precious seconds before she quickly turned and left.

She opened the door and a sigh escaped her as she was engulfed in the comforting smells of cinnamon and coffee. The aroma covered her like a warm blanket, and having just seen Shayla, she felt calmer than she had in over a month. Her boot tapped and she couldn't help but smile as she waited in the long line to get her coffee.

Her stomach rumbled as she watched Sandy and Mac walk between tables, delivering lunches that consisted of either sandwiches or pizza. Another growl from her stomach alerted her to the fact she had skipped her own breakfast since she had been helping Morgan get ready for work. She didn't have anywhere to be. Work was going smooth and the edits were going great.

As she reached the counter, she decided on a sandwich to go. The take out was protection from Shayla wandering in and catching her. There would be no way she could explain how she didn't visit her if she was sitting and enjoying lunch right next door.

"Hey there, stranger, it's been a while since you've been out this way. Is everything all right with

Morgan since our last visit?" Dion asked.

"Oh yeah, she's fine. Sorry I've been absent. It's just the writing and deadlines. You know how it is," Bailey said.

"You don't have to tell me. I can't wait till we can finally retire. Maybe just travel with no responsibilities," Dion commented, pushing over a large paper cup.

"Hey, I was wondering if I could get a ham and cheese on rye to go." Bailey played with the sleeve on her coffee. She eyed the cup as if it had been made of gold. After the first sip, she made a noise that made the older woman blush.

"Sorry, it's been a while since I've had a good cup of coffee," Bailey said, unable to contain her own blush.

"Don't worry about it. Did you want everything on that sandwich?" Dion asked, unable to meet Bailey's eyes.

"Yeah."

"Coming up. It might take a few minutes to get ready. We're a bit busy, you know," Dion said and filled out the order form.

Bailey didn't know how long she had and didn't know if she should chance it. The rumbling of her stomach answered Dion before she could finalize her decision.

"Don't worry, I'll try and hurry it up," Dion said.

Dion disappeared into the back but just as quick she returned. Before Bailey could pull out her card to pay Dion shook her head. "We got this, but you'd better prepare yourself. There's one pissed bookstore owner heading your way."

"How did she know I was here?" Bailey asked.

The coffee in her hands began to shake. She was unprepared for this meeting. If Dion spoke the truth, there was no way she could avoid the angry woman. With one more sip of the flavorful brew, she prepared herself.

Dion sadly looked to the empty cordless phone hanging on the wall. The sound of clanging bells and Dion's quick disappearance told Bailey Shayla had arrived.

Bailey couldn't blame Dion as she had caused the mess herself. After one deep breath, she turned to meet her friend. She put on her best smile and tried to stop the barrage before it hit her full force.

"Hey there, I was just coming over to see you." Bailey hated to lie. It was partially the truth. She was going to try to catch a few more glances of Shayla through the window before she headed home.

"I think we need to talk," Shayla said through clenched teeth. Bailey had never seen Shayla like this. She didn't know if she liked it or not. Since they were younger, Shayla had always been in control. Even when facing bullies at school she had never lost her temper.

Before she uttered a word, Shayla grabbed her arm and dragged her to an empty booth. Even though she was in for an ass chewing, Bailey couldn't help but think about the hand that clutched her arm. Guilt ran up her spine as she enjoyed the touch and didn't want it to stop. She would walk miles, as long as Shayla continued to touch her. Sadly it only lasted a few steps. Confrontation had never been something Bailey was good at. The clock ticked as she waited for Shayla to start. The more silent moments that passed, the more she knew she had made a mistake keeping her distance.

A few more seconds passed before Shayla finally spoke. "Where the fuck have you been?"

Bailey looked at her friend with both eyebrows racing for her hairline. She had never heard her friend curse. A saint Shayla was not, but there were certain things she just did not do. If Bailey thought she was in trouble before, she knew now she was so deep she may not make it out alive.

"I've been at home working," Bailey said. Her fingers picked at the top of her coffee lid. Anything to avoid looking into the pained eyes she couldn't help but look into earlier.

"Too busy to pick up the damn phone. You didn't even come to the last group meeting. You can't take one fucking moment out of your precious little day to stop by?" Shayla asked.

"I'm sorry, but I'm under a lot of pressure to get things done. I might work from home but I still have to work. Plus I've been trying to take care of the house by myself and help Morgan. It's been rough since she had her surgery. It wasn't easy and she's still recovering. She's also a bit down about having to take leave so early and it's getting close to her delivery day. I didn't have much time to myself before and I'm going to have less of it in the future." Bailey knew using her sister as an excuse was a low blow. The look that passed through Shayla's eyes told her she had successfully knocked the wind out of her sails. It was a crappy thing to say and it just piled on more guilt to what she was already feeling.

"I'm sorry. I should've known you were helping Morgan. But I'm here and I can help too you know," Shayla apologized. Bailey watched Shayla back down.

For the second time in months, Bailey felt like shit on the bottom of a person's shoe. Shayla had every right to her feelings. Bailey had avoided her and hurt her again. She knew what she had been doing, and Bailey should have taken everything that Shayla had to dish out.

"No, I'm sorry. I should've at least picked up the phone. I just was overwhelmed. I know Morgan relied on you last time and I wasn't here. I just wanted to be the one to be here for her now. I guess I just felt like I had to shoulder it all," Bailey said.

"I got scared. I mean, I just got you back and I was afraid you would bolt again. I'm sorry, I don't know why I felt like that. I mean, I know you won't leave Morgan. I'm just so confused. I still don't know why you left the first time. I thought you were leaving again. When Morgan said she didn't know why you weren't answering the phone or stopping by I just got scared," Shayla said and wrapped her arms around her body.

Bailey didn't know if it was a talent Shayla had, but again she felt like scum. She had been selfish. She had assumed Shayla would be too caught up in her new romance to even miss her. "I'm sorry. I just thought you would be too busy with Dana to even notice I wasn't around."

"That's not possible. Plus that's a whole other subject," Shayla said and slumped into the booth.

It wasn't hard for Bailey to hear the change when Shayla spoke about Dana. Gone was the dreaminess and excitement that had been there in the prior months. Bailey wanted to be happy but she actually felt sad for her friend. She never wanted Shayla to be unhappy. Dana was not her favorite subject but she needed to know why the change. She knew she would not try to influence her friend one way or the other, but she would listen to what she had to say. Her desire for Shayla put her on a fence she wasn't comfortable sitting on. She knew she couldn't help her friend decide what to do because of her own feelings. If she told Shayla to stay with Dana, she would betray her own heart. On the other side, if she told Shayla to end it with Dana and then it came out that she wanted Shayla to dump her over her own feelings, Shayla could end up resenting her. The only thing she could do was listen to her friend and be impartial but supportive.

"Sounds like trouble in paradise," Bailey said. It was hard to try to suppress the glee she felt, but she was able to keep her face neutral.

"Well, there are good times. It's just when we go out I find she isn't the person I met. When it's just the two of us and we're in my apartment and I'm making dinner it's really nice. She's really sweet and attentive."

Bailey wanted to roll her eyes but decided to focus on the tepid coffee in her hands. Dion silently delivered her sandwich on a plate before she returned to her place behind the counter. Bailey had asked for it to go but guessed Dion knew she wouldn't be going anywhere for a while. She dug into her sandwich as Shayla continued. It was just a sandwich but since someone other than her made it, it tasted like ambrosia.

"I mean it's great, we just eat and talk. She's very....interesting. I've learned a lot about her. Then we usually end up on the couch and watch TV or a movie on the television I bought a few weeks back. If she gets her pick, it's usually a horror or action. I don't like either, so I end up reading a book until the make out sessions start." A dreaminess started to edge back into her voice.

Bailey set down her half eaten sandwich as her appetite flew out the window. "But everything sounds like it's going great," Bailey said after she swallowed her last bite.

"Not really. She seems really eager to take the relationship to the next step. I've been taking it slow. I don't know why, but something's missing," Shayla said as she tore up a napkin she found on the table to shreds.

"You've been with her for a while now and haven't had sex?" Bailey asked. There was slow and then there was snail pace. Even though Bailey didn't want to think about Shayla and Dana having sex she couldn't blame Dana for not wanting to crawl beneath the sheets. Mac had told her how she liked to get women in bed and move on but maybe this time was different, unless the chase truly excited Dana.

"Well, I didn't think I would wait this long either, but in the past month things hadn't been that great," Shayla admitted.

"Not all relationships are great. They take work. When you know you can work through things, that's when you know you'll make it," Bailey commented.

"I understand that. I mean I read a lot of romance novels, and I know what it takes to make a relationship work," Shayla said.

"My god, Shayla. Life isn't a book. You can read a thousand romance novels but they are not road maps to a good relationship. They're called fiction for a reason." Bailey instantly regretted the words that caused the hurt look heading her way. She slumped back into the booth.

"I know that. I'm not stupid," Shayla spat back.

"I'm sorry. I shouldn't have said that. It's just that this is life and life is tricky. There are twists and turns that no book can prepare you for. I know you read romance novels and I'm not sure why you're so drawn to them, but just remember sometimes life does not turn out the way we hope or want."

"I know. I'm sorry."

"Don't apologize. I'm the one who's sorry. But you were saying," Bailey said. Once again she found her coffee cup interesting.

"Right, as I was saying, things are not all roses. We don't have dates on Fridays or Saturdays anymore because Dana's always at the club. I mean that's ok and all, but I've stopped going with her. The last time I went with her I felt like I was her ATM. The first few times I picked up the tab, and not just for us, but for a lot of her friends too. I mean I know I can say no, but I didn't want to upset her."

"Then don't go anymore," Bailey stated.

"I don't, but for the past few months she's asked to borrow my car so much it's almost like I don't even have one. For example, I need to go to the post office today and I can't because she has my car. It was ok because I was just going to drop off the package with the delivery guy but I missed him. Now I'll have to wait till tomorrow," Shayla said.

"I can take you to the post office," Baily suggested.

"Would you please? That would be great, but you haven't finished your sandwich." Shayla mentioned the forgotten meal.

"It's ok. I can get Dion to wrap it up. It was supposed to be to go anyway."

"If it's no trouble?"

"None at all," Bailey said and stood. "I'll meet you at the bookstore in a few minutes?"

"Perfect. I'll see you there," Shayla said and hurried out the door.

Bailey handed Dion the half-uneaten sandwich. "Could you wrap this after all?"

Bailey waited for Shayla outside the store. It was a lovely day and she didn't feel the need to spend any more time indoors. The next nice day could have been weeks away, and she wanted to enjoy this one as much as possible. The sun felt good on her bare arms. She couldn't wait until she could start working on her tan again. The flowers were in bloom in the pots that surrounded the lampposts. Mothers sat in the shade while their young children played in the freshly cut green grass. Bailey hoped that one day her sister would be able to sit on one of the park benches and watch her own kid play.

"You ready?" Shayla asked and pulled Bailey out of her musings.

"Yep, here, let me get that for you," Bailey said. Her arms strained against the weight of the few packages. "Wow, this is heavy. It's going to cost a fortune to mail."

"Nope. Flat rate box. It's almost as good as media rate, but I have more than just books in there, so I have to go this route." Shayla followed Bailey to her truck.

"There you go." Bailey used the bed of the truck to take some of the weight so she could unlock and open the door for Shayla. When she made it to her side, she slid the boxes in-between them before taking her seat. She didn't trust the packages wouldn't get dirty in the bed of her truck. The bag with her sandwich was smashed between the windshield and the dashboard.

"I can hold that for you." Shayla retrieved the battered sandwich.

"Thanks."

"So how is Morgan doing? I haven't seen her since the last book club. She looked tired. I have been meaning to stop by since her surgery but haven't had enough free time," Shayla said. The brown bag crinkled as her fingers played with the paper.

"Yeah, she gets tired really easy now. I basically do everything around the house, but I don't mind as long as she rests and gets better." Bailey paused as a lump had formed in her throat. It took a few seconds for her to clear it. "I just want her healthy. I know that's asking a lot, but I don't want to lose my sister."

Bailey shifted into second. Before she could remove her hand, Shayla covered it with her own. Surprised by the touch, Bailey snatched her hand back and quickly placed it on the steering wheel. Shayla was slower to remove her hand from the shifter.

"So, uh, why do you let Dana borrow your car so much?" Bailey asked, thrown by Shayla's touch. No matter how innocent the touch was, she couldn't help but feel guilty by her feelings.

"She's been interviewing a lot and her car's broken down. Both her parents work, so I let her borrow mine."

"But if she gets the job how is she going to get there?" Bailey asked.

"I'm loaning her some money to fix her car," Shayla said.

Bailey bit her tongue. It hurt, but was necessary to hold back a response she was sure would start another fight. It was hard for Bailey to understand why Shayla couldn't see how she was being used. She wanted to tell her friend, but again she didn't want to seem like she was trying to break them up.

"I know things aren't perfect. Just like in stories, they're not flawless, but she's wonderful to me. She's attentive, beautiful, strong, and caring. She's already told me she loves me," Shayla said. The dreamy tone had once again made its way into her voice.

Bailey found breathing difficult and was thankful they had arrived at the post office, or she would have had to pull over. "Here you go."

"I'll be right back." Shayla scooted off the seat and reached back in the cab to grab her boxes.

Bailey watched as she made her way into the old one story brick building.

Bailey had hurt Shayla before by not talking to her. Now that she was back for good, maybe it was time she found her voice. Bailey decided that she would have to talk to Shayla, and soon. But first, she would give Mac and Sandy a few more weeks to get more information. If they didn't come through by then, she would just have to go by what she already knew. By what Shayla had recently told her she tended to believe what Mac had told her already.

Shayla practically skipped back to the truck. Bailey didn't want to be the one to ruin her good mood and shelved her current thoughts.

"Well, we'd better get back. I have to go and pick up Morgan for her doctor's appointment. I didn't realize how late it was getting." Bailey didn't wait for an answer before she pulled away from the curb.

"Bailey, if you ever need any help, I'll do whatever I can." Shayla held on to the door as Bailey took a turn too fast.

"I know. I appreciate that, but we don't know how bad it's going to get," Bailey said and took her foot off the gas. Going just a few miles over the speed limit was not a smart idea with the police headquarters just a few streets over.

"That's not what I mean," Shayla said. "I mean if you need anything. I already talked to Morgan. But I want you to know that if you need anything. Just a friendly shoulder, someone to talk to, anything. I'm here for you."

"Thank you. And the same goes for you. You know I'll always be here for you, right?" Bailey asked Shayla. Stopped at a red light, she took a few moments to look at her friend. "I'm different then I was ten years ago. I won't go anywhere. I'm here if you need me. I'm not the same person I was in high school."

Shayla smiled. Bailey's breath caught in her throat as she watched her friend's eyes travel over her body and linger on her lips. She had never felt so on display. She couldn't help but enjoy the way Shayla was looking at her. Just the way her eyes dilated made Baily's heart race.

"I know," Shayla said. A few more seconds passed before she turned to look out the window, a slight rosy hue graced her cheeks.

Bailey blushed, startled by her friend's actions. The light turned green and she returned her focus to the road.

"Here you go, sorry I can't stay longer," Bailey said before she pulled up to the store.

"It's ok. I understand. Go take care of your sister. Don't be a stranger," Shayla said. Slowly she exited the car.

"I won't," Bailey said after Shayla had already

disappeared into the store. She couldn't help but allow a tiny bit of hope to blossom in her chest at the way Shayla had looked at her lips.

Chapter Fifteen

Shayla sat perched on her work stool with the latest book club novel nestled in her hands. No matter how hard she tried, she couldn't comprehend the words on the page. Never had she had such a hard time immersing herself into a book, but in the past ten minutes, she had read the same page three times and still couldn't remember one thing. Words swirled before her. Frustrated, she closed the book. Months had passed since they had played truth or dare and still Shayla couldn't get Bailey out of her head. The previous months where Bailey had again been absent from her life had just reinforced her obsession. The way she shamelessly stared at her yesterday in the truck had her more confused than ever. She had been upset with Bailey when she missed the book club, but furious when she didn't go to the sleep over. Morgan had made some excuse for her, but no amount of words justified her actions. She tried to counter her feelings by spending more time with Dana, but no matter how hard she wanted things to move in the right direction, she felt as if whatever they had was crumbling around her.

At night when Shayla would put her book down, she started to think about how things were progressing with Dana and what to do. But eventually her thoughts would wander to her friend. Every time she was near Bailey, she longed to touch her, to confirm if the spark she had felt was real. Dana had still yet to come close to making her feel the way she did for Bailey, and now months later, she was thinking about ending it with the young woman.

She enjoyed her time with Dana but recently she realized something was lacking. Almost every story she read spoke of sparks, fireworks, and butterflies, and with Dana she had felt butterflies but for months they had laid dormant. Dana had confessed her love weeks ago. She thought she would have felt something more when she heard those words pour from her luscious lips, but she had felt empty. Sadly, most of their nights together would end with her phone in hand as she called a cab for the drunk woman. She wanted to take the next step, but every night they started to move towards the bedroom, something didn't feel right. Soon she would have to take the next step or walk away. Every time she looked at Dana she couldn't help but be drawn to her beauty. But was that enough for her? She craved the all-consuming love she read in books. The more she thought about it, the more Shayla realized that it possibly wasn't in the cards for her, but could she settle for just being in a relationship?

With a heavy sigh, Shayla tried once again to resume her book. Seconds later the bell sounded and seeing the customer, she couldn't help but smile. "Hi."

In an attempt to make up for the months she had been absent, Bailey decided to surprise Shayla. When greeted with a large smile, Bailey couldn't help her own grin as she walked through the door. The store was extremely quiet. Bailey knew Shayla couldn't be making any money. She wished there was something she could do to help the struggling store, but Shayla was doing what she loved, and that was the important part.

"Hey there, what are you doing here in the middle of the day?" Shayla asked and set down her book.

"I just thought I'd stop by. I'm caught up with everything at home, finally, and I wanted to pick up something nice for dessert. Since I was going to be next door I figured I'd stop in for a few minutes," Bailey said. She leaned on the counter. Her blunt nails drummed against the wood counter. "So, anything new since yesterday?"

"They pushed back Allura's new book. They're not sure when it's going to come out now," Shayla said. Not the kind of news Bailey had been looking for but it was apparently something important to her friend. But still she couldn't control her eye roll.

"Hey, I love her. She's my favorite author," Shayla said, a rosy color rising to her cheeks.

"Whoa, settle down. You don't even know that she is a she."

"She's a female. I'm sure she's a lovely woman. I can tell by her writing style that she is kind and caring. I get a feeling when I read her words that I don't get with anybody else." Shayla defended the author.

"I think that's gas." Bailey threw her head back and laughed. The look on her friend's face and silence informed Bailey she didn't think too much of her joke.

"Kidding. But really. I mean, you've never met the lady. Plus she doesn't do showings, she doesn't even have much information on her website. She probably only has it because her publisher made her create it. I'm willing to bet she's a lonely woman who's been pining after the same person forever. That's what her books read like. They all follow the same formula. Nothing original about them whatsoever. Every time I've picked up one of her books I feel like I've read it before."

"But isn't that romantic? Can you imagine loving someone for so long and to write about it? To be able to draw from something so real. Her books are all about unrequited love, but then they end up together in the end. That's so romantic." The voice Bailey had come to associate with only Dana suddenly made an appearance. She smiled, knowing Dana wasn't the only person that could make Shayla sound like that.

Honestly, Bailey could understand that type of longing. She had been living it for the past thirteen years. She knew exactly what the author was writing about. She hated reading those books and having to relive every painful feeling they stirred in her. The only thing she didn't have from the books was the happy ending. No matter how hard she tried to write her own happy ending it just wouldn't come. She wished there was some way for her to be able to pick up a pencil and edit her life. But in a way, she was, and she knew there were some mistakes in her past that she couldn't change, but she sure hoped that she could turn around most of the mistakes she had made.

She had insulted Shayla's favorite author and Bailey realized it was time to change the subject. "So any plans for this evening? If you're free, you could come over for dinner."

"Sorry, but I already have plans. Dana is coming over. I think it's long past time for kissing. It's time we moved on to something else. Really make this relationship work," Shayla said. Nimble fingers played with the corners of her paperback book.

Dana was not a subject Bailey ever wanted to talk about and now was no exception. But with the words she just heard from her best friend, Bailey knew that the time for telling Shayla about Dana had finally arrived. If she waited any longer, her friend might do something she could end up regretting. It wasn't going to be a short or sweet conversation. She knew if she was going to get through this, she would need some coffee to keep her wits about her.

"Hey, I'm going next door to get some coffee. Do you want some?" Bailey asked.

"Nah, I'm fine. It feels like I've already had a whole pot today."

"Ok, I'll be back," Bailey said and escaped next door.

The bakery had a line but all the tables were empty. Mac was just inside the door, picking up baskets.

"Hey there, haven't seen you for a while," Mac said as Bailey passed, her busy hands continuing to wipe down an empty basket.

"Yeah, I know I've been absent for a while, but I should be around more."

"It's a good thing you showed because I have something to tell you, come here." Mac pulled Bailey to the booth by the window. "I found out some more stuff about Dana."

"Hold that thought. Let me get a coffee." Bailey hurried to the counter and retrieved the coffee that was already waiting for her.

When she returned to the table, she didn't waste any time getting to the point. "Did Sandy find out anything either?" Bailey asked.

"Nah, she's too busy with school. She actually went back full time and it has eaten into her free time," Mac said. Pride in her friend caused her eyes to sparkle. Bailey knew how it felt to talk about the person you loved to others. Mac leaned forward and a few blond strands escaped from her ponytail. Quickly she brushed them behind her ear. As soon as they were seated, she jumped into what she needed to say. "I went out a few weekends ago and saw Dana out. I was invited to join their group for a few drinks. Dana had stumbled away drunk, and I do mean stumbled. I looked for Shayla but couldn't find her. I thought she was there since I saw her car in the parking lot. Dana didn't come back so I asked someone where she went. They said she probably went home, or to her new girlfriend's house. Nobody knew I knew Shayla so I asked about her girlfriend. Most of her friends were also drunk and they had very loose lips so I took advantage of that. They said she was just using her for her car and money. They said Shayla was paying for Dana to get her car fixed, and she was letting Dana use her car. They laughed because they said Dana didn't even have a car. She had totaled it when she was drunk last year. They said she used the money to buy an Xbox and buy the booze they were drinking. The worst part was she was driving with a suspended license because of DUI's."

The longer Mac kept talking, the more anger boiled Bailey's blood. She wasn't just mad at Dana; she was mad at herself. Her stupidity and fear had stood in the way of helping her friend. Earlier she had decided to tell Shayla what she knew. Now she realized she should have been a true friend and told Shayla what she knew a long time ago. She decided to make sure Mac did the right thing too.

"Thanks Mac. That's just the info I needed. Now allow me to butt in here. I don't think I'm off base when I tell you, you should tell Sandy how you feel about her."

The look of fear that passed through the young woman's eyes told Bailey she was spot on.

"Don't say anything. Just think about it. You have nothing to lose and everything to gain. I lost a lot because I didn't say something to the person I loved years ago. And from one mute to another, I just don't want to see you go through the same thing I did."

Bailey looked at the clock and saw that more time had passed then she thought.

"Shit. I got to go. Think about what I said and thank you for everything you did," Bailey said before bolting out the door.

Nobody was at the counter when she entered the bookstore. Quickly, she walked the small store in search of her missing friend. In the last row, she found someone and it wasn't the person she was looking for.

"Hey Bailey," Ivy said, her arms loaded with books. "Shayla's already gone. She said she had to leave early for a date. She said if you showed up to tell you she was at her apartment getting ready. The door should be unlocked."

"Thanks. It's good to see you, Ivy," Bailey said.

"You too."

"Bye." Bailey quickly made her way to the exit.

"Bye." Bailey heard from behind the shelf.

As quick as she could, she ran around the corner and took the stairs two at a time. She hoped she still had some time.

Chapter Sixteen

Shayla had just pulled on her tee shirt when she heard a loud knock at the door. Bare feet padded their way across the hardwood floors. She smiled as she prepared to greet her guest. Dana fell on Shayla as the door flew open. Surprised, Shayla barely had time to grab her before she hit the floor.

"Whoa, are you ok?" Shayla asked. The strong scent of booze wafted up from the young woman. It would be another night that would end with Shayla pouring Dana into a cab. Nights like tonight were becoming all too frequent. Something had to give. The relationship wasn't going anywhere but it wasn't fair to discuss it with Dana in the condition she was in.

"Yeah, just lost my footing." Dana struggled to get to her feet. "You look good."

Shayla backed away. She saw something in the young woman's eyes, and she wasn't sure she liked it.

"How did your interview go?" Shayla distanced herself from the drunk woman by moving into the living room.

"Not good. I don't think I got the job," Dana said and stumbled after the shop owner.

"How did you get here?" Shayla asked, afraid of the answer. Slowly, she continued to back into the living room.

Dana held up Shayla's keys. Shayla grabbed her keys out of the larger hand.

Dana studied her empty hand.

"That was irresponsible," Shayla said. Her legs hit the couch and she fell back. Dana plopped down so close she was almost in Shayla's lap.

"Well, I needed a way to get here."

"You could've called a cab. Speaking of a cab, I think I'm going to go call one for you now." Shayla attempted to stand. An iron hand grabbed her wrist and kept her from rising.

"I don't think so. We could still have fun." Dana leaned in to kiss Shayla. The force of her weight caused Shayla to fall back into the couch. Dana's weight kept her pinned. Shayla struggled beneath her captor. She turned her head when Dana attempted to kiss her. Rough lips bruised her cheek. Dana left a slobbery trail leading to Shayla's mouth. Trapped under the younger woman, Shayla was afraid of what could happen. Fear coursed through her imprisoned body as she tried to avoid booze-tainted lips. She bucked under the woman, trying to free herself. Dana's only response was a laugh and the hand that held her captive tightened around her wrist.

"Get off me," Shayla demanded. Hard as she tried, she couldn't keep a tremor from her voice.

Her demands fell on deaf ears as Dana's free hand pulled at Shayla's shirt. A large hand pawed at her breast and again Shayla struggled to extricate herself. Neither woman heard the door open or the coffee hitting the metal deck. It wasn't until strong arms pulled the large woman off Shayla they realized they had company. Bailey was quickly at Shayla's side. Shayla shrunk back when she saw the fire in Baily's eyes.

Bailey saw Shayla move away from her. She closed her eyes and took a steadying breath. Slowly she reached up and placed a gentle hand on Shayla's cheek.

"Are you ok?" Bailey asked as calmly as she could. Her hand shook and it took everything in her to focus on Shayla and not to beat the piece of shit that was still lying on the floor.

"Hey! What do you think you're doing? We were having some fun," Dana said. She attempted multiple times to try and pull herself from her prone position on the hardwood floor. Eventually she had to use the chair for support. Before she could fully stand, Bailey was at her side. The fire had returned to her eyes. Even though she was smaller than Dana, she hauled the woman to her feet and pushed her to the door.

"I think your fun is done for the evening," Bailey said through gritted teeth.

"Hey, you can't do that. You don't live here, Shayla does, and only she can tell me to leave," Dana said. She struggled to escape Bailey's grasp.

Bailey turned and looked at Shayla, her eyes silently pleaded with her to agree.

"I think you'd better leave," Shayla said and looked away from the women.

Bailey wanted to go to the woman who sat huddled in the corner of the couch with her arms wrapped around her legs.

"How am I supposed to get home?" Dana asked.

"I'll call you a cab." Shayla still was unable to meet the young woman's eyes even as she reached for her phone.

"I don't think so." Bailey dug into her pocket and pulled out two wrinkled bills. She shoved the money in to Dana's outstretched hand. "You can take the bus."

"But I live more than a mile from the closest stop," Dana complained.

"Then I suggest you get exact change so you can call someone when you get off the bus," Bailey said and pushed the woman out the door and slammed it in her face, stopping any rebuttal. She knew Shayla would eventually have given in and paid for a cab. Shayla had already been used and abused enough. Quickly Bailey returned to her shaken friend and knelt by her side.

"Are you all right? I was told you were here and the door was unlocked. I was about to turn around and leave until you asked her to get off," Bailey said. When she heard her friend cry out it didn't take but a second before she hauled Dana off Shayla. She didn't think she would have been able to pull her off if Dana hadn't been drunk.

"I'm fine. I'm glad you showed when you did. I don't know what she would've done. I don't know if I would've been able to fight her off." Shayla continued to shake.

Bailey watched a shiver run through her friend.

"I know you would've been able to get away from her. You're stronger then you think. I'm going to make you some tea," Bailey said and hurried to the kitchen. She wanted to give her friend some time alone to process what had happened. Her plans to talk to Shayla hadn't changed. Now she regretted not saying something earlier. The longer she stood waiting for the water to boil, the more she thought tonight may not be the best time to talk about Dana. Maybe they could talk tomorrow. Bailey didn't want to admit to Shayla but the experience had also shaken her. She couldn't help but think that by trying to keep neutral she might have allowed one of the people she loved the most in her life to get hurt by her silence. Again because of fear. The teakettle whistled and pulled her from her thoughts.

With two cups of tea in hand, Bailey returned to the couch. When the offered cup of tea went untouched, she set both mugs on the table. Unsure of how much space to give Shayla, she decided to sit in the middle, hoping she was close enough to let Shayla know she was there for her, but far enough to give her some space. Suddenly she found herself slammed against the back of the couch with Shayla's head buried into her shoulder. Tears dampened her shirt. Concerned and worried for her friend, she wrapped her arms around Shayla before she pulled her close. She wove her fingers through Shayla's long silky hair just like she used to when she was younger. Bailey hadn't noticed that she had left it down.

Guilt engulfed her as she couldn't help but enjoy the feeling of her friend in her arms. It was something she had longed for since high school, but the actions that led them to the situation could have been avoided. Minutes slowly ticked away as Bailey rocked Shayla, giving silent comfort. Eventually Shayla's tears dried up but she didn't pull away. Bailey didn't want to break contact but in time, Shayla pulled away, apologizing for her actions.

"Don't be sorry. You have nothing to be sorry for." Bailey tenderly reached out and pushed a few loose strands of Shayla's hair behind her ear before she cupped her cheek. Shayla leaned into the comforting hand.

"I'm glad you were here," Shayla whispered.

"I am too," Bailey said, trying to control her raging hormones. So many nights she had dreamt about holding her friend like this.

"Bailey, can I ask you something?" Shayla asked so softly Bailey almost didn't hear.

"Of course. You can ask me anything." Bailey felt so guilty that she could have prevented this she was willing to do anything or say anything to help her friend.

"There's been something I've been thinking about for a while. A few months ago, when we were playing truth or dare, you avoided answering the question about your first love. Will you tell me who your first love was?" Shayla asked. Her eyes pinned Bailey to her seat.

Seeing the ledge in front of her, Bailey knew it was time to jump. Her heart pounded in her chest but this time she wasn't scared. "You. It's always been you. And had this been one of your story romance books, this is where we would kiss passionately before heading into your room and make love. But this isn't a book and we are not going to do that, right?" Bailey said ruefully. A small part of her still held out hope Shayla was working off a script. To her vast disappointment, Shayla did not move in for the earth-shattering kiss most authors would have written.

Instead Bailey found hurt, anger, confusion, and acceptance flash quickly through chocolate eyes.

"Why didn't you ever tell me?" Shayla scooted away from Bailey.

This was not the direction Bailey wanted her to move. She wanted to reach out and pull her back before she moved further away, but realized her friend might need some time. Bailey had years to come to terms with her feelings.

Bailey rubbed her face, trying to plan her words and rub away the frustration she felt. She had gotten herself into this mess and she had to be the one to get herself out.

"I did tell you. I told you on the last day of high school when I gave you that." Bailey pointed to the necklace that had reappeared on Shayla's neck.

"I remember that day. You said you love me and I said I loved you too," Shayla said. Her fingers brushed against the metal that hung from her neck.

"Right, you said you loved me like a sister. And I don't know about you, but I wouldn't date my sister." Tears blossomed in her eyes. The sting of rejection was as acute today as it was all those years ago. It was more intense since Shayla sat next to her.

"I don't know, your sister is kind of cute," Shayla said, smiling at Bailey. The smile quickly vanished when Bailey didn't respond. "I'm just kidding."

Bailey's head snapped up and her hands slammed against her jean-clad thighs. "I'm being serious. This is something I've had to live with for years. I loved you then, I loved you when I was in the service, and I love you now. I've never stopped loving you," Bailey said. A huge sigh left Bailey and she felt like the weight of the world had just been removed from her shoulders. She hid her eyes in her hands as she again slumped back into the couch.

"Then why did you go? Why didn't you give us a chance?"

"Because there was no chance. You never looked at me like I look at you. You never wanted me that way," Bailey said and continued to hide her eyes. She felt it was easier to pretend it was dark then try to look Shayla in the eyes while she bared her soul.

"That's not true," Shayla said. She reached up and pulled Bailey's hands away from her face, waiting until Bailey's eyes met hers. "I've loved you since forever. It took your leaving for me to really realize how deeply I truly loved you. When you left I was hurt, but more than that, I missed you. I missed you every day you were gone. I didn't think I would make it through school. I didn't want to go on without you."

"Why didn't you say something?" Bailey's head couldn't comprehend the words that were coming from Shayla's mouth.

"Because you never gave me the chance. You abandoned me. Then whenever you came home, I somehow always seemed to be gone. When you did finally come home, it felt like things had changed between us. I knew how I still felt about you, but you were so distant. I couldn't stand that. You were so near, but still out of my reach."

"I'm sorry. I've been so stupid. I thought I was giving you space. I kept my distance because I knew I was still in love with you and I didn't want to get too close. I knew I would lose my heart again. But in the end it didn't matter because even though I stayed away the feelings didn't stop."

"I didn't say anything to you either because I was afraid if I told you how I truly felt it would end up pushing you further away. I had lost you once and I wasn't willing to lose you again. That's why I didn't even confront you when you came back. I was just happy to have you back. I was content to be your friend." Shayla scooted closer. She took Bailey's hand in hers. “Did you feel it?”

“Feel what?” Bailey asked. At that moment, she couldn’t feel anything but the thumb Shayla was slowly rubbing against her knuckles that caused fireworks in her head.

“When we kissed. Did you feel anything?” Shayla asked.

Bailey couldn’t help but see hope in liquid brown eyes. Her eyes moved down to the pink lips that had caused feelings inside her she had never felt before.

“Yes, I’d never felt anything like that,” Bailey finally admitted. Her eyes moved to meet Shayla’s before moving back to her lips.

“Me too. I’d like to feel that again.” Shayla whispered the words but Bailey heard them nonetheless.

Without a word, Bailey leaned in and lost herself in Shayla’s soft lips. She disengaged her fingers from Shayla to reach up to thread her fingers into soft locks. The moan that escaped Shayla reverberated through her lips. Bailey’s head felt empty of anything but the sensation running through her body. Time seemed to stop. When she felt a tentative tongue touch her lips, she didn’t hesitate to allow access. After a few minutes, she reluctantly pulled away for fear she would pass out.

Her eyes opened and found ones dark with desire. Bailey leaned back into the arm of the couch. Shayla removed her glasses and tossed them onto the table before she snuggled into Bailey. Strong arms pulled her close. Silence absorbed the two women. Bailey reveled in the feeling of being so close to the only person she had ever loved. No words were needed. Silent moments passed as the two women just held each other, but when Bailey felt Shayla yawn against her chest, she gently pushed the tired woman away.

"It pains me to say this, but I should be going." Bailey stretched her cramped arms.

She attempted to stand, and Bailey found herself pulled back to the couch by insistent hands. "Please stay. I don't feel safe right now. Dana had my keys a lot and I don't know if she made duplicates or not. I would feel safer if you were here with me."

Bailey wanted nothing more than to spend the night with Shayla. Her body hummed with anticipation of what could happen, but she had two people at home depending on her. Morgan was six months pregnant and Bailey wanted to help. Sometimes more than what was needed. The surgery had gone well and the chemo was going well, but she never knew when her sister would really need her.

"I have to call Morgan and see how she's doing today," Bailey said.

"Oh, I understand if you're needed elsewhere." Shayla reluctantly let go of Bailey's hands.

"Just let me call her. I want to be here, but I also need to be there for my sister."

"Really, if you need to go I'm sure I can just lock my bedroom door," Shayla said.

"Please, just give me one minute." Bailey leaned in and gave Shayla a quick kiss. "I want to be here."

Before Shayla could say anything, Bailey pulled out her cell phone. Morgan was on the other line before she was five steps away.

Five minutes passed before Bailey returned and took her seat next to Shayla. She opened her arms. It felt wonderful when Shayla curled up and laid her head on her shoulder.

"Is everything ok?" Shayla asked. Her hands played with the buttons on Bailey's shirt.

"Everything is great. Morgan said to go ahead and stay. She said she would be fine. She was getting ready for bed anyway. Buddy was already fed and waiting for her. I'd already prepared everything for tomorrow morning so she said she would be able to take care of herself for the night. She assured me if she needed me she would call," Bailey said as she ran her fingers through Shayla's hair. Even though she was comfortable, she could feel Shayla didn't seem quite as relaxed as she had earlier.

"That's good. Uh, Bailey, I just want you to know..."

Bailey heard hesitation in Shayla's voice. "Don't worry, I know nothing will happen between us tonight. I wouldn't want you to do anything you're not comfortable with," Bailey assured the woman in her arms.

"Thank you," Shayla said. Bailey smiled when she felt Shayla relax.

"Do you think you have something I could possibly wear tonight because I'm not prepared to actually stay over?"

"I'm sure I have something," Shayla said. Slowly she disengaged herself from Bailey's arms and pulled her to the bedroom.

"Why don't you take your shower and I'll get you something to wear," Shayla said and disappeared into her walk-in closet.

"That sounds great," Bailey said.

"The towels are in the closet." Shayla said from the closet.

"Thanks," Bailey said and made her way to the

bathroom. She quickly stripped and set her clothes on the counter. She turned on the shower and waited a few minutes for the water to warm up before she stepped into the glass stall. She felt exposed by the glass. The shower was one of the quickest she had taken since boot camp. Steam filled the room as she exited the shower. She wrapped a large fluffy blue towel around her body and exited the room with a smaller towel still attacking her short hair. It was one of the perks of the haircut. Instead of having to blow dry it, all she had to do was run a towel over it and wait ten minutes and it would be dry.

"Here, these should fit," Shayla said and thrust an old pair of shorts and threadbare tee at Bailey.

"Thanks. Hey wait, isn't this my old B.U.M shirt from high school? I couldn't find it when I left for Europe," Bailey said. She held up the shirt, amazed that it found its way back to her.

"Could be. I use it to sleep in," Shayla said before disappearing into the bathroom. Bailey waited for the doors to close before she dropped both towels in the hamper.

Twenty minutes later, Shayla exited the bathroom dressed in shorts and a tee, but had her hair still wrapped in a towel. "Do you think we can talk a while? I have to let my hair dry or I'll never get a comb through it tomorrow."

"Sure. I think there's still a few things we need to talk about, and no time like the present. I want you to know as of now, I'm an open book. You can ask me anything," Bailey said, folding the covers back on the queen size bed. "I hope you don't mind if I take the left side?"

"No, I actually sleep on the right. Well, more in the middle but that's fine too," Shayla said.

Not quite ready for bed and with the knowledge they had plenty of time before the lights would be extinguished, Bailey sat against the headboard and pulled Shayla's head into her lap. Shayla turned so she was looking up at Bailey and reached around to slide her hand under Bailey's leg. Her fingers tingled as they played upon the smooth exposed flesh.

"So, you said you would answer anything, right?" Shayla asked as Bailey's fingers once again found their way into her hair. She had always loved the feeling of Bailey's fingers threading through her hair. If she were a cat, she would be purring now.

"Yes. I've kept silent long enough and now I don't want to keep anything from you."

"This is something I've wanted to ask for a long time, but always been too afraid to," Shayla said. She turned on her side and faced the foot of the bed and softly rubbed Bailey's exposed legs.

"Ok." Bailey drew out the word.

"Why did you live with your grandparents?" Shayla asked.

Bailey's fingers paused in her hair. Shayla realized she may have asked something too personal and already stepped over a line. "I'm sorry, you don't have to answer that."

"No, I said I would answer anything. It's just…I wasn't expecting that, is all. I've never talked about what happened back then. I just need to actually figure out a way to say it so it makes sense," Bailey said.

Shayla waited. Silent moments stretched on

before she heard Bailey take a long breath before starting.

"Well, I don't know how much you have talked to Morgan about our childhood but I'm going to let you know it was probably worse then what she even remembers. I tried to shield her from most of the scum that our mother brought into that house. At times, it felt like we had a revolving door with the way she went through men. Some were nice but often they were nothing but drunks and druggies. Even at that age, I knew to keep my distance. Morgan was more trusting and I was scared that something would happen. I had started to have her sleep in my bed to try and protect her as much as possible. I think I had started to beg my grandparents to let us move in with them when I was just ten, but they wouldn't. Then I don't know what happened but one day Nancy dropped us off at our grandparents' and never came back. I know I had asked for that but somewhere deep down I hated her for abandoning us." Tears started to run down Bailey's cheeks.

Shayla sat up and pulled her into her arms. The room was silent as she rocked Bailey in her arms.

"I don't know why it still gets to me. It was so long ago," Bailey said and used the back of her hand to swipe at the drying tears.

"I'm sorry that happened. Come here," Shayla said and scooted down on the bed before she pulled Bailey into her arms.

"Is this ok? I'm not too heavy?" Bailey asked.

"It's perfect." Shayla ran her fingers through Bailey's soft curls. She realized they were softer then they looked.

"Have I told you lately I love your hair? It's so

soft," Shayla said and let the short strands fall through her fingers like sand.

"Thank you. I love your hair too. I used to braid it just so I could feel it slide through my fingers," Bailey admitted.

"I loved it when you would braid my hair too."

Shayla watched Bailey try, and fail to stifle a yawn. The evening had been extremely emotional. She had lost a lot of time with the woman in her arms, but hopefully they would have plenty of time to make up for what they lost. But now they needed to get some sleep.

"It's ok, Bailey, you can go to sleep," Shayla said and tightened her hold. "I'll be here when you wake."

Chapter Seventeen

Bailey woke with an unfamiliar weight against her chest. Fear ripped through her until she felt a strong arm pull her close. Slowly she opened her eyes to see disheveled brown hair splayed across her body. She wanted to pull Shayla closer but didn't want to wake her. Even though they had spent the night together, she was still unsure where they were going, if anywhere. All that mattered to her at that moment was how she enjoyed the feeling of waking up with Shayla in her arms.

Gently she attempted to lift Shayla's arm and slide out from under the unconscious woman. Moments later, she had successfully extracted herself, instantly missing the contact. Ever so quietly, she tiptoed to the bathroom and changed her clothes before she splashed some water on her face. The reflection in the mirror continued to smile at her when she thought about who was in her arms just moments earlier. She checked on Shayla after she exited the bathroom and found her snuggled up to the pillow she had used. It took a few minutes to find her socks and shoes. She quietly exited the apartment, leaving the door unlocked. She hurried down the steps and rounded the corner to find the bakery empty of any customers.

Dion met her at the counter with one to go cup.

"Hey Dion, can I get another to go cup and.... how about two chocolate croissants?" Bailey asked and wrapped her hands around the hot cup. Fingers tapped on the mug as she waited for the pastries.

"Sure kid. Who's the second one for?" Dion asked.

"Shayla."

Bailey laughed at the surprise she saw in the older woman's face.

"Wait," Dion said, her hand hovered over the baked goods.

With the pastries forgotten, she disappeared into the back. Seconds later, she returned with a latte and Connie. "Sorry, I just thought Connie should be here."

"What am I here for?" Connie asked as she wiped her hands on a dishtowel.

"I don't know," Bailey said with a look of innocence. "I'm just here picking up coffee and pastries."

"Come on. What's going on?" Dion asked.

Bailey wanted to continue to string her along but she couldn't hide the smile that had been plastered on her face all morning.

"I don't know, but all I can say is I just spent the most wonderful night in the arms of the most amazing woman," Bailey teased the older women with a crumb.

Connie made a little squeak. Her rotund body gave a small bounce before she scrambled around the counter and engulfed the younger woman in powerful arms. Bailey felt as if the life was being squeezed out of her. "Oh honey, I'm so happy for you."

"Thank you, but I don't know what's going on yet. All I know is I finally admitted to her how I feel," Bailey said.

"How you really feel?" Dion asked with a quirked

brow.

Bailey's nod was all the women needed.

"Good girl. I'm proud of you. Now I wonder where those two slackers are. I'm supposed to teach Sandy how to keep the books this morning," Dion said and ran a cloth across the already sparkling counter.

As if on cue, Sandy and Mac wandered through the door. "There you two are. You're late."

"Sorry. We were up late last night," Sandy said and kept her eyes on the tile floor.

"Yeah, we were uh…talking," Mac said. Her eyes never made it off the floor either.

Bailey tried to catch the younger woman's eye but Mac and Sandy hurried past the three women.

"I wonder what's gotten into those two," Connie asked before she hurried after them.

"Kids these days," Dion said as customers came into the shop.

Bailey had an idea of what might have the two women distracted. But at that moment, she had her own life to worry about. She hoped it was good news and as a line started to queue up behind her, she looked at the clock and realized she needed to get back to her sleeping beauty. "I hate to grab and go but I need to get back. She was still sleeping when I snuck out."

"Well, don't let me keep you, but I expect you to come back here when she opens shop and tell me all the dirty little details," Dion said and allowed Bailey to exit.

"I will," Bailey said. Even with the promise hanging in the air she knew there were things she wouldn't be sharing. There were still some things she was not willing to tell anybody.

Afraid Shayla had woken up, Bailey ran around

the building and took the stairs two at a time. In her rush, she was relieved she had not spilled the hot coffee on herself. The door was still unlocked. As she passed through the metal door, she locked the deadbolt. Silently she kicked off her shoes. In her bare feet, she made her way back to the room to find Shayla unmoved. Bailey set the bag of pastries and Shayla's coffee on the nightstand. In the light of the morning, she was nervous about how to act. She didn't know if they were actually a couple, or if they would revert back to being friends. Her immediate reaction was to lean down and kiss Shayla. When she looked back at the woman of her dreams, she saw concerned eyes watching her.

"Hey. I woke up and you were gone. I thought last night had been a dream," Shayla said. Her lean body stretched like a cat. Bailey couldn't tear her eyes off the perky breast that pushed against worn fabric.

"Like what you see?" Brown eyes twinkled in amusement.

Bailey blushed at the question. Bailey smiled. "Yes." She had been caught, so why lie. "Oh, here, I brought coffee and pastries."

"Mmmmm, thank you. This is wonderful. Here. Sit." Shayla patted the bed next to her. Bailey didn't waste any time before she crawled onto the bed.

"What's wrong?" Shayla asked between sips.

Bailey cradled her coffee in her lap. Her head fell against the headboard before she lazily turned to look at Shayla. "What are we doing here?"

A simple question, but had so many different answers.

"I thought we were having coffee and pastries," Shayla answered the most obvious one.

Bailey couldn't help but smile. "You know what I mean. What are we doing? What's going on with us?"

"Well." Shayla set her coffee in her lap. Bailey patiently waited for her to continue. "I thought maybe we could try dating."

Bailey shook her head. She cringed at the hurt she saw in Shayla's expressive eyes. "I'm sorry, but I don't want to date. I don't want anything short of commitment. I know I don't want anybody else. I've never wanted anybody else and I don't want you to want anybody else either. I know commitment is a big word, but I've been committed to you for years now already."

Shayla set her cup on the nightstand and snuggled into Bailey. "That sounds good to me."

"I know this is quick, and you haven't even officially dumped…I'm sorry, I don't even want to say her name, but I won't settle for anything less."

"I won't even call her. I'll text her. That's how people break up these days, right?" Shayla asked.

"Right." Bailey didn't want to talk about Dana any longer. "Has anybody ever told you that you're adorable when you sleep?"

"Nope."

"Well, I'm telling you. You're adorable. I know we just said we're committed to each other, but I still want to go slow. I want this to grow between us. I don't want to jump right into bed," Bailey said before she looked at where she was presently seated. "You know what I mean."

"I agree, but right now I want to go brush my teeth so I can kiss you properly," Shayla said and tried to scoot away.

"That's not really fair. You get to have minty

fresh breath and I don't. I think I'll take my chances." Bailey pulled Shayla back into her arms to kiss her properly. It wasn't a long kiss or a deep kiss but sweet nonetheless.

Bailey reluctantly pulled herself from her new snuggle toy. "Do you think I could take a shower before I head home?"

"Sure."

Bailey was already in the shower when Shayla returned with a few clean towels. She stopped at the door and listened to Bailey's crystal voice belt out one of her favorite songs from Les Misérables. Silently, she opened the doors and deposited the towels on the counter. She returned to the room and got comfortable on the bed to listen to the concert in her bathroom.

A few minutes later, a clean Bailey exited the bathroom.

"You have a beautiful voice," Shayla said. Her eyes roamed freely over her new girlfriend. It felt great to finally be able to say that.

"Thank you." Bailey blushed as she continued to dry her hair.

"I didn't know you liked Les Miz."

"I don't, I love it. It's my favorite show." Bailey made her way to the edge of the bed.

"I saw it once in Portland."

"I was dragged to a show in London, and saw it with a few friends from the ship."

"Have you seen other shows?"

"Yeah, a few, but none of them touched me the way Les Miz did," Bailey said.

"How?"

Bailey sat down and scooted back until she rested against the headboard. "I don't know. I guess when I was watching it I could just relate to so many of the characters in different ways."

"Who did you relate to the most?" Shayla asked. Her coffee remained nestled in her hands.

"There were so many. Initially I found a lot of myself in Jean Valjean and Javert. Well, I wasn't Javert but the Navy was. This was during Don't Ask, Don't Tell era, and Javert was the Navy just waiting for me to do something so it could toss me out for being gay. I was Jean Valjean hiding in plain sight but with this big beacon pointing me out. I mean, here I was gay, and if I just messed up once I was out. I was so afraid of being caught I didn't even step foot in a gay club. I didn't do one thing that they could say was homosexual activity."

"Wait. You're saying you had done nothing during your time in the military."

"Nope. I was too scared. I was so paranoid of being caught I didn't want to do anything that they could use against me." Bailey reached for her warm coffee and took a sip.

"So answer me this. How many women have you ever kissed?"

"Why?" Bailey asked.

"Just curious," Shayla said and scooted closer. Her hands moved over Bailey's fabric covered abs, delighted to feel them tremble beneath her fingers.

Bailey turned away. "Four."

"You've kissed four women. So I'm one and who are the others?" Shayla asked.

Still looking away, Bailey whispered, "My

grandmother, mother, and Morgan."

"Wait. So you're telling me that outside your family I'm the only other person you've kissed?"

"Yes."

Tired of looking at the back of Bailey's head, Shayla turned Bailey to face her. "How can that be? You're an attractive, desirable, sexy woman. The other ladies must have been falling over themselves to get at you."

"Like I said, I didn't want to get caught."

"But they repealed Don't Ask, Don't Tell before you got out. You could've been with someone then." Shayla saw something she had never seen in Bailey's eyes before. Desire. And she loved the way it made her feel. If she didn't have to go to work, she would have jumped Bailey then and there.

"Why would I do that? I'd already started the discharge process. I was leaving. Why would I want to start something with someone when I was in the process of coming home? On my way back to the only person I'd ever loved. Why kiss someone just to kiss someone? I wanted to kiss the person I loved and the only person I had ever loved. I didn't want to waste my first kiss on just anybody. I wanted it to mean something," Bailey said and leaned into Shayla and kissed her. Shayla moaned into the kiss. She had to pull away to catch her breath.

Shayla looked into Bailey's eyes and all she saw was love reflected back. Nothing Shayla could say could express how much that first kiss had meant to her. There was only one thing she could do to show Bailey how she felt. She leaned in and captured the former sailor's lips with her own. Sparks flew as the two women continued to kiss. Grudgingly, Shayla again pulled back.

"Thank you. I'm glad I was your first kiss. I have to go to work soon, but before I do, I want you to finish your story."

"I'll try, but I think I might need another shower. A cold one this time."

Shayla grabbed the pillow beside her and flung it at Bailey, happy with the grunt that it caused. She smiled, thinking about the fact that the woman sitting next to her was finally hers.

Bailey removed the flying projectile and placed it behind her back before getting comfortable. "Ok, ok. Where was I? Oh yeah, next I would have to say Fantine, not the whole prostitute thing, but the idea of my life not turning out the way I had planned. On the last day of senior year, I had all these grand ideas in my head of telling you I love you. Then we would be happy and go off to start our life in college. But that didn't happen. So I hardened my heart to life and lived every day a shell of the person I once was. Life had turned into just making it one day at a time with no happiness in sight."

Shayla lay down in Bailey's lap and relaxed as long fingers threaded through her hair.

Bailey continued. "Next I related to Marius. When he fell in love with Cosette at first sight, I knew how that felt. Granted I didn't know it at the time, but when I saw it on stage, I realized that it was what happened to me. Eighteen years ago, standing in Mrs. Wetzler's fourth grade class in my new jeans and purple polo shirt, you walked into my life. You were wearing a yellow dress. You had on these big red glasses and your hair was pulled back into a ponytail. I remember thinking at that moment I was going to be your best friend. There was no question."

Shayla laughed. "I know. That's what you told me when you walked over to me."

"I didn't realize it then, but I know now that I fell in love with you at that very moment. I remember the first time we played house and thinking I never wanted it to end."

"Funny, I didn't want it to end either," Shayla said. "Sorry, continue."

"I guess the person I really connected with was *Éponine*. I had been really into the show, but when Samantha Barks stood on that stage and sang On My Own, I could have sworn she was singing it to me. Well, not to me but she had looked in my soul and found my deepest darkest secret. That she had reached into my chest and pulled that song from my heart. At that time there wasn't a night you were absent from my dreams. Each night I lay down, I was happy because I knew that once I closed my eyes you would be there. Every time I closed my eyes, you were there to grab my hand and walk with me through every minute of my dream. For just a few hours, you were mine. I was happy to have you in my arms if only for those moments. I feared morning because I knew I would be waking and again you would be gone. I loved you and in my dreams, you loved me too. When I woke, I still loved you but in the dawn of morning your love for me was gone and so were you." Tears streamed from Bailey's eyes as she told her story. Shayla reached out and brushed away the wet trails.

Shayla couldn't help the dampness that pooled in her own eyes. Now she understood why the voice she had heard earlier that morning was so soulful. It wasn't just the words and the voice; it was the passion.

She looked at the woman who had just bared her soul. Shayla said the three words she hoped would take away some of the pain Bailey had lived with. "I love you."

"I love you too." Bailey pulled Shayla into her arms. The two women stayed wrapped in each other's embrace until Shayla again was forced to pull away.

"I'm sorry, but I really need to hurry so I'm not late opening the store."

Shayla slid off the bed and disappeared into her closet.

"Uh....do you think it would be ok if I stopped by tonight and took you out on a real date?" Bailey asked from the bedroom.

"That would be wonderful." Shayla beamed as she exited the closet with her clothes in hand. She made her way to Bailey still lounging on the bed and gave her a quick peck. "I hate this but I really need to get ready." Shayla started to lift her shirt and watched Baily start to blush again. She laughed when her girlfriend bolted off the bed.

"Well then, I'll grab my pastry and be on my way. I'll be back at six to pick you up. Dress casual," Bailey said and hurried out of the room.

Shayla enjoyed teasing Bailey but when she looked at the clock, she started to strip in earnest. Shayla knew she should already be down at the store but still didn't want the morning to end. The story had enchanted her as she sat and listened to her new girlfriend talk about Les Miz. There was such passion in her words. The longing in her voice reminded her of her favorite author. Again she looked at the clock and hurried to get out the door.

After she left Shayla's, it felt like her feet barely touched the ground as she made her way back to the bakery for a fresh cup of coffee. She needed one more jolt before she headed home. Even though she had just told Shayla some of her darkest secrets, she felt like she was floating on a cloud.

The atmosphere of the bakery had drastically changed from earlier. Content to wait in line, Bailey smiled and nodded at everybody who passed. A hot cup of coffee was waiting for her when she arrived at the front of the still extremely long line.

"Thank you," Bailey said and turned to leave.

"Don't think you're getting off that easy. Wanda has a table waiting for you. When I finish this line, Connie and I will be over there to join you, so you might as well take this with you." Dion passed over a warm gooey cinnamon roll.

Bailey knew not to argue. With a nod, she accepted the coffee and pastry. Even though she had a croissant in her hand, she welcomed the warm one. She could just take the other one home for Morgan or a late snack.

"Hey Wanda," Bailey said as she slid into the booth. "You're here early."

"Well, Connie called and woke me up a little after seven. She told me I had to get over here. So here I am," Wanda said and attempted to stifle a yawn behind a recently manicured hand. "I don't know what the fire is and I've been sitting here for a while. This coffee isn't doing anything to wake me up either. So what's going on? Don't tell me you're bolting again. I promised your grandmother I would take care of you two and I can't do that if you leave."

"Don't worry, I won't be going anywhere," Bailey said, unable to stop the smile that spread across her face as she caught sight of Shayla hurrying past the large window. Her eyes followed the shop owner until she was gone. It wasn't until she turned to Wanda that she found the older woman studying her.

"Hot damn, you finally told her, didn't you?" Wanda slapped the table. The sound resounded through the small space, causing a few customers to jump.

"Shit. Did everybody know?" Bailey asked. She tried to hide her blush by digging into the gooey roll.

"Anybody who has eyes knew you were bat shit crazy for that girl," Wanda said. With a smug look, she took a few sips of her coffee. Bailey didn't mind the look the older woman gave her. She was happy and nothing could diminish that.

"Well, guess I don't have to try and hide it now," Bailey said.

"Wait, don't say anything yet." Neither woman had seen Dion approach. "Let me get Connie and I'll be right back. Sandy and Mac can watch the store for a while."

It only took a minute for both women to return to the booth with coffee and breakfast.

"Ok, continue, and don't leave anything out," Connie said and tore into her own cinnamon roll.

There was no way Bailey would say everything that happened the previous night. Some things would remain between her and Shayla. The few minutes she expected to be in the bakery stretched out to an hour. It took making a promise to tell about their date before the women would allow Bailey to leave the shop. There were only a few hours left before she had to be back to pick up Shayla. She had a lot of planning to do to give Shayla the date she deserved. Dates had never been high on her priority list, but she would be able to remember a few she had read in books. She was sure she could come up with something that would make her new girlfriend happy.

Chapter Eighteen

Bailey's mind wandered; unable to concentrate on the words on the screen, she pushed away from the desk. After an hour of not one word being added to the page, she finally gave up and shut down the computer for the day. Frustrated over not getting any work done, she leaned back in her chair and allowed her mind to continue to obsess over the one thing that had dominated her mind since waking up.

Girlfriend. One simple word, but until that day had only existed in her dreams. She hoped, but never believed that she would ever be more than a friend to Shayla. For years, she had been stupid and pushed the only person she ever loved away. Now in a few hours she was going to finally be able to take that one person on a real date. Not just another dream. Excitement bubbled within. The night held so many possibilities and all she needed to do was chose one.

With time to spare, Bailey spent the afternoon doing housework and even gave Buddy a bath. Not that it was voluntary on either of their parts. When she let him in after vacuuming, he brought in a horrendous stench. Before he could mess up what she had spent the past hour cleaning, she coaxed him back out with a few tasty treats. Buddy was quickly captured as he licked his chops. She picked up the little guy and carried him, at arm's length, to the sink to give him his weekly bath a few days early. Laughter erupted from Bailey as she watched him prance around the house. A little after three, she headed upstairs to get ready.

An hour later, dressed in jeans and a light blue sweater, she placed a casserole in the oven. Bailey sat at the table when Morgan trudged into the kitchen. Instantly Bailey was at her side to assist her to the kitchen table.

"Want me to fix you some ginger tea?"

"That would be great. You look nice," Morgan said. The wear of the day was evident by the heavy bags that hung below her eyes. Wisps of long blond hair had escaped her ponytail and accentuated her frazzled look.

"Thank you. I have a casserole going and it should be done in about thirty minutes," Bailey said. She grabbed the kettle and held it under the faucet. Her sister had started drinking so much tea Bailey had considered taking stock in Lipton.

"I don't feel so great. I don't know if I could eat," Morgan said and laid her head on the table.

Bailey's heart went out to her sister. The job of a teacher was hard enough without having cancer ravaging her body, and a small baby sapping her remaining strength. Maybe that night would not be the best for her first date. She wanted to be able to focus on Shayla on her first date. With the condition her sister was in, there was no way she would be able to concentrate on Shayla with Morgan home alone.

"Morgan, you have to eat. You have to keep up your strength," Bailey said and situated herself so she could rub some of the tension out of her shoulders.

"That feels so good. I could get used to this," Morgan said, allowing her head to fall forward, giving

Bailey access to her neck.

Bailey took the hint and used her thumbs to rub the tension from her sister's neck. Guilt surged through Bailey. She had spent the previous night blissfully wrapped up in her girlfriend's arms, but her happiness from the previous evening had now been shadowed by her sister's pain.

All day she had been looking forward to her evening with Shayla. When she saw her sister's slumped shoulders and weary look, Bailey's happy mood deflated like a popped balloon. Her plans with Shayla swirled down the drain. She would have to postpone the date. She looked at how run down Morgan was and considered pushing it back to the weekend. Hopefully the time would fly, but with Bailey's luck, she wouldn't bet on it. A few days would be a cakewalk compared to the thirteen years she'd already waited.

"Hey, I have some news to tell you, but I need for you to give me five minutes," Bailey said as she continued to try and work out the knots bunched along her sister's shoulders.

Morgan nodded. Bailey left the room to make a phone call, somewhat relived she got Shayla's voicemail. She left a quick apology and explained why she had to cancel. The call ended with a promise to make it up to her. Her phone flipped shut as she entered the kitchen. The whistle blew on the kettle. Two cups were placed on the counter and soon filled with tea and water. Lemon and sugar joined her cup and honey was drizzled into Morgan's.

"Here, just like you like it," Bailey said and handed over her sister's mug.

"Thanks. Who did you call, and what did you have to tell me?"

"My girlfriend." Bailey hid her smile behind her mug.

Morgan answered with a simple arch of her eyebrow. No words were needed for Bailey to continue.

"I canceled our first date," Bailey said. A smile stayed on her face even though it was forced. She didn't want her sister to feel any worse than she already did.

"That's great about the girlfriend and I'm really happy for you, but you don't have to cancel your date. Please don't do that on my account. I'll probably go to bed and rest. I'm beat, is all," Morgan argued.

"It's ok. We'll have plenty of time for dates. You're important and I need to keep you healthy for that baby."

"Really Bailey. I'll be fine. I'll even promise to eat." Morgan took another sip of her tea. Her slim fingers tapped against the ceramic.

Normally Bailey would have been annoyed but she had found herself making concessions where Morgan was concerned.

"I'm not worried about that, because I'm not going anywhere." A shrill ring interrupted their argument. The display lit up on Bailey's phone and she couldn't hide her smile.

"Go take it."

Morgan laughed as Bailey practically skipped out of the room with the phone to her ear.

"Hi," Bailey said.

"Hi. I just got your message. Is everything ok?" Bailey smiled at the sound of her girlfriend's voice. Her heart swelled when she heard the concern for her sister and fell even deeper in love.

"Yeah, Morgan isn't feeling so hot. It would be best if I stayed home. Today looks like it was rough."

"Well, I could come over there. I'm sure you had something lovely planned, but honestly at this point, I really want to spend time with you. I might even be able to be of some assistance to Morgan and give you a break," Shayla suggested.

"Really?"

"Sure, is there anything I can bring?" Shayla asked.

"No, we have everything. I already have dinner warming in the oven so whenever you can get here that would be great."

"Ok. Well, Ivy just walked in. Let me tell her she can close the store and I'll be on my way," Shayla said.

"I'll see you soon," Bailey said, unable to contain her smile. She was a little relieved since she still hadn't made any plans for the evening.

"I'll be there as fast as I can. Bye," Shayla said. The line went dead before Bailey opened her mouth to reply.

She rejoined Morgan and she couldn't hide the smile that became a constant fixture since the previous night.

"I take it Shayla's on her way?" Morgan asked between sips.

"Yep. Damn. I didn't have time to get her flowers. I was going to pick them up on my way to her place," Bailey said. Her smile finally deflated.

"There's always next time. I'm sure this won't be considered a first date since I'll be in the middle of it. Really, you don't have to stay here," Morgan said.

"I know I don't have to. I want to," Bailey said. She reached across the table and took her sister's hand in hers before giving it a squeeze. "I wasn't there for you once and I'll be damned if I'm not going to be here for you again. I better start a salad." Bailey released her hand and went to the fridge.

"What did you make tonight?"

"I was kind of stir crazy earlier so I made a lasagna."

"But I never taught you how to make one," Morgan said. Slowly she made her way to the stove, turned the kettle back on, and added a new bag to her mug.

"I know. I did a simple internet search and presto. You would be surprised at the five star recipes you can find online. I hope you like yours really meaty because you need protein. I also put some spinach in it. I thought it might taste good that way," Bailey said. Her fingers tore at the romaine lettuce. She filled a medium size bowl and put it aside before heading back to the fridge to pull out a cucumber, tomato, and a few radishes for the salad.

"It should be about done. So I'm going to set the table after I feed Buddy." Bailey grabbed the needed dishes and silverware and looked at Morgan when she heard the door.

"Go. I'll feed Buddy and take care of the table." Morgan shoved her out the kitchen door.

Bailey checked herself in the mirror by the entryway. She took a deep breath. Her nerves a little calmer, she opened the door. The smile that had been on her face most of the day returned instantly when Shayla stood at the door with a bouquet of flowers.

"These are for you," Shayla said and handed Bailey the colorful arrangement.

"They're beautiful, thank you," Bailey said. She buried her nose into the blossoms.

"Just like you," Shayla said and leaned in and

kissed Bailey. "Was that ok?"

"More than ok. I hope to do more of that tonight," Bailey said and leaned in for another kiss.

"I missed you," Shayla said when they parted.

"I missed you too." The two women were still embracing when Morgan made her way into the living room

"Hi Shayla." Morgan eased into the couch.

"Hi Morgan. How are you doing?"

"Ok, a little run down. I'm sorry I ruined your date," Morgan apologized.

"Don't worry about it. There's bound to be many more so this is fine," Shayla said and shrugged out of her light coat before handing it to Bailey.

"Can I?" Shayla asked. Her hand hovered over Morgan's belly that had started to steadily grow the past few weeks.

"Of course. She's been rather fussy today," Morgan said. Shayla kneeled in front of Morgan and gently placed her hands on the bump. Bailey watched the woman interact. It occurred to her she hadn't thought to ask to feel the baby. It hadn't crossed her mind that the life inside of her sister was moving and listening to them.

"You found out the sex?" Shayla asked, not taking her eyes off the miracle growing in Morgan's belly.

"No, but your girlfriend has been calling it a she so I went along with it." As Morgan said the word girlfriend, Shayla's head turned. Her eyes found Bailey's and held them.

"I like the sound of that, girlfriend," Shayla said, her eyes never leaving Bailey's. Silent moments passed before she broke contact and looked at Morgan. "Have you thought of a name yet?"

"Yeah, I've been pondering it and I'm leaning towards Angelique Allura Hutsell. She's going to be my little Angel and if it's a boy I'm going to name him Gabriel, no middle name yet."

"Very nice names. Strong names, for a strong person. So what's for dinner?" Shayla removed her hands. She scrambled to her feet and held her hands out to help Morgan extricate herself from the couch.

"I made lasagna and a salad. I hope that's ok?" Bailey said and led the women to the dining room.

"That sounds wonderful," Shayla said.

"Oh damn. I forgot to make garlic bread," Bailey said.

"That's fine. I'm sure there will be plenty." Morgan looked at the bubbly gooey goodness her sister placed on the table. "Wow, Bailey, this looks really good. I'm impressed. It seems you might surpass me soon in the cooking department."

"Thank you. But I'm sure that won't happen. I actually took a few different recipes and mixed them together. I hope I can remember the formula so I can make it again some other time," Bailey said and dished out large squares of pasta for the women.

"I agree, this looks wonderful." Shayla took a large bite. The moan that escaped her made the sisters blush. "It's really good. The sausage is really sweet and complements the sauce very well."

The three women enjoyed the meal. The conversation was kept light. They avoided any stressful topics. Bailey finished first and started to clear the dishes. The evening couldn't have been better. True, she would have preferred a one-on-one date with Shayla but she had a wonderful time with the two people she loved more than anything. Even the little scavenger sitting at Shayla's side got to enjoy a few scraps from the meal. Soon Bailey heard the tick tick that preceded Buddy into the kitchen.

"I better let Buddy out. How about I put this away while you two get set up on the couch and we'll play a game. I'll even put on another pot for tea," Bailey said and escaped into the kitchen.

"That sounds wonderful. Plus I need to talk to Shayla about the book we're reading. I have a few questions," Morgan hollered at Bailey.

Shayla watched her girlfriend disappear into the kitchen. It had been a wonderful meal and she truly enjoyed the company.

"Great," Shayla said and aided Morgan to her feet. The younger woman looked like the walking dead. It hurt Shayla to see how Morgan struggled through her pregnancy because of the cancer treatment. This was supposed to be a joyous time. The only thing that should have been making her miserable was the baby playing the bongos with her bladder. Unfortunately, the baby was both a blessing and curse. Through the joy of watching the baby grow and blossom, Shayla often forgot Morgan was still battling cancer, but as she watched the younger woman struggle to get up she remembered that not only was a life growing inside her, but death continued to ravage her body.

"I really don't need the help," Morgan said but took the offered hand. "But I do appreciate it. I get tired easily. I have to admit, I'm scared of what's to come. If it's already this hard I don't think I'll be able to make it through the school year."

"Maybe you should be on bed rest? I know you still have three more months, but your case isn't normal," Shayla said.

"I know, but I keep pushing myself. Sometimes I feel I'm trying too hard, but I love those kids. I only have another month and a half to go until summer break. I would feel bad leaving them so close to the end of the year. They don't know about the cancer, just the pregnancy. The principal and I thought it best not to tell them."

Shayla couldn't ignore the unshed tears in Morgan's eyes and pulled her close. She held on to the younger woman. Warm caring arms gave silent strength. Soon Morgan pulled away. Slowly Shayla trailed the younger woman into the living room. Silent minutes passed before Morgan broke the silence.

"There's something I do want to ask you. I wanted to talk to you after the last book club but you seemed a bit upset," Morgan said.

Shayla looked towards the kitchen. "I was, but I'm better now. What can I help you with?"

"I need for you to promise me something," Morgan said.

"Of course. It doesn't matter what it is. If it's within my control to do it, I will."

Morgan covered Shayla's hand. "I hoped you would say that." Morgan glanced at the kitchen. No sound came from the kitchen and she continued, "I need for you to promise me that if something happens to me you will be there for Bailey."

Shayla's head snapped back. Not once in the years since the cancer first appeared had Morgan ever talked about not emerging cancer free. Now hearing the defeat in the young woman's voice, it scared her, but for both their sakes, she had to stay positive. "You're going to beat this again. We will do everything we can to help."

"Shayla, listen to me. I don't know if I'm going to beat it this time. It's different. I can feel it." Morgan wiped away a tear that slid down Shayla's cheek. "Please don't cry. Promise me you'll be there for her. This is going to be hard on her. If she loses me, she'll think she's alone, but she won't be. She'll have you and my little angel to watch over her. She needs people to be there for her. Bailey's life hadn't been the easiest, and she has a tendency to make it worse. I want your promise that it won't happen."

Shayla had to clear her throat a few times before she was able to speak around the lump that formed. Tears continued to pour from her eyes. "Of course. Of course I'll be there for her."

"Now dry those tears because I don't want my sister coming in here and seeing you cry."

Shayla stood and hurried from the room.

A few seconds after she heard a door close, Bailey entered the living room with a tray loaded with snacks and tea. "Hey, where's Shayla?" Bailey set the tray of goodies on the coffee table and sat in the open chair.

"Bathroom."

"Ok, hey, are you ok?" Bailey asked her sister. The light atmosphere that had been there during dinner had disappeared. In its place was something heavy. It felt like she was sitting outside during a Florida summer. She didn't like it.

"I'm great. I'm tired and I still have a few papers to look over. I'm going to take my tea and head up to bed."

"Are you sure? I thought we might be able to play a game or something."

"Nah. I'm good, plus you deserve a little alone time. I'm sure you'd like that better than me kicking your ass at Scrabble," Morgan said and pulled herself from the embrace of the couch.

"You're right. Here, take your tea at least," Bailey said. She held out a large mug. Morgan wrapped both hands around the cup. Bailey enveloped both of her hands around her sister's. "Are you sure you're ok?"

"Yes. Thank you, and good night. Don't do anything I wouldn't do."

"I'll try and restrain myself," Bailey said. When Morgan laughed, Bailey realized she couldn't remember the last time she heard the small sound from her sister. She had been so involved in her drama and taking care of her sister the only emotion she could recognize was stress. Laughter would need to be something she infused into the household more. For both their sake.

"Good night," Bailey said to Morgan.

"Good night, Shayla," Morgan said as she passed Shayla on her way upstairs.

"You're going to bed?" Shayla asked as she entered the room.

"Yeah. I'm tired and hope to get some extra sleep tonight. Plus I have a few papers to grade." Firmly Morgan grasped the banister as she made her way upstairs.

"Good night. Sleep well." Shayla watched Morgan disappear upstairs until there was a click of the door closing.

No words where needed as Bailey held out her arms. Shayla quickly crossed the room and dissolved into her embrace. “I want to kiss you.”

“What’s stopping you?” Bailey asked.

Bailey crawled onto the couch and again opened her arms. She enjoyed the weight of Shayla’s body as it pressed down on her. Then she kissed Shayla with a passion she didn’t realize she possessed. Everything she had she put into that one single kiss, hoping Shayla could tell how much she loved her. Time slipped away as two friends became so much more. Every feeling they had ever felt for each other exploded while their lips moved together. Two bodies came alight. Skin seared with each caress of roaming hands. Forever could have come and gone and both would have died happy as the two women tried to convey their love through one searing kiss. Neither wanted the kiss to end but oxygen was necessary for their survival.

Shayla pulled away. Bailey whimpered when their lips separated. Shayla rested her forehead on Bailey’s while she tried to calm her ragged breath. “I have never felt anything like that.”

“Me either,” Bailey admitted. “Are you ok?” She had expected to see something in Shayla’s eyes but sadness was not it.

“Yeah, I’m fine, I’m just a little emotional. I mean with everything that’s going on right now,” Shayla said and turned her back to Bailey. She grabbed her arm and wrapped it around her middle.

With her arms wrapped around Shayla, she pulled her as close as their bodies would allow. Lazily she allowed her hands to roam over Shayla’s stomach. With a sigh Bailey responded, “I know. I’m so extremely happy but yet I have this fear right here," Bailey touched her own chest for a second before she once again reached out and pulled Shayla close, "that won't go away."

"I have to admit I was a little shocked at how Morgan looked today. We talked a bit about how she was doing at work. What do you think about her and work?"

"I don't know. Even though she sits most the time, it's still a lot of work for her body to handle. I don't know how much longer she can do it. She wants to be there for those kids but I really don't think it's going to happen. At the last doctor's appointment, they said the baby was on schedule and looked healthy. I'm happy about that, but I'm more than a little concerned about Morgan. Don't tell her but I talked to the doctor and asked if there was any way there was a possibility of delivering early."

Shayla turned incredulous eyes to her girlfriend. "Bailey, you can't do that. It's not your body. No matter how much you want to protect your sister it's still her baby and her body."

"I know." She looked into Shayla's caring eyes, ashamed she had even thought about asking her sister to deliver before the baby was ready. "But she'll have better odds if she can deliver the baby soon. We need to see what's going on with her body. I hate being in the dark," Bailey said, defeat evident in her voice. "I can't lose her."

"Right now you're doing the only thing you can, and that's to simply be there for her. Help her when she needs it. Give her enough space so she knows she still has her independence. Continue to love her and support her through any decision she makes."

"How did you ever get so smart?" Bailey asked and kissed the crown of Shayla's head.

"I read a lot."

Bailey laughed. Today had not been what she had thought when she woke up but she was still happier then she had been in a long time. For a while, she didn't ever think the bad news was going to stop. Now as she felt her arms wrap around Shayla she had finally turned a corner. Hopefully it was a path she continued to travel.

"I was thinking about moving her into Gram's old room. It'll be harder for her to go up and down the stairs the further along she gets. Plus it has its own bathroom with a large tub. I think she might like that." Bailey wiggled until she was lying under Shayla again. The bookstore owner rolled on to her stomach, folding her hands over Bailey's chest and resting her chin on her hands. Bailey reached up and wrapped her arms around Shayla.

"I think she'll like that too. When do you plan on doing it?" Shayla asked. Her fingers lazily stroked Baily's skin at her throat.

"Well, we have next month's sleep over coming up and I talked Dion into having it here again. I figured the morning after I would ask Mac and Sandy to help move everything." Bailey closed her eyes, reveling in the sensations Shayla's fingers were causing through her body. Goose bumps exploded on her arms.

"That sounds like a good idea. And don't think I forgot how you missed last month's book club and sleep over. I'm still unhappy about that. I looked forward to those sleepovers. It was nice to be able to watch you sleep," Shayla said. Her nails dragged across the exposed skin.

Bailey couldn't stop the moan that escaped. She did get some satisfaction when the nails stopped. The blush that also graced Shayla's cheeks made her feel a little better. She took a moment before replying. "I'm sorry, it was too hard to see you with Dana all the time. I didn't think I'd be able to escape with my skin if I showed up for the sleepover and then disappeared again. Believe me, it was just as hard on me as it was you. And did you say you used to watch me sleep?" Bailey quirked her eyebrow at the woman in her arms.

"Yep. You like to sleep in. I usually woke up first and would watch you sleep for a while before the others started to stir. Did you know you drooled? I'm so not looking forward to that," Shayla said and her nose bunched up.

"I do not drool. And even if I did drool you snore." Bailey huffed.

"I admit that." Shayla giggled.

"But I think it's cute. It's not bad. It's not like the logs Sandy saws but you have this little soft sound that seems to escape," Bailey said.

"So you watch me sleep too?" Shayla's fingers returned to Bailey's neck.

"Yeah, guilty. You're usually the first out. I lay there listening to you. I find your snores comforting. Even in high school when we would have our sleepovers I would stay awake and let your snores lull me to sleep. I always seem to sleep the best when you're with me," Bailey admitted and captured Shayla's hands.

"Speaking about sleeping, I hate to do this but I should get going. I didn't get much sleep last night," Shayla said. Strong arms halted her attempt to get up.

"You can stay here," Bailey whispered in Shayla's ear. She kissed the nape of her neck, causing a slight shiver to run through Shayla.

Shayla's tone had become huskier when she replied, "Amazing as that sounds we both agreed to take things slow. I really should go home. I find it so hard to sleep when I'm in your arms. I'm afraid to wake up and find this whole thing is a dream."

"Ok, but can I stop by tomorrow and talk about the possibility of taking you on a real date?" Bailey asked. Reluctantly, she allowed Shayla to escape her grasp. With weak arms, she pushed herself off the couch to follow Shayla to the door.

"I would love it if you stopped by the bookstore tomorrow. I'll be counting the minutes," Shayla said and wrapped her arms around Bailey's neck. "Is this ok?"

"No, but it will be in a minute," Bailey said. She leaned in and tenderly kissed Shayla. It was a quick kiss, but left both woman wanting more. When Shayla leaned in for another kiss, Bailey backed up. "If we continue on this course, you'll never make it out that door."

"You're probably right, but I need one more."

Bailey didn't want to deny Shayla anything, and the short kiss she had planned never happened. Long passionate minutes later Bailey found herself backed against the wall and Shayla's hands freely roaming her body. Her plans for the evening hadn't included a cold shower but as she watched Shayla walk out the door she knew one would be in her immediate future.

She returned to the living room. Drained from the day, she picked up the tray that held the cold tea. Sharp nails clacked on the floor as the only two people in the house still awake made their way to the kitchen. Bailey let Buddy outside as she made sure the kitchen was cleaned and coffee was ready for the morning. Bailey let Buddy back in and knelt down to give him some puppy love.

"Hey there pal, how about you keep me company for the night? I won't be sleeping for a while."

He answered with a couple kisses and an energetic tail wag that shook his whole back half. "I know you just went out but it's still early and I don't want to come down again, so you had better do your business."

The night was substantially cooler from earlier. Bailey stood on the back stairs and looked at the inky black sky that was littered with bright stars. They were the same stars she gazed at when she was a kid in high school. Back then, she continuously wished on them to have the confidence to tell Shayla what she truly meant to her. Now staring at the stars, she thanked whoever answered her wish. It didn't matter that it had taken years longer than she wanted; they had still been answered. Buddy made one final loop to make sure no stray animals entered his domain and pranced back to Bailey. He leaned against her leg and let her know he was ready for bed.

"Well, come on, Buddy, let's do some edits and see what we can get done." Bailey entered the house. Another long night stretched before her. She hadn't been sleeping well thinking about the two women she loved. For some reason she didn't think this night would be any different.

Chapter Nineteen

Time seemed to fly as Bailey and Shayla fell into the motions of dating. The first date Bailey had stressed over had come and gone. Now the bulk of their time was spent with Morgan. By the end of May, Morgan had finally been informed she would have to go on bed rest. On her last day, she was surprised when her third graders held a going away party. The principal called Bailey early to pick up Morgan. Everything had overwhelmed Morgan to the point that she couldn't stop crying. Bailey kept Morgan at her desk while she packed up her personal belongings. Even as they exited the building, tears continued to stream down the teacher's cheeks.

Bed rest was not something either woman was looking forward to. Days spent alone had become Bailey's escape. Now she found herself busy with work and taking care of Morgan. Not that Morgan wanted to be taken care of. The constant attention annoyed her. More than once Bailey found herself in her truck on her way to the grocery store or bakery for her sister. The more this happened, the more Bailey came to understand her sister's need for space, and left the house willingly.

Shayla spent most of her evenings at Bailey's house playing games and spending as much time with the sisters as possible. The women fell into a pattern where Morgan would turn in early to allow the two women some time alone. It was during one of these evenings Shayla finally confronted Bailey about how she smothered her younger sister.

"Honey, I think we need to talk," Shayla said. She lay in her favorite position wrapped in her girlfriend's arms.

"Is it about moving on to the next stage in our relationship, although I'm not complaining at the speed we are taking?" Bailey said as she squeezed Shayla and wiggled her eyebrows.

"No, but we'll talk about that soon enough. What we need to talk about is Morgan." The arms around Shayla tensed. "I know you're doing your best, but honey, you really need to back off a bit. There's such a thing as doing too much."

"Did she say something to you?" Shayla could hear the hurt in Bailey's voice.

"Well no, not in so many words. The last book club she pulled me aside and said you did mother her a bit too much. She said she was surprised you didn't try and wipe her face with a spit damped napkin. I'm sure she was kidding, but there was some truth behind her words."

Bailey laughed. "Ok, maybe I have been a bit too attentive. But I don't want her to hurt or strain herself."

"I understand, but she still can do some things. I understand not doing any housecleaning or anything too strenuous, but she still needs to feel useful. Maybe she can cook a simple meal or two. Just let her feel like she's not a burden. She needs to feel like she can help or at least take care of herself."

"I understand. I'll back off. But I still won't allow her to do any cleaning."

"Fine, I'm sure she won't argue with that, but

I have another idea. I was thinking maybe she could come and spend a few days with me at the bookstore."

"But she can't really get around. She's supposed to be on bed rest," Bailey argued.

"Honey, bed rest doesn't mean she has to be in bed all day. It simply means she needs to take things easy and rest. I was thinking she could sit behind the counter and greet customers. Maybe she can check them out. We have a comfortable rolling chair. She can spend most of her time just sitting. Plus I'll always be there if she needs anything."

"I don't know." Shayla could hear the hesitancy in Bailey's voice.

"This will allow her to get out, and even interact with people. I'm sure she enjoys Buddy and your company, but I think she might be going stir crazy. I think it might be best if we head her off before she gets to that point. She can also spend some time with the ladies next door. They miss her. It's hard for them to get out here, and she isn't going anywhere so I think this will be best for everybody's sanity." Shayla crossed her fingers and snuggled back into Bailey's embrace.

"I guess it wouldn't hurt to ask her opinion," Bailey agreed.

"Good. Now, that other thing I brought up." Shayla turned in Bailey's arms and silenced her with a toe-curling kiss. They had yet to move their relationship to the next step and Shayla was still hesitant. Even though she knew Bailey loved her and wasn't using her for anything, she just didn't want to jump into bed. Out of all the stories she read, she disliked the ones where the main characters jumped right into bed. She appreciated the dance leading up to the sex, the anticipation for that one special night when two people truly in love come together for the first time. Those were the stories she loved. To her, those sex scenes were the ones she felt to her core. She could sense every emotion and touch, and those were the ones that made her want to smoke after reading, and she hated cigarettes. That was the type of buildup Bailey and she had. It was something she felt from her fingertips to her toes to the tips of her hair. Sometimes she thought about going out and buying a pack of cigarettes for the night her and Bailey would finally come together.

"I don't want to give you the wrong idea but how about I start staying over?" Shayla said and rested her head on her folded hands that lay on Bailey's upper chest.

"Really?"

"Really. I have a bag out in my car. I figure I can take Morgan with me tomorrow. And give you some time off," Shayla said.

"If she wants to that would be great, but even if she doesn't, just to be able to sleep with you in my arms would be wonderful. How about you go get your bag and I'll let Buddy out. Then we can get ready for bed."

"It's still early," Shayla said.

"That's ok, we can just crawl into bed and talk."

"Talk?"

"Well, we'll be using our lips but there may not be many words uttered," Bailey said with a smirk.

"Sounds good to me," Shayla said and bolted for the door.

"Hey Buddy, hurry it up. I don't think you're going to be able to do three rounds tonight. Out and in tonight," Bailey said and ushered the dog out the back door.

Morning came faster than Bailey expected. Disappointment surged through her when she reached out to find Shayla's side was considerably cool. Silence hung in the air. There was no doubt the house was empty of any other person. It wasn't until she searched for Buddy that she realized she was more alone than she thought. The moments ticked by and after the first hour, she discovered she missed her family. She forced herself to work a few more hours. Time dragged by until she finally pushed herself away from her desk. When she walked into the kitchen, she decided to fix a lunch for her family.

It was a great plan. The simple action allowed her to be able to check on her sister, to see that she wasn't pushing herself too hard. It wasn't until the last few weeks flew by that she realized how much she had really missed her alone time. She had a pattern, and since Morgan had been around, she found herself out of pace. Even her job was starting to suffer. Her boss asked her if she needed to take some time off. Of course she declined. She needed to be the strong one. She had to prove that she could do her work and take care of her sister. The past few hours she had worked proved that her girlfriend was one smart cookie. She had done more work in those few hours then she had done the previous few weeks.

In no time, Bailey had the car loaded with three sandwiches, a bag of pita chips, and hummus. She didn't forget little Buddy when she added a treat of chopped chicken and rice. Music blared from the radio and she sang along at the top of her lungs. It was something she only did in private. Once she tried with Buddy and he howled the whole time. With a sparkle in her eye, she made quick time arriving at the bookstore. Luck was on her side when she found a spot outside and expected to see Morgan sitting at the counter, but she was surprised to find Shayla bent over talking to a customer. The longer she stood and looked at the stranger at the counter, the more she realized it wasn't just any customer.

Bailey burst through the door. The women at the counter jumped when the door crashed against the wall. She didn't even pause when she slammed the cooler on the counter and headed straight for the taller woman.

"What the hell do you think you're doing here? I can't believe you have the audacity to show your face here after what you did," Bailey entered Dana's space and backed her away from her girlfriend.

"Bailey!" Shayla shouted.

The blond woman ignored her girlfriend. Rage simmered in her body as she waited for a response. It wasn't long in coming.

"I stopped by to talk to Shayla." Dana continued to back away from the irate woman.

"What gives you the right to talk to her?" Bailey asked. With clenched fists, she stood between Shayla and Dana.

"Bailey, stop," Shayla said. Deceptively strong hands reached out to grab one of her clenched fists to keep her away from the younger woman.

The single touch threw water on the fire that simmered in Bailey's eyes. She loosened her fingers and threaded them through her girlfriend's.

"I know what I did was wrong," Dana said, her eyes quickly glancing at the joined hands.

"What one? Using her, or forcing yourself on her?" When Bailey heard Shayla gasp, she knew she had crossed a line. She felt the fingers laced with hers attempt to pull away but she held them tighter. If she didn't have the connection grounding her, she wasn't sure she wouldn't throw a punch.

"Bailey, I know you're upset and I'm sorry. That's why I'm here. I'm here to apologize for everything I did." Dana took a tentative step closer to the woman.

"She's here to make amends. She's on step eight and came here to apologize," Shayla explained. "She was just about to tell me what happened to get her to this place before you barged in."

"And what got you to this place?" Bailey asked. Again she squeezed the hand twined with hers. She couldn't help the smile when she saw Dana look at their clasped hands again.

"Honestly?" Dana asked.

"What the hell is up with that saying? Has anybody ever said 'no, lie to me'? Of course honestly," Bailey said, frustrated with the whole situation. She didn't like the woman who stood before her. More than anything, she just wanted her to get on with her story so she could leave.

"It was because of you, and what you did. You stood up to me. That's something nobody's ever done," Dana said. Her eyes turned down and didn't leave her scuffed boots.

Now Bailey was intrigued. The woman who stood before her was a shell of the cocky twenty-something she met a few months ago. Her clothes hung limp from her frame; her slumped shoulders and back spoke of a woman defeated.

"That day you threw me out and handed me those two dollars was the day I hit rock bottom. I was sitting at the bus stop with just those two bucks to my name. I didn't have a job, a car, real support. The only friends I had were people I would party with. There was not one person I could ask for help and know they would be there. But as I sat waiting for the bus, I realized the only friend I had was a bottle. Hell, the reason I didn't have a car was too many DUIs. That was the other reason I didn't have a job. My parents were also pressuring me, and I think they were at the point where they were going to kick me out. They were all I had and I was about to lose them too. On the long walk home, I realized I needed help. When I arrived home, I found my things boxed up. I begged my parents to help me. That night I checked into rehab, and now here I am at step eight. It's a long list and I'm just getting started. I knew I needed to start here," Dana explained. Bailey waited for her to look up and was surprised to find tears in her eyes.

Bailey knew how hard it was to dig their way out once someone fell into a bottle. She lost her mother to the bottle and she admired the young woman for taking the steps to reclaim her life. Even though she admired Dana for her recovery, she knew they were still never going to be friends.

"I just wanted to say my piece and not keep you from your day," Dana said. "Plus I have a bus to catch if I'm going to make it to work on time."

"I'm glad you got your life in order," Shayla said. She reached out with her empty hand and took Dana's hand before giving it a squeeze. "I wish you all the luck in the world."

"Thank you again for accepting my apology," Dana said.

Words froze on Bailey's lips by the slight squeeze from Shayla's hand still entwined with hers.

After Dana left, Bailey turned to Shayla. "You accepted her apology after what she did to you?"

"Yes," Shayla said. She took back her hand and folded them over her chest.

"Why?" Bailey asked. She knew Shayla was a nice person, but she had been used and hurt. It would have served Dana right to hold back her acceptance and let her squirm, knowing how she had hurt someone.

"Because she needs it if she's going to be able to heal and get on with her life," Shayla said. She started to straighten the counter and avoided meeting Bailey's eyes.

"But she hurt you." Bailey reached out and grabbed Shayla's hands to get her to look at her.

Eyes almost black with anger turned to her. "What would have been gained if I had held back and not accepted her apology? It takes more energy to hold a grudge then just get over it and move on. Plus you hurt me too."

The words Shayla said hurt worse than if she had actually slapped her across the face. Finally the truth of how she felt was out. But Bailey couldn't see how the two things were similar.

"How can you say that? I never used you. I've only loved you."

"You abandoned me. I loved you and you just left. You didn't even give me any warning."

Bailey watched tears form in her girlfriend's eyes, extinguishing the fire. Shayla swiped at them but they continued to fall. Bailey tried to go to her but Shayla held up a hand. Feet from her distraught girlfriend, she stopped.

"But that's nothing close to what she did to you. It's apples and oranges." Bailey didn't understand how her leaving compared to being almost raped.

"Honey, apples and oranges are both fruit. They're not the same thing but they're close. Granted you didn't use me or force yourself on me, but you still hurt me. When you left, you didn't give me any warning. I had to live with what you did. You ripped out my heart and didn't tell me why. At least with Dana I had choices. I knew what she was doing, but I allowed it. That's the difference. Knowledge. I knew she was using me, but I was using her too. I voluntarily handed her my car keys and money. In return, she made me feel wanted, and loved, and at that time in my life I needed it. You know how much I read. People say when you're in a situation like that you have blinders, but I didn't. I saw everything, and even had you told me about what Sandy and Mac had told you about Dana I still would've gone through the same thing. At that time, she was able to give me what I needed. If I was able to give her something that she needed too it was a win-win. She didn't use me, because I willingly gave to her. So you ask me how I can forgive her, because the only hurt she gave me was when she tried to force herself on me, and that didn't happen because you were there to rescue me." Shayla's tears never stopped. Her face hid behind her hands finally allowed Bailey the opportunity to take her into her arms.

Bailey's heart hurt knowing that her actions had wounded the woman she loved. Each tear that fell on her shirt burned, knowing she caused it.

"If I forgave you then I have to forgive her," Shayla whispered into her chest. "I love you. I've loved you for years, and everything that happened before this day is in the past, and that means nothing to me. The only thing that matters to me is you and our future."

Bailey took a few deep breaths before she replied. "I love you. I'm sorry if I overreacted. It wasn't my place. It's just I saw her in here and I couldn't help but think back to the last time I saw you two together."

"It's ok. I kind of liked it actually. It's nice to know you're there for me," Shayla said as nimble fingers started to play with Baily's exposed throat.

Bailey blushed. "Hey, where's my sister and dog?" Bailey said before she pulled away.

Shayla rubbed her face before answering. "Buddy needed a potty break and Morgan wanted to get out for a while. She took him for a walk. She should've been back by now. So my guess is that they're both next door."

"Ok. Well, I fixed lunch for the four of us. I'm going to go and get them so we can eat," Bailey said.

"You seem to be getting more and more domesticated in your old age. I kind of like it," Shayla said and ran her fingers through Bailey's short locks. "Before you leave, can you do me a favor?"

Bailey knew she would probably have to carry a large box of books and didn't mind it. She would do anything for the woman she loved. "How can I help?"

"Can you bring those two lips over here and give me a kiss? I've been waiting all day for a kiss since you didn't wake up when I left." Shayla's fingers grasped Bailey's hair and pulled lips to her. She didn't pull away until the doorbell sounded.

"Sorry," Bailey said before she backed away.

"Don't ever apologize for being a good kisser. I expect more when you return," Shayla said and tuned to welcome the customer.

Bailey hurried to the bakery and found it doing stiff business. The person she was looking for was in a booth with Wanda and Buddy. Buddy was on the older woman's lap and his long tongue lapped at the fingers feeding him bits and pieces from her personal pizza.

"Hey, you guys," Bailey said.

Morgan slid further into the booth and gave her sister room to sit.

"What are you drinking?" Bailey asked her younger sister.

"An almond latte with cinnamon," Morgan said. A tiny smile appeared after she took her sip.

"But you're not supposed to have caffeine." Bailey said and reached for the drink.

"Hey, back off and get your own. It's decaf," Morgan said. She pulled the drink away from her sister's outstretched hand.

"Here you go." Connie said. Two cups were placed before Bailey. She rolled her eyes at Bailey's inquisitive look. "One for you and one for Shayla. She just called and said you were on your way and asked if we could have a cup sent over. Oh, and she said to hurry because the sandwiches looked so good she didn't know if she was going to wait for you two."

"Come on. We'd better get over there before she eats Buddy's chicken and rice too." The small dog's head snapped up upon hearing his name. "Yes, I brought you lunch too. Are you hungry?"

The question was rhetorical. He was always

hungry.

"Well, come on then. I'm starving myself." Morgan pushed at Bailey until she slid from the booth.

"Ok," Bailey said and acquired Buddy's leash from Wanda. "Sorry to take her from you but we need to feed Angel."

As if the baby had known she was the topic of conversation, she decided to get into the action by kicking. Bailey's eyes grew to the size of saucers as she saw the foot outline.

"Can I?"

Morgan laughed and grabbed her sister's hand, placing it on her belly. "She's been really active. I think everybody here has felt her already. Here," Morgan said as she felt her kick again.

"Soccer. Definitely soccer," Bailey said. She smiled when she felt another well placed kick. "Crap. We need to go. Here, take Buddy and I'll get a carrying case for the coffee. I'll be there in a minute."

With drinks in hand, Bailey made her way back to the bookstore to find Buddy already finished with his meal. Sad eyes watched as Morgan and Shayla set out the sandwiches and sides. Those big browns were his secret weapon and he knew how to use them.

"Thanks for setting this up," Bailey said before she bent down before Buddy. She grabbed his face and placed a quick peck on his nose and was rewarded with a kiss of her own. She gave him another quick scratch before making her way to the food.

"No problem, it was rather selfish. I was starving," Morgan said. A chip loaded with hummus was already half way to her mouth.

"Well, we have to keep you nice and fed. Don't want you getting weak. I think next time I'm going to make sure I'm up so I can make you lunches to take," Bailey said. White teeth sunk into her chicken salad sandwich.

"This is really good. I didn't know you were so good in the kitchen." Shayla said around the bite she had just taken.

"Neither did I," Bailey admitted.

"So what are you doing for the rest of the day?" Morgan asked Bailey, who had just taken her own a mouthful.

Bailey held up a finger and swallowed before answering, "I thought I would just chill here and help set up for the book club. I still have a chapter or two to read before tonight."

"I like the sound of that," Shayla said and leaned her head on Bailey's shoulder. Bailey turned and kissed her girlfriend's forehead. Another smile blossomed on her face, knowing she could do that any time she wanted.

Bailey spent the rest of the day on the couch with a book in hand and Buddy on her lap. Since they had bought him, he had never really been out in public except his walks around the neighborhood. The pet owner couldn't have been more proud of the way he was acting. He alerted them when he needed to go to the bathroom, and left the customers alone. Every once in a while, a child would cautiously approach him and he graciously allowed them to hug and pet him. He would thank them with the same puppy kisses Bailey enjoyed.

When people started to arrive for the book club, Buddy remained next to Bailey as she prepared the store. He only left her side when she assisted Morgan with getting comfortable on the couch, at which time he switched allegiances and snuggled up to the pregnant woman. Bailey couldn't blame him; she had a much bigger lap now.

As the women strolled in, Bailey realized Amanda was not in attendance. It worried her to think she was the reason for her quitting the book club. She might have caused her girlfriend a possible sale.

Women stood around drinking coffee and eating pastries while they waited for the group to start. It seemed every woman had placed a hand on Morgan's bulging belly, asking how she was doing. It warmed Bailey's heart to think these women cared about her sister. Bailey had actually stayed to monitor her sister to see how far she pushed herself. To her surprise, the most strenuous thing Morgan did all day was push herself out of the office chair to make her way to the bathroom. Bailey had to agree she was doing less at the bookstore then she was at home. Maybe her working at the bookstore was a good thing after all.

Before the group started, Bailey noticed how Sandy and Mac attempted to slip quietly into the building, not an easy task when there is a small bell above the door. It didn't surprise her as they were always cutting it close, but what did surprise her was the hand holding. The little display was something new. She caught Mac's eyes and a small thank you was sent her way. It made her feel good to know she helped a couple come together.

Shayla sat next to Morgan and Bailey sat on her other side, perched on the arm of the couch. The rest of the group settled and Bailey was happy to see a few new faces. Shayla started by giving a brief background of the author and the book. Sandy was quick to jump in once she opened the discussion.

"I thought this book was great. It had everything, action, romance, sex, twists, and turns. I couldn't put it down. It took me only two days to get through the whole thing. I would have gotten through it faster but my miser of a boss kept making me actually work."

"Damn right," Connie said before the room erupted in laughter.

"But seriously, I loved this book. I wasn't expecting the ending. The romance was subtle enough to be enjoyable. It didn't over power the real adventure that we were on. It was there the whole time like a backpack but it didn't weigh the story down. I really didn't want it to end. When it did, I felt a sudden loss. Like I was losing two of my best friends," Sandy added.

The women sat silent. Never before had they heard Sandy talk so passionately about a book. In the few months Bailey had been attending, all she ever heard from the young woman was complaining. She had never understood why she actually attended the book club. She had always thought Mac was the only reason she made the meeting.

"Thank you, Sandy. Does anybody else have anything to say?" Shayla asked.

The women continued to break down the book for the next hour and a half. Morgan had started to slump in her seat and had Shayla not called the meeting to an end Bailey would have taken her sister home.

"Well, I think that about does it for this evening. Before we break up, I wanted to let you know that I had said a few months ago that Allura Williams would be releasing another book soon. I know a few of you were looking forward to it but the publisher had released a letter stating that they were pushing it back a few more months. I decided to slip in another action book for Sandy. Now if anybody doesn't have the next book I have a stack at the register if you need it," Shayla said. Gently, she pushed the pup that had made his way onto her lap and stood to make her way to the front of the store. A few women followed her to the register while the rest of the group stayed to talk to Morgan.

Bailey watched her sister smile, trying to ease everybody's concerns, but the bags under her eyes and slump of her shoulders told a different story. Only four more weeks until her due date, but Bailey knew they could have a new book club member sooner than that. Two more weeks and they would be hosting a baby shower. After that, Bailey's spare time would be spent setting up playpens, bassinettes, and cribs. They had agreed to turn Morgan's old room into a nursery. Even though Morgan's new room was on the first floor, Bailey had argued that Morgan would need her sleep. With the baby across the hall from her, it would be easier for her to take care of the night time feedings. In the morning when Bailey started work, she would take the baby downstairs and place her in the bassinette in Morgan's room.

"Are we ready?" Shayla asked after the last customer left.

Morgan nodded and tried to push herself out of the couch. Bailey saw her struggle and scooted over. While Shayla pulled, Bailey lifted her off the old sunken couch.

"Thanks."

Bailey snapped on Buddy's leash and grabbed the cooler now filled with books. Since her truck was higher and easier for Morgan she had Shayla take Buddy and the cooler while she drove her sister.

"Tired?" Bailey asked as she pulled onto the road behind Shayla.

"Yes and no, my body is tired but my mind is wide awake. You know the saying 'the mind is willing but the flesh is weak'? I finally know where that comes from. Plus I think I've had more hands on my belly today then I have in my whole life."

Bailey watched as Morgan wrapped her arms around her stomach, protecting her little package. It's something Bailey saw Morgan do a lot. She came to realize that it was subconscious move her sister made. When Bailey asked Morgan about it she denied she did it that often, but whenever Bailey looked at the mom to be her hands were somewhere on her front bulge.

"How about we pick something up on the way home? You pick," Bailey said.

"I know it's not good for me because of the sodium but I could kill for some Chinese right now," Morgan said as her head fell back on the seat.

"That sounds good. I'll just call in an order. I'm sure Shayla will be fine with whatever we get."

They arrived home not too long after Shayla. The food was quickly consumed and the house was shut up tight as everybody settled into bed. Buddy had taken to sleeping at the foot of Morgan's bed.

Shayla lay in her usual position with her head on Bailey's shoulder. Her fingers drew lazy patterns over Bailey's tee shirt-clad stomach.

"You're driving me crazy." Bailey captured the wandering hand.

"I'm sorry. Is my staying here a bad thing? I mean I know we agreed to take things slow, but with me practically living here and us still not making it past first base has to be hard."

"I knew when I asked you to move here it might be a challenge, but having you with me is totally worth it. I can stand a little torture now and then."

Shayla laughed and cuddled closer. "I love you. I don't mean to torture you. I just can't keep my hands off you."

"I love you too and I promised when I asked you to stay here that I would not push you."

"Thank you."

Soon both women were asleep. Bailey knew that their life was going to get more hectic as the due date came closer. They were not ready for the little bundle of joy and now it was a race to the big day.

Chapter Twenty

The old house was bursting at the seams with the number of women who had arrived for Morgan's baby shower. The warm June day allowed Bailey to move the party to the back yard. As the women ooo'd and ahhh'd over the presents Morgan opened, Buddy kept a steady watch. He was diligently making sure no uninvited furry animals invaded the party while periodically making stops to receive a treat or two.

Sandy and Mac pulled Bailey aside when she emerged from the house with another platter of food.

"We've been talking, and for our present we'd like to paint the baby's room," Mac said.

"That would be nice. We haven't really had any time to get to it yet. We've at least cleared it out." Bailey couldn't help but feel relieved. There was still so much to do and time was short.

"That's great, so it shouldn't take us much time to get everything painted and set up," Sandy said.

Months had passed since Bailey had been introduced to the girls. Mac had not changed much externally but internally, she saw confidence radiate from the young woman since she had started to date Sandy. But Sandy had finally dropped the crazy hair and settled on a light brown that complimented her features. The loss of a few facial piercings also had a drastic transformation. Bailey didn't know if it was the influence of her girlfriend or her dedication to the bakery. Either way, she enjoyed watching the two women bloom in front of her.

"You're going to set up too?" Bailey questioned and shifted her grip on the heavy platter.

"Yeah. You're going to get a lot of gifts that need to be assembled. We'll do that and have it all done in a day, possibly a day and a half at most," Sandy said. The young woman took pity on Bailey and relieved her of the food tray. She walked it to the buffet table.

"Thank you. That would be perfect. Maybe you can get the painting done tomorrow. Then set everything up on Monday while she's at the bookstore. I'll talk to Dion and Connie to see if they can let you off a little early. I think Morgan would love that," Bailey said. Her forearms burned from the strain of holding the heavy platter. Gently she rubbed them to try to get some feeling back.

"Great, we'll go and bring around the dresser we refinished. We'd planned on that being enough, but then we heard Morgan say something about the nursery not even being started. We thought we could help," Mac stated.

"I'm sure she's going to love it. Do you need any help with the dresser?" Bailey asked.

"Nah, we got it. Can you just make sure the back gate is unlocked and Buddy isn't close so he won't bolt?" Mac requested and wrapped her arm around her girlfriend when Sandy rejoined their conversation.

It took a few chicken treats before Bailey could grab her sentinel. He had a fit when she locked him inside. After he was secure, she unlatched the back gate. He was only appeased when she again bribed him with a few treats. A few minutes later, she was able to rejoin the group. She stood next to Shayla, who wrote down a list of who gave what, so Morgan could send off thank you cards later. A huge pile of gifts sat on the back lawn. Bailey didn't know what else they could possibly need for the first few years of this little baby's life. Even though they had been calling the baby a girl, she was relieved to find the bulk of the baby's clothes were in colors for both boys and girls. There were not very many blues or pinks in the growing stack.

The large group of women were now playing the first of many games when Bailey heard the two women bicker while trying to get the dresser into the back. Before she could reach the side yard and offer assistance, they emerged with a beautiful dresser. They struggled under the weight of a heavy sturdy dresser that the baby would be able to use for a long time. It was not some new piece of furniture made of particle board, but hand crafted, made of solid oak. She wasn't surprised to hear gasps from the women on the lawn. Mac and Sandy progressed slowly until they were able to set the dresser on the back porch.

"Oh my God, it's gorgeous," Morgan said and struggled to extricate herself from the plush chair they had brought out from the living room. Bailey was quickly at her side. Morgan waddled over to the dresser. Manicured nails traced the ornate detail on the dresser. The stain on the wood was beautiful, causing the grains to pop against the rich color.

"Oh, thank you so much," Morgan said. Suddenly she pulled the two women in as close as her bulging belly would allow. Tears sprang to her eyes. Mac and Sandy blushed as Morgan clung to them, thanking them profusely.

"It wasn't anything. We found it at a garage sale.

A few hours with the sander and some stain and this is what you get." Sandy tried to sound like it was no big deal, but Bailey knew there were plenty hours of love and sweat in the tall bureau.

"I'm sorry, everybody," Morgan said after she released the women. She pulled a hanky from her pocket. It wasn't the first time she had to dry her tears. It probably wouldn't be the last either. "I'm sorry, it's the hormones, but I really do love it."

A few hours later, the party broke up and Bailey and Shayla moved the presents into the living room. The three women stood in the living room and looked at the piles of gifts. They realized there was nothing else they could possibly buy for the baby. Everything on Morgan's wish list and then some had been purchased.

"Thank you for a lovely day." Morgan hugged her sister before moving on to Shayla. "I wish I could stay out here and visit some more but think I had better get to bed. I've felt a bit off today and think I should turn in."

"Are you all right?" Bailey asked and hurried to her sister's side. In the past few weeks, it seemed she was at her sister's side more than her girlfriend's.

"Yeah, I just think it was the excitement, and heat," Morgan said. One hand continued to rub her bulging belly as the other hand found a new home on her lower back.

"I knew we should've done this sooner. We shouldn't have waited so long." Bailey paced the room as her fingers ran through her hair.

"Bailey, it's fine. I'm fine. It was a beautiful day. I'm just ready to have this little one out of me and meet her. Hopefully she'll be on time, and in two weeks we'll be meeting this little one," Morgan said.

"You go to bed. I'll take care of her," Shayla said from the couch.

"Good night," Bailey said. She followed Morgan to the hall.

"Will you look at all this stuff? I think that baby is going to be set for the next few years," Bailey said when she returned to the living room. With her hands on her hips, she surveyed the gifts that littered the living room.

"Well, that one year of diaper service that Wanda purchased is worth its weight in gold," Shayla agreed as she flipped through the pages of gifts she had written. She set the book down and kicked off her sandals before placing her bare feet on the old coffee table.

"You mean poo." Bailey laughed. "I think the dresser is beautiful. What nobody else knows is that Sandy and Mac are coming over tomorrow to paint the nursery. Then Monday, while you and Morgan are at the bookstore they're going to come back and set up the whole room. And let me tell you I'm thankful because I know I couldn't have carried that dresser upstairs by myself."

"Let's head upstairs ourselves," Shayla stretched and tried to stifle a yawn. She stood and reached for Bailey's hand.

Bailey took the offered hand and kissed her knuckles. "Are you tired?"

"Not so much. I was thinking we could do something else," Shayla said. She pulled Bailey behind her as she made her way to the stairs.

"Are you sure? I don't want you to do something you're not ready for, or want to do," Bailey hedged. She stopped at the bottom of the stairs. Shayla paused on the first step and turned to her girlfriend.

"Don't worry. Right now there's a lot I do want to do, and the quicker we get up there the quicker we can start doing it," Shayla stated as she pulled a reluctant Bailey behind her.

"Shayla, I think we need to talk before we do anything," Bailey said when they entered the room.

"I can think of something better you could be doing with your lips. Talking is ok, but it's normally done after. But if you want to talk we can talk," Shayla agreed, but still pulled a surprised Bailey onto the bed with her.

The two women got comfortable on Bailey's new queen size bed. The double had been tight and after a month of tight quarters Bailey realized it was time to get a grown up bed.

Bailey picked at a hangnail while she tried to gather her words. She grabbed Shayla's hand. A few more silent seconds passed before she started.

"I know you read a lot. I want you to have all the love and passion you've read about, but I'm afraid I'm not going to be able to give you that." Bailey gently ran her thumb over Shayla's knuckles. Their eyes hadn't met since they walked through the door.

Shayla forced Bailey to look at her. "Hey, listen to me. I do read a lot, and yes, I want what I read about, but I don't expect it. Just being with you is better than anything in a book. It's not the sex but the emotional part. You already give me that. You make me feel things I've never felt, and that's just by kissing me and being near me."

"I feel the same, but I have something to confess. I guess it's something we should've talked about before we got to this point but…." Bailey paused and looked away. She was self-conscious and couldn't tell Shayla what she needed to while looking in her trusting eyes. It was embarrassing. She didn't want to see Shayla laugh at her. "I uh... I've never been intimate with anybody."

"Bailey. I kind of figured it out. If I was your first kiss, I didn't think you had been intimate with anybody else either. So is this why you really have been ok with taking things slow?" Shayla asked. Soft fingers caressed Bailey's cheek urging her to look at her.

"Yes and no. I mean, I respect you, but I'm also afraid I'm not going to be able to please you, but really I do want this," Bailey said. She leaned into Shayla's touch.

"Good, because I don't care that you're a virgin. But if I were honest about it, I would say I'm honored to be your first. I've only been with one more person than you have, so I only have a little bit of an edge on you," Shayla said.

"So it's really ok? You really want to do this?" Bailey asked, hope evident in her eyes.

"Yes. I want you. I've made you wait long enough. I love you and want to show you how much," Shayla said. Not giving Bailey a chance to reply, she leaned in and captured her lips with her own. Slowly she edged off the bed to stand in front of Bailey's parted legs.

"Is this all right?" Shayla asked.

Bailey nodded.

"Good."

They only broke eye contact when Shayla removed her tee. Bailey let her eyes roam Shayla's creamy skin. She leaned in and kissed the birthmark located directly above her belly button. Since high school, she had wanted to do that. She couldn't stop smiling as she was finally able to do one thing she had thought of doing forever. Her breath caught when Shayla reached back and unfastened her bra, slowly peeling it down her shoulders. The last time she had seen Shayla in any form of undress was over ten years ago and the woman baring herself before her had changed. Her breath paused as skin was uncovered.

Bailey sat silently as she looked at the beautiful body before her, unable to speak. Her mouth was dry. All the moisture in her body had moved south. Slowly Bailey reached out and ran her fingers up silky skin. She felt Shayla shiver at her touch. When she came to the bottom of Shayla's breasts, she ran her fingertips along the underside of soft mounds and reveled in the way her nipples pebbled. Gentle fingers brushed the tip of the hard nipple. Shayla hissed in response to the touch. Her legs started to shake so she crawled onto Bailey's lap. Quickly Bailey removed her fingers and reached around to keep Shayla from falling.

"You're killing me," Shayla said before she bent down, once again capturing Bailey's lips with her own. Their lips moved as if they had known the feel of each other for years. Too soon, Shayla broke their connection, her breath ragged.

Shayla slid off Bailey's lap. Before Bailey knew what was had happened Shayla had removed her shirt and was attempting to undo her bra.

"Here, I got it," Bailey said and reached around to undo her bra, letting it fall to the floor.

Shayla silently undid her jeans. Pushing them and her panties off her hips, she allowed gravity to do the rest before stepping out of the pile of clothes. With a flick of her foot, she sent the garments flying across the room. She reached down and rested her fingers on the button on Bailey's jeans before she paused. Brown eyes asked what words could not. The only response she received was a nod. Slowly she unbuttoned then unzipped the pants. Bailey raised her hips off the bed, allowing Shayla to pull them off.

Bailey's heart pounded a mile a minute. All the nervousness she thought she would have felt never appeared. She had waited and dreamt of this moment forever, and now that it was here, she wanted nothing more than to please the woman who held her heart. Sitting naked in front of Shayla, she felt comfortable and loved. Silently she slid onto the middle of the bed and lay down. A few more seconds passed, while Shayla simply looked at Bailey's exposed body before she crawled onto the bed to lay down next to her. Again she kissed Bailey as she rolled on top of her. Both women couldn't control the moan that escaped when their naked bodies came in contact for the first time. No more words were uttered as the women came together to do what both had longed to do for so very long.

"I love you," Bailey heard from the body that her head rested on. She also thought she caught something else but she couldn't catch it over the beating of her own heart.

"I love you, too," Bailey said as she lazily ran her fingers along Shayla's back. "That was just…Wow. I'm glad I waited."

Shayla laughed. "I'm sure there are women out there better than me, but thank you. It meant a lot to me too."

"But it meant everything to me because it was you," Bailey said. She turned to look at Shayla. Bailey rolled Shayla on her back. She placed her hands on Shayla's chest and rested her chin on her entwined hands. Her eyes traveled down and landed on the necklace she had given Shayla in high school.

Suddenly Bailey rolled over, opening the drawer to her nightstand. She had something she wanted to show Shayla. Now felt like as good a time as any.

"Remember this?" Bailey asked, holding out a long white box.

"You didn't," Shayla said.

"No, I didn't. This isn't for you. It's for me," Bailey said before opening the box. Inside sat a necklace matching Shayla's.

"What's this?" Shayla asked.

"I bought it for me when I bought yours. I wanted matching ones so people knew we were a couple, or well, you know," Bailey said. "I know, the stupid thinking of some teenager."

"No, I think it's sweet. Here, turn around." Shayla nudged her.

Bailey did as instructed and soon felt the metal of the heart land on her chest. It had taken years for it to get there, but it felt good, right, and warmed her heart that Shayla wanted her to wear it. She turned and wrapped Shayla in her arms. "Thank you,"

Shayla laughed. "You bought it, but I wish you would've told me back then. I would have asked you to wear it then."

Bailey knew that she had made a mistake running when she was younger, but as she lay naked in her lover's arms, she knew that her track days were over. She wasn't going anywhere. No matter what, her lover was stuck with her. She rolled Shayla on her back, intent to continue with their night, but again she heard a noise.

"Do you hear that?" Bailey strained to hear the sound.

Both women waited silently until they heard the noise again.

"It sounds like scratching," Shayla said.

Bailey reluctantly rolled off Shayla before making her way to the door. Buddy stood on the other side, and ran to the stairs, turned and waited for Bailey to follow.

"It's Buddy. I think he has to go to the bathroom," Bailey answered. Before leaving the room, she slipped on her jeans and tee.

"Hurry back," Shayla said before she lay back down. A thin sheet draped across her waist as she put her hands behind her head to wait for Bailey's return.

Bailey looked over her naked body, unable to help but leer as she said, "I'll be right back."

Buddy scrambled down the stairs. Bailey was hot on his tail when she suddenly stopped. The sight at the bottom of the stairs froze her blood. Morgan stood on the landing in her nightgown, holding her stomach, standing over a puddle. Bailey's heart went out to her sister. It wasn't the first time she had lost control of her bladder.

"Morgan, are you all right?" Bailey asked as she rushed to her sister's side.

Morgan clutched her hand, almost breaking her bones when she squeezed. Bailey was forced to her knees and instantly knew she was not. She gritted her teeth against the pain and seconds later Morgan's iron grasp eased.

"I think I'm in labor," Morgan said through clenched teeth.

"SHAYLA!" Bailey yelled. When she was able to get back on her feet, Bailey helped her sister to a chair. "How far apart are the contractions?"

"I think about five minutes," Morgan groaned. Bailey used the hem of her tee to dab at the sweat that peppered her sister's brow.

"Why didn't you call earlier?" Bailey asked and rubbed her sister's hands that were still held between hers.

"Because I thought you were asleep. I didn't want to worry you. They started about an hour ago but they've been getting closer. The thing that scares me is I think my water broke." Morgan indicated the puddle.

"Oh shit. We need to get you to the hospital. SHAYLA!" Bailey yelled, helping her sister up.

Shayla appeared a second later, barely dressed. She took one look at the situation before she turned and bolted back upstairs. "Let me get some pants on. I'll grab the suitcase. You get your sister to my car and we'll get her to the hospital."

Morgan leaned on Bailey as another contraction hit. She doubled over and let out another gut wrenching moan.

Bailey had never felt so helpless in all her life as she watched her sister deal with the pain. She stopped and reached over to gently rub her sister's lower back. It was all she could think to help. Everything they had learned in the birthing class had vanished from her memory. They had barely made it out the door before Shayla raced past them with Morgan's suitcase and keys in one hand, two pairs of sandals in the other.

The car was started and ready to go before Bailey was able to settle Morgan in the front seat and buckle her in.

Shayla ran every yellow light. Bailey had never known the woman to speed but was thankful she pushed the limit the whole way to the hospital. The only time her foot hit the brake was when she pulled up to the emergency room. "You get her checked in and I'll park and be in as soon as I can."

Bailey was out the door the second it stopped and ran in to get a wheelchair. Quickly she had her sister seated and pushed her into the highly illuminated emergency room. A sigh of relief escaped her when she saw that the room was practically empty.

"I need help. My sister's in labor. The contractions are now only about two minutes apart and her water broke already," Bailey informed the nurse on duty.

Soon an orderly came in and whisked Morgan away through doors Bailey couldn't get past.

"We need you to fill this out." The nurse handed Bailey a clipboard.

"I don't have all her information but I'll do my best," Bailey said and accepted the clipboard with shaky hands. Before she put pen to paper Shayla ran through the doors.

"Is she all right?" Shayla asked. She bent at the waist and grasped her knees, breathing as if she had just finished a mile.

"I don't know. I have to fill this out, but we have to wait and see," Bailey said. They had the whole place to themselves. Shayla pulled her over to two hard plastic chairs. Bailey immediately started filling out empty boxes, surprised to discover she knew almost everything on the forms.

After she returned the stack of paperwork, they silently watched the local news before they were called to the desk. The nurse informed them that Morgan had been moved to the fourth floor. They were given instructions at the nurses' station to find out what room she had been checked into. They were then directed to a bank of elevators. Bailey grabbed Shayla's hand as they walked to the elevators. Silently she pressed the up button and pulled Shayla in for a hug. "I'm sorry our night was cut short."

"Oh honey, it's fine. We have so many more nights to come. This night was already special, but now it's more important. It seems like someone else wants our attention right now." Shayla pulled away when she heard the ding. Hand in hand, they entered the empty box. Again Bailey pulled Shayla in, kissing her, trying to tell Shayla that their night was to be continued.

"I love you," she said when she pulled back.

"I love you too," Shayla replied.

The doors opened and they quickly were on the fourth floor. They found the correct room, but it was empty. At the nurses station they were directed to an empty waiting room. Bailey began pacing. Her mind started to wonder about what was going on. She was Morgan's birthing coach. With every step she took in the small room, her training came back. She was supposed to be there for her. It was her job to make sure her sister was comfortable. To do everything she could to help her sister keep her mind off the pain. By her side was where she was meant to be. After countless trips around the waiting room, she made her way back to the nurse's station, demanding to speak to someone.

"I'm sorry ma'am. There should be a doctor out

to see you soon," the nurse said, again instructing Bailey to be patient and return to the waiting room.

The nightly news blared from the TV hanging on the wall opposite where they sat. Shayla finally pulled Bailey to an empty seat. She held her hands, trying to soothe the distressed woman. Moments before Bailey was ready to make another visit to the nurses' station a small balding man with thick glasses entered the room. "Are you waiting for Morgan Hutsell?"

"Yes," Bailey said. Like a rocket, she popped up from her seat before bolting to the man's side. Shayla quickly joined them and placed a hand on her lover's back. The small circles helped to calm Bailey's frazzled nerves.

"I'm sorry it's taken me this long to get to you. We've had three deliveries tonight and your sister's is unfortunately not easy. The baby is in distress and we're currently prepping her now. We need to do an emergency c-section. It seems the little one has the cord wrapped around its neck and is losing oxygen. We need to get the baby out. I'll be back as soon as I have any more information," he said before hurrying off. Even if they had any questions, they didn't want to hold him up from getting back to Morgan.

Bailey sank into one of the plush chairs. "Oh God. I hope nothing happens to Morgan or the baby."

"I'm sure they'll be all right. Soon we'll have a little visitor and everything will be fine," Shayla said. "Why don't you call Dion and the girls? I'm sure they'll want to be here for this."

"You're right. I totally forgot. They would kill me if they missed this." Bailey pulled her phone from her pocket. She was happy to have something to do to keep her mind off her sister and what was going on down the hall. Ten minutes later, she shut the phone and waited with Shayla. Dion and Connie were on their way to pick up Wanda. Dion said they would call Sandy and Mac since Bailey didn't have their number programmed into her phone.

"Everything's going to be fine," Shayla said. She reached over and planted a kiss on Bailey's head.

"I hope you're right. I really do."

They moved to the couch. On autopilot, they assumed their normal position. Bailey wrapped her arms around Shayla and pulled her close. Heat radiated off the bookstore owner and Bailey remembered the heat they had created earlier that night. She had waited so long to be with her. Now it was both heaven and hell to hold the woman in her arms. The urge to touch her continued to raise. Her hands started to snake under Shayla's shirt, creating little moans from the woman in her arms. Her desire skyrocketed. Thankfully, before she actually acted on the craving, the waiting room erupted as three harried looking woman rushed in.

"Is everything all right? Did we miss it?" Wanda asked, rushing over to the couple. Bailey tried not to laugh at the frantic woman. Wanda had always been poised, dressed to the nines, but the woman who stood before her with curlers in her hair and slippers on her feet was something she never thought she would see in public.

"Uh, Wanda, why do you have tin cans in your hair?" Shayla asked.

Bailey looked harder and realized the older woman did have four or five tin cans wrapped in her hair.

"I saw it on Pintrest. They're cheaper than curlers and they give bigger bounce. Now you know my secret." Wanda patted the cans.

Dion hid her smile behind her hand and Connie swatted at her partner.

"And to answer your earlier question no, you're fine. We're just waiting on the doctor," Shayla said, before the door opened again. The women assumed it would be Mac and Sandy, but the doctor came in wearing disheveled scrubs.

The women surrounded Bailey like soldiers protecting their general. Bailey squeezed Shayla's hand before letting her know she was ok.

"Well, great news. Both ladies are doing just fine. We're just getting them cleaned up before moving them back into their...."

"Ladies? It's a girl?" Bailey asked. Her voice hitched at the news.

"Yes, a healthy little girl. Ten toes and ten little fingers," he said. "Give us ten minutes. A nurse should be in with a room number." The doctor scribbled something on the clipboard as he exited the room.

Shayla pulled Bailey in for a bear hug. A few seconds later Bailey had to beg her to ease up for her ribs' sake. The group was still high-spirited when the door opened again. Mac and Sandy entered and their face fell as they took in the women.

"We missed it?" Mac asked. Mac looked like Bailey had just taken her only puppy away.

"We were just told. She had a little girl. They're both fine. They're moving them to a room now. We have to wait a little while so you didn't miss meeting her," Dion replied and pulled the girls into a hug.

Soon the women found themselves crammed into a small room. Six pairs of eyes misted as they looked at the little baby with a head of thick black curly hair and cobalt eyes.

"She's beautiful," Bailey said.

"Do you want to hold her?" Morgan asked as she smoothed down the still wet hair.

"Oh, I don't know. I'd probably drop her. It's all right. I'm sure everybody else wants to hold her," Bailey said. She wrung her hands, not taking her eyes of the little bundle. Each second she would reach out just to snatch her hands right back.

"It's ok. You're not going to drop her. Here, just cradle her head in your arm like this. Now hold her bottom with your hand and you'll be fine," Morgan instructed before she handed over her baby girl. When her daughter was out of her arms, she fell back into the bed. Bailey looked at her sister and her heart went out to the woman. She appeared as if she had just run two marathons back to back. There was not an ounce of strength left in her fragile body. Now that the baby was born, she still couldn't rest as she had to fight the cancer that still inhabited her body.

Bailey cradled Angel as if she was precious china. When the little hand grabbed her finger, she knew she had also grabbed her heart. She was so in love with the little girl she couldn't have loved her more if she were her own child. Unknown to Bailey a certain pair of eyes watched her, knowing she possibly would be the one to hold Angel's hand through her life if Morgan couldn't.

"Stop hogging her. Hand her over." Dion demanded her turn. Nobody held her longer than five minutes before the next person stepped up and wanted to hold the new bundle. The little group had left for a few minutes while the new momma attempted her first feeding.

Bailey hovered around the baby until she noticed Morgan fighting to stay awake. It wasn't until then that she realized how late it had gotten. The sun was already starting to peek through the windows.

"We should go and let you and the baby get some sleep. It's been a long night and you need all the rest you can get before you start your treatment," Bailey said as they followed the baby being wheeled out of the room.

Morgan didn't reply. She simply nodded and closed her eyes. Everybody had quietly slipped out of the room. The small group made their way to the big pane window, joining other strangers gathered around to look at their new bundle of joy.

"She's beautiful," Wanda gushed again for the hundredth time.

"I'm just glad she's here so Morgan can start her treatment. It's going to be a long battle for her to be able to watch this little one grow," Bailey said. She didn't know if she was saying it for her benefit or those standing around her.

"And we'll do whatever we can to help," Connie stated. The woman hung on Dion, not taking her eyes off the little bundle behind the glass.

"That reminds me," Mac started. "Tomorrow we're going to come over to paint the room. We got the eco paint that doesn't have any fumes but we're going to bring a few friends so we can get the room painted and set up in one day instead of taking off Monday."

"That would be great. If you're there by eight I'll let you in and feed you," Bailey offered.

"Sounds perfect," Sandy said.

The small group pulled themselves from the

viewing area and slowly made their way to the elevators.

"You girls get home and get some sleep. I hate to say it, but it might be the last one you get for a while," Wanda said while she pulled the cans from her hair.

Bailey wanted to go home to continue what they had started earlier, but knew Wanda was right. Resigned to one more night of simply cuddling, Bailey and Shayla made their way home.

Chapter Twenty-one

Two days later, they were finally able to bring Morgan and Angel home. Angel had been able to leave the next day but nobody wanted to separate mother and daughter. The doctor requested Morgan stay another day just as a precaution. The extra days allowed Sandy and Mac enough time to complete the room. Bailey did her part by setting up a bassinette in Morgan's room. When the new mother walked through the doors and saw all the work done, nobody thought she would be able to stop crying.

As expected, the only person getting any sleep besides the baby was Morgan. Nobody faulted her. Everybody knew she still had a hard road ahead. Life had turned into long nights of feedings. Bailey and Shayla had agreed to alternate nights so at least one of them was getting enough sleep. Their night of romance when Angel had been born had been the only time the two had been able to connect. Work and taking care of Morgan and Angel had not allowed the two women much alone time. Bailey was afraid Shayla would pull away but each night she laid down and Shayla snuggled in her arms, she knew they could weather any storm that came their way.

When they had left the hospital, Morgan had set up an appointment for her cancer test. She decided to wait a week to recover from the delivery. The days ticked by to the appointment and everybody had bit their nails to the bone. Except Wanda; there was no way she would ruin her manicured nails. When the day finally arrived, Bailey was pissed she couldn't attend due to a mandatory meeting. Shayla agreed to accompany Morgan while Wanda watched Angel.

Shayla and Morgan had been whisked into the doctor's office when they arrived. Morgan had been ill since returning from the hospital and nothing they did helped the young mother. Shayla sat next to Morgan and her heart went out to her. Even though she was the only person in the house to sleep through the night she looked drained. A sickly pallor replaced her previous rosy color. It scared her to think her girlfriend might lose her younger sister, whom also happened to be one of her best friends. They had spent many a night tangled in each other's arms discussing what their future might hold.

A few minutes passed before the doctor walked through the door. He acknowledged the two women as he took his seat behind the desk.

"I know we've been here a few times already so I'm just going to come out and say it. The results are in and I'm sorry, but even though we removed the breast, the cancer has spread. When you mentioned having a pain in your shoulder, we checked and unfortunately we found that the cancer has moved into the bone."

Shayla reached out and took Morgan's hand. She hadn't expected the prognosis to be great, but she had hoped. Since they had removed the breast and surrounding tissue, there had been the possibility that they had gotten everything. Just hearing the doctor say the "c" word hurt and she couldn't stop the tears that sprang to her eyes. She squeezed the small hand in hers. Silently she listened as the doctor continued.

"As you know we gave you a heavy dose of radiation then gave you an x-ray so we could see where the cancer had spread to. Don't give up. There are still things we can do. Have faith. What we need to do now is decide how you would like to attack this."

The doctor went into different options; as he prattled on Shayla didn't know how he could give that type of news day in and day out. He saved lives, but often he had to tell someone they were going to die, unable to do more than give a time frame. It would kill her to tell someone their days were numbered, being unable to give them a shred of hope. With each word that passed through his lips, Shayla could see a change in Morgan. The woman who sat in the uncomfortable chair next to her reminded her nothing of the young lady who went through the same fight years ago.

The only signal she received from Morgan, who quietly sat next to her, that she heard the doctor was the slight slump of her shoulders. Defeat radiated off the young woman. She wanted to shake Morgan, urging her not to give up hope. She knew she couldn't. Support was what she was there to give, no matter how scared she felt. Shayla would help her no matter the cost. They had been prepared for this news since they had been told the first time. Shayla had researched the possible outcomes and not one was positive. When Morgan had decided to fight for Angel's life, Shayla knew Morgan was playing an aggressive hand of all or nothing with lady luck. It appeared Morgan had a few more hands left to play.

"How long will I have if I choose not to go

through treatment?" Morgan asked.

Shayla couldn't stop her gasp. She turned to look at the woman sitting next to her so fast her neck cracked. Ignoring the pain, she watched the stoic woman look at the doctor. Silence permeated the air and she wanted to reach out and shake her. Never had Shayla thought Morgan would give up. If Morgan did nothing she would never see Angel say her first word, first haircut, first step, walk her into her first day of school, get married. There was even the possibility her daughter would go through life and never know the love she had for her. What she had sacrificed to make sure her daughter had a fighting chance. There was no guarantee with any treatment, but with no treatment it was accepting a death sentence. Everybody eventually dies, and Shayla knew that, but not in their twenties with a new baby.

"I would advise against that, but if that is what you choose you would probably have just a few months, six at most. I know many women who have had the cancer spread to their bones and recovered. We just have to find a treatment that is aggressive enough," Doctor Harrison replied.

Shayla couldn't believe what she had heard from the person seated next to her. She bit at her lower lip to stop the pleas from tumbling out of them. The idea of her not getting treatment hadn't even entered her mind. It would be suicide. A metallic taste appeared on her tongue. The pain from her cut lip did nothing detract her from the knowledge that Morgan was choosing to die, leaving her sister, new baby, and all her friends. It was selfish. She wanted to say something to her, but in front of the doctor would not be appropriate. If she waited a few more minutes, she would have a captive audience in the car. Even though confrontation was something she disliked, she could not allow Morgan to do what she was thinking. It was her life but there was no reason she couldn't give her opinion. She didn't want to watch her friend die. She needed more time, for herself and her lover. It hadn't even been a year since Bailey and Morgan lost their grandmother. The loss of her sister would devastate her girlfriend.

"If this is the route you choose we can set up another meeting to discuss your options. We'll do everything we can to make sure you're comfortable. I just want to say that I'm very much against this option per my medical opinion. All I ask is that you at least take one night before making your final decision. Talk to your family and then please call us," the doctor said before closing his file.

"Thank you, doc. I'll have to think this over then get back to you. I'll call your office when I've made my decision," Morgan said. With her shoulders back, she rose to shake his hand.

The two women walked to the car in silence. Shayla didn't know how to approach Morgan about what they had just heard. They were pulling out of the parking lot before Morgan broke the silence.

"Shayla, I have to ask a favor. Can you please take me downtown? I have another meeting. If you have to get back to the bookstore, I understand. I'm sure I can call someone to pick me up if you can't stay," Morgan said.

"That's fine. I took the rest of the day off. I can take you," Shayla agreed. Her lip was now raw. She could no longer hold her tongue. "Morgan, how can you do this? How can you think about refusing treatment?"

"Chances are I will die sometime. We all will."

Shayla was surprised at the calm in the young woman's voice. There was no quiver, just stoic acceptance. Shayla had never stared death in the face but Morgan had. It was the second time, and now it sounded like she walked up to the grim reaper and spat in his face, tempting him to take her. Soon he would have her, but Shayla realized it would be on Morgan's terms.

Hearing the words caused tears to suddenly appear in Shayla's eyes. To hear those words pass Morgan's lips so calmly, it felt like a knife to the back. Shayla knew Bailey had lived the last six months with the hope her sister would be able to fight and win. It dawned on Shayla that Morgan knew her time was short. It made sense now. Morgan had asked her to take care of her sister and be there for Bailey, knowing she was not going to be able to do it herself.

"I just didn't know when or how soon. I know I should do the treatment, but knowing it's moved to my bones is a death sentence. Doing treatment would just prolong the inevitable. I know you're going to tell me I should still do the treatment, but I want to live the last of my days and be able to hold and love my daughter, knowing what's going on around me."

"What do you mean?"

"The last time I went through treatment I thought it was bad. I mean they're pumping my body full of toxic chemicals. I was miserable for days afterwards. Then just as I started to get better, I had to go right back in and do it all over again. It was awful. I had so much radiation in me I couldn't wear anything heavy. If someone touched me, it felt like a thousand needles were pricking me. That was to cure the cancer, now they say it is going to have to be more aggressive, and that's just to prolong my life. What kind of life is that? I can't do it. I want to be able to hold and love my little girl for as long as I can. I don't want to be throwing up or living with constant pain when all I want to do is hold my daughter. If she cried, I wouldn't even be able to take care of her. Just to have her in my arms would be heaven and hell. It would be torture just to hold her. I want to enjoy the same feeling I get now when she is near me."

"I understand." Shayla accepted things were not going to change no matter how much she argued. She didn't know what it had felt like for Morgan to go through what she had been through, and now that she knew, there was no way she would try and talk her out of it. It made sense to her, but she didn't know how she was going to be able to help Bailey understand. They were going to have to work together to get her sister to comprehend the decision Morgan was making. Shayla knew Bailey would focus on the single fact her sister was choosing death over life.

"I know this will be hard on everybody but it's something I have to do. I know I'm dying. It's something I've already come to terms with. Don't think I'm not afraid because I am. I'm scared about what will happen to Angel and Bailey once I'm gone. I'm not going to be there for them. That scares me more than death." Morgan's voice quivered.

Shayla continued to drive in silence, allowing Morgan a few minutes to get her emotions in check before her next meeting.

"You can park anywhere," Morgan choked out when they pulled into town.

Shayla parked, shut off the engine, and turned to the devastated woman sitting next to her. She needed to try to alleviate the fears that Morgan had.

"Don't be afraid of what will happen once you're gone. I'll be there for both of them. I'll take care of them," Shayla reassured her friend.

Shayla intently watched blue eyes. Defiant eyes finally crumbled as tears blossomed and rolled down Morgan's cheeks. Not once since they had heard the news had Shayla seen Morgan lose control. Shayla pulled Morgan into her arms, holding her until the tears dried. Her own tears fell freely.

Morgan pulled back and dabbed at her eyes. "Thank you for being here for me."

"I'll always be here for you," Shayla whispered and wiped at her own tear-stained face. "You're family."

"I don't know how long I will be. If you want, I can call or you can wait here. It's up to you."

"I'll be fine. Bailey insisted on downloading some books on this pad thing. If I can figure out how to work it, I'll do some reading." Shayla pulled out her birthday present.

"All you do is turn it on and find the book icon," Morgan informed her.

"Yeah, turning it on, that's the first thing I'm not sure about," Shayla said and turned the pad over in her hands.

Morgan giggled before she reached for the pad. "Here, first you press the button on the top to power it on, then you press this button at the bottom, then when the page lights up like this you put your finger here and pull this bar across the screen. Now we have the main page and here is the icon I told you about."

Shayla watched and listened as Morgan turned on the tablet. She had started to carry the device to appease her girlfriend, but she knew a book would have been easier. She didn't need instructions on how to turn a page.

Morgan handed the device back to Shayla and showed her how to turn the pages before she crossed the street and disappeared into the only lawyer office in town.

Fifty pages later, they were headed back to the house. They found Angel in Bailey's arms as she sucked on a new bottle. Bailey turned to the women when they passed through the door but continued to rock and feed the little one in her arms. The women had not even taken their seats before Bailey asked about the appointment.

Shayla took a seat next to Bailey. She reached over and played with the soft dark curls that covered Angel's head. She watched Bailey's eyes track her sister as she paced the floor.

"Not as well as we had hoped for," Shayla finally said. She placed an arm around Bailey.

Bailey looked at Morgan and continued to silently wait for her sister to continue.

"We tried, but it's moved into the bone," Morgan finally said

Shayla felt Bailey tense. She rubbed her lover's back. Her hands traced small circles, feeling the muscles start to bunch up.

"What are they going to do?" Bailey asked.

Shayla could hear her lover try to keep her voice quiet. The baby in her arms continued to pull at the bottle.

"Well, of course he suggested we start treatment,

but basically all it would do is prolong the obvious. As I understand it I would be doing treatments until…"

Morgan didn't need to finish the sentence; the three women knew what was unsaid.

"Or?" Bailey asked and set the empty the bottle aside. She laid Angel against the towel protecting her shoulder.

"Or I do nothing. The doctors do what they can to make me comfortable, letting it run its course," Morgan said.

"You chose door number one, right?" Bailey said before she cooed at the baby who had let out a burp that could rival any man.

"I didn't give him an answer yet. I wanted to weigh my options," Morgan stated.

"But it's an easy answer," Bailey replied.

"No, it's not. You don't know what it takes to go through that. You don't know what I went through the first time. I don't know if I could do that again. And it's not even what I went through then. It'll be a lot harder this time and for what? A little time? Bailey, we know we are all going to die sometime. Mine just might come sooner than later," Morgan said.

It was the truth. Shayla and Bailey could do everything in their power to be supportive. They did not know what it felt like to have poison pumped into their body to try to kill cancer. Shayla had promised to be there for Morgan and that was what she was going to do. If she had to fight with her girlfriend to make her understand her sister's decision then she would.

Shayla watched tears spring to Bailey's eyes. Her heart went out to the women.

Two women in the room held their breath and watched Bailey continue to rock Angel. They had no idea what was racing through her head. Neither knew what her next reaction would be. Morgan and Shayla were both prepared for a fight when Bailey finally looked up with unshed tears. Clearing her throat, she waited a few more seconds before she spoke.

"I know this is hard for you. It's just as hard on me too, but whatever you decide I'll be there for you. I won't be happy if you choose to pass on treatment. But you have to understand I love you more than anyone in this world. Besides this little one in my arms, you are the only family I have. I'll admit that I want to beg and plead for you to at least try, but I know no matter how much I wail, you'll just do your own thing. But I'll be here for you." Bailey stood and handed Angel to Morgan before she headed for the stairs. No more words were needed.

Shayla turned to follow her. A deceivingly strong hand caught her arm. She knew Bailey finally realized that Morgan had more than likely already made up her mind. They would have to stand by and watch Morgan's body deteriorate. No matter what Morgan decided, chances were that in a month, or few years, there would be a funeral. The slam of the bedroom door hurt her heart. Shayla knew her girlfriend was behind that door all alone in her grief but a strong hand still kept her downstairs.

"Give her a few minutes. She needs time to absorb this."

Shayla nodded. Again she reached out in a vain attempt to control unruly curls. The shaggy hair reminded her of the woman above them alone in her grief.

"I'm so sorry," Shayla said.

"So am I," Morgan said. She pulled her daughter

tight. "I know I've been asking a lot of you lately but I was wondering if you could do one more thing for me."

"Sure." Shayla watched mother and daughter. A smile appeared on her face even though a dark cloud hung over the home.

"I was wondering if you could take me to an electronic store. I'd drive myself but I haven't been feeling well. Please don't tell Bailey that, she worries enough as it is. I want to get a camcorder. I want to tape my little girl a message before I get too weak," Morgan stated.

It pained Shayla that Morgan spoke of the end so candidly. It was as if the young woman had already given up. She didn't like the attitude Morgan had taken but there was not a lot she could do. She was close to Morgan and a few things would fall on her shoulders. It was understandable since nobody knew how much time Morgan had, and what little of it she did would be focused on her daughter. Shayla would do what she could to try to shelter Bailey from Morgan preparing for the end.

"Don't worry, I have one. My parents gave it to me for Christmas last year. I haven't used it. I think you already know how good I am with electronics. I'll bring it over tomorrow after work," Shayla said.

"That would be great. I just don't want her to forget me. I mean, I might not be around to watch her grow up." The force of hearing it aloud again brought on the tears. The baby started to fuss. Within moments, both women had tears flowing down face.

"It must be residual hormones," Morgan said, trying to wipe away the tears.

"No, it's just emotions. It's ok to be scared,

Morgan." Shayla hugged her friend, trying to be careful of the baby between them.

"I am scared," Morgan whispered.

"We all are, but the best we can do right now is just live one day at a time. Try and make the best of every minute we have left. You know what. I've made you a few promises today and I would like for you to make one for me," Shayla said.

"Ok."

"Promise me you won't give up. Just do some research, hear what the doctors have to say, think about everything, and then make up your mind. Don't sign your death warrant tonight." Shayla continued to lavish the baby with attention. By the time she was ready to leave, at least one person had a smile on their face.

"Ok, I promise," Morgan said.

"Good, now I'm going to go talk to your sister. I need to see how she's doing." Shayla pulled away from the mother and daughter and knew they would be ok. There was someone else in the house that needed her at that moment.

The few steps it took to get to the top of the stairs felt like an eternity as Shayla slowly made her way to the bedroom she now shared with Bailey. Quietly she opened the door to find Bailey on the bed, curled into a tight ball, her shoulders heaving. Small sobs were heard coming from the woman. Shayla hurried to the bed. She sat down and gently pulled Bailey to her. Bailey tried to pull away but strong arms held her close.

"Don't pull away," Shayla cooed. "I know this is hard but we have to be strong for Morgan and Angel."

"I know, but it just hurts so bad. It feels like a

part of me has been ripped out. She's still alive and walking around downstairs, but knowing someday she won't be is killing me," Bailey wailed.

"I know." Shayla attempted to fight her own tears. She couldn't break down now. Later when she was alone she would cry the tears she fought against, but now she had to be strong for Bailey. "My heart hurts too, but we have to be supportive. We have to be here for her, let her know we'll be fine."

"But I won't be. She won't be here anymore. I'll be alone." Bailey continued to cry.

Shayla forced Bailey to look at her. "You'll never be alone. Do you hear me? You'll always have Angel, our friends, and me. Morgan will always be here." Shayla softened her voice as she placed her hand on Bailey's chest, then her head. "And here, you have to keep these fresh because when Angel is older you'll have to tell her all about her mother. Every story you have up here, about Morgan, you'll have to remember so you can tell her daughter. You have to be strong, for Angel. She will need you more than anybody."

"I don't know if I can."

"I do. I know you can. You were just a kid when you took care of both you and your sister. You knew what you had to do and you did it. Just like now. All you have to do is be there for her. You have to make sure she stays up beat and keep the house filled with as much happiness as possible. There will be rough patches, but we'll get through them. And I'll be here with you every step of the way, so will the other ladies. You're not alone and never will be."

"Whatever did I do to deserve someone as wonderful as you?" Bailey asked.

"You came back to me. I love you," Shayla replied

before she kissed Bailey.

"And I love you. More than ever," Bailey said. "We have to tell everybody else what she's decided to do."

"She hasn't made her decision yet. I think it would be ok to tell them about the cancer, but until Morgan decides what to do, I think we should wait for Morgan to let them know. I'm sure they will be supportive and do whatever they can to help."

"I know. They're wonderful women. I know they'll help, but it's going to be a hard dance to try and help Morgan, but still try and give her as much independence as possible. I've already tried that but I didn't do so well," Bailey said.

"Well, last time you were doing it alone. This time I'm sure you'll have more help. We might be able to spread it out more."

"I hope you're right. We all still have our lives to live. We have to continue to do that and try and make sure Morgan and Angel are taken care of." Bailey rolled on her back and opened her arms. Shayla crawled into them. She felt guilty taking comfort in Bailey's arms when Morgan was downstairs all alone.

"I don't think we have to worry about Angel. I know if we call Wanda she'll be here in a second."

"I know. I love to watch the changes that come over everybody when they're in Angel's presence. Even Sandy has started to mellow. At least now, her hair is a normal color and she's even removed all her piercings. She actually looks respectable." Bailey pulled Shayla closer.

"Honey, I think Mac has a little more to do with that. I heard Dion and Connie have talked to the girls about selling them the bakery, or allowing them take it over for a while so they can either retire, or do partial retirement."

"I didn't know that."

"Well, it's not like they were keeping it from you. Everybody just knew you were under a lot of stress. We haven't had much time to sit down and talk is all." Shayla let her fingers play across her girlfriend's flat stomach. It felt good to feel Bailey shiver under her touch. It had been a long time since they were intimate with everything going on around them.

"Well, I think that needs to change. No matter what happens in the next few months we still need to make time for each other. Morgan is important and the time we have left with her is precious, but you're important, too. I don't want you to think I don't have time for you."

"Honey, I've never thought that. I love you. I was just giving you some space and time for yourself. We have forever to spend together. Our time with Morgan might be limited. I want us to make the most out of what time we do have left." Shayla scooted up and kissed Bailey.

Bailey laid her head on Shayla's shoulder. Shayla ran her fingers through Bailey's hair, enjoying the feeling of being able to give her partner comfort when she needed it. Within a few minutes, she felt Bailey's breathing even out. Gently she untangled herself before making her way downstairs to see if Morgan needed anything, sure it would be the first of many more to come. She found Morgan still on the couch with a sleeping Angel in her arms. Buddy had settled on the couch nestled between arm of the couch and Morgan's feet.

"Do you want me to put her down for the night?"

Shayla asked.

"No. I think I want her to sleep with me tonight. I know I'm not going to be much help with her in the coming months. Even if I choose treatment, I'll still be of little help. I'll take her tonight. You go back up and get some sleep," Morgan said.

"You have a good night," Shayla said. With one more look at the mother and daughter, she turned to lock the front door.

"You too, Shayla, and thank you for being here."

"There's no other place I would want to be," Shayla said, meaning it with every ounce of her being. She left Morgan alone on the couch as she locked up the house before she headed back to her partner.

Chapter Twenty-two

Life continued to go on for the Hutsell household. Angel flourished with all the attention she received. Women were in and out of the house at all hours to help the three adults. Morgan's summer off had come and gone and the school had graciously allowed her to take the year off to continue treatment along with the extended maternity leave.

When Morgan had told Bailey and Shayla she had agreed to attempt treatment on a trial basis, the house had erupted and nobody felt guilty when they had woken up the sleeping baby. The treatments had been hard on the young woman. Bailey did not know how difficult it would be. It was difficult to watch her sister deteriorate. She had hoped and expected to see her sister get better but to watch her sister struggle just to pull herself from bed was hard on Bailey.

The baby's first Christmas was fast approaching and the tree that stood in the middle of the living room held ornaments that had been hidden for well over a year. Now the noble fir was pregnant with presents for everybody in the household. Even though Morgan was not doing as well as they had expected, Shayla had convinced Bailey they should do what they could to keep everybody in a festive mood.

Bailey attempted to set another box under the tree. The box was small so she placed it on a branch heavy enough to carry the weight of the gift.

"And who is that for?"

Bailey jumped at the voice and turned to find her sister sitting on the couch wrapped in a new blanket. "Shit, you scared the life out of me."

"Sorry. I just wanted a change of scenery. I was getting tired of sitting in my room and watching TV day after day."

"Can I get you something?" Bailey asked and settled into the chair. It felt good to get off her feet. She had been up and running around for hours. Her work had started to suffer from lack of sleep and she still had at least five more hours of writing to complete her latest assignment.

"I'm good. I know you've been busy but I was wondering if you have a few minutes to talk," Morgan said and attempted to sit up.

"Here, let me help."

"No, it's ok. I'm fine. I can do this. But do you have a few minutes?"

"For you I have all the time in the world."

"I'm not doing well...."

"You're fine. You're getting better," Bailey argued.

"I'm not. You know that and I know that. But that's not what I want to talk to you about. I need to talk to you about Mom," Morgan said but a cough stopped her.

"I don't want to talk about that woman," Bailey said after her sister calmed down.

"Fuck Bailey. Shut up for a moment."

Bailey sat back, struck by her sister's words.

"Please. You have to remember the world does not revolve around you."

"This isn't about me. It's about you and getting

better. We don't need to talk about this right now. Actually we never need to talk about this," Bailey said, crossing her arms over her chest. There would have been a lot of subjects she would have liked to talk about but this was the last one she ever would want to have.

"You don't understand. I need to talk about this. I need to explain a few thing about Mom."

"What is there to talk about? She left, she hadn't come back, there's nothing else to talk about. I wish she was dead."

"Well then, Merry fucking Christmas, you got your wish," Morgan spat.

Bailey didn't know what to think. People say they wished someone was dead all the time but it was never true. Morgan was just upset and saying that to hurt her feelings. "What the fuck are you talking about? You're lying."

"I'm not," Morgan yelled at her sister.

"You are. You're lying. Someone would have said something by now." Bailey sprung from the chair and started pacing the small room.

"No, I'm not. Every time anybody brings her up you shut down. You don't want to hear anything and walk away." Morgan closed her eyes and leaned her head against the back of the couch.

"No, no, no, no, no. This isn't possible. I would know something. Someone would have said something." Bailey gripped her hair and shook her head as her feet continued to propel her around the little room.

Silent minutes passed while Bailey continued to tromp around the room. Morgan sighed then situated the blanket around her legs as she waited for her sister to calm down so she could continue. Ten minutes passed before Bailey fell back into the chair. Tears slid down her cheeks. She didn't know why she was crying. She had spent over half her life hating the woman who gave birth to her, but when she heard that she had died she couldn't stop the tears. She hated herself for crying over a woman who didn't care about her.

More silent moments passed before she finally spoke. "What happened?"

"She died in a car accident. She was on her way home when she was hit by a drunk driver," Morgan said.

Bailey couldn't stop the bark that escaped her lips. "That's rich. She spent her life drunk and she gets killed by a drunk driver. She was probably drunk herself."

"She wasn't, she had just spent thirty days in rehab and was on her way home in a cab," Morgan defended her mother. "I know you didn't like Mom, but she was still our mother."

"The only good thing she ever did for us was give birth to us. When she left, she gave up any rights to be called mother," Bailey said. Her hands continued to run through her hair. She pulled at her curls until they were straight before they sprang back to her head.

"Actually, you don't know the full story. Before Grandpa passed he let me know what had happened."

Morgan's words were met with silence.

"Fine. Let me tell you what he told me. He said you had been asking them to let us stay with them. When she dropped us off the last night, they had decided it was time to take some control. Mom had shown up the next day and waited for us to get off school. He gave Mom a thousand dollars to take some time away and get her head straight. Months passed by and then years and she continued to keep in contact but wasn't ready to come back. He said that she finally came back at your graduation."

"Pfft. That's just convenient," Bailey cut off Morgan.

"Are you going to let me finish?" Morgan asked. Bailey could hear frustration seep into her voice.

Bailey knew she was being unreasonable. She nodded and Morgan continued.

"You don't know this but Mom was actually at your graduation. I was there, this I know is true. She didn't look good. She had lost a lot of weight and she looked nothing like I remembered. When she saw you walk across the stage, she broke down and started to cry. It got so bad Grandpa had to take her out into the hall. He came back alone and then left. That's why he wasn't there when we met up with you afterward. I guess they had talked and she wanted to come home. Grandpa said that in order for her to come home she had agreed to go to rehab. I know she went because I visited her once. It was during a family visit. I also received multiple letters from her."

"So you're telling me she changed?" Bailey asked.

"I can't tell you that. I can tell you that she went through some hard times. I'm not going to tell you what my letters said. Those are for me. You have your own set. I've kept them for you. They have never been opened. If you want them, I'll tell you where they are. If you don't then they will remain there until you're ready. All I do know is that she was on her way home from rehab to start her life over and she never made it back."

"I don't know what to say," Bailey said. Bailey

had always resented her mother for what she had done to her youth, but now that she knew this what was she supposed to think. She had been trying to edit the mistakes she had made in the past, but she didn't know what to think about what she just heard. She wished there was a delete button so she could just forget what her mother had done but she couldn't.

"You don't have to say anything. You just need to know. I'm not giving up but if something did happen to me you had to know."

"Thank you for telling me."

Morgan coughed and shifted again. Bailey realized how much it had taken out of her sister to tell her that story.

"Here, let me help you back to your room so you can take a nap." Bailey pushed herself from her chair.

"No, it's ok. I think I'll just take a little nap here. I like looking at the tree and watching the snow fall outside. This is my favorite time of year and I don't know if it will be my last but I want to enjoy it as much as I can." Morgan slid down onto the couch.

"Ok. That's fine. I'll just check on Angel and try and get my work done."

"Actually, Wanda had come and picked Angel up and took her to the bakery for the day."

"Oh, well then, I guess I'll just head upstairs. Yell if you need anything."

"Actually I want to ask one last thing," Morgan said. Her eyes never left the window.

"Anything."

"Promise me you will tell Shayla about....well, you know." Morgan bent her head back to meet Bailey's eyes. Before Bailey responded, she turned to look back out the window.

"I promise. I was going to anyway." Bailey stopped at the steps and just watched her sister as she gazed out the window. She had to digest what Morgan had told her. She had never thought of her mother when she thought of family but now knowing that her mother truly would not be there for her she could only hope that Morgan would get better. If not, then she would only have Angel. As she turned to trudge up the stairs, with each step she took, she prayed to a god she had not prayed to since she was a child not to take her sister. Before disappearing upstairs, she took one last look at her sister, realizing the end may be near for her, and once again prayed that the last chapters of her life were not ending soon.

Chapter Twenty-three

Shayla practically danced around the bookstore. She had to make sure everything was just right. Finally she was going to be meeting her favorite author. She didn't even know Allura Williams lived in the same state, let alone the same city. When the publisher had called and asked if she wouldn't mind hosting a reading, Shayla couldn't say 'yes' fast enough. It had shocked her to know Allura was local. For the past four weeks, she had looked at the face of every woman who wandered into the store, wondering if she was the elusive author.

The night she had told Bailey of the reading, her partner had not shared her enthusiasm. Bailey didn't think it would be too exciting to sit around while Allura read a few pages from her new book, and then answer questions from the crowd, before signing a few books. She wasn't even sure a lot of people would show up. She hoped the turn out wouldn't disappoint Shayla

When the day finally arrived, the store had gradually started to fill. Every available seat had been occupied, leaving standing room only. Shayla was so thankful the bakery had closed early. The women from next door were currently busy filling cups of coffee and handing out pastries. She couldn't thank the women enough. They had showed up early with the pastries, coffee, and small sandwiches. When Shayla asked them how much she owed, Mac sent her away, claiming it was good for business. Shayla didn't know how giving away food was good for business, but Mac said when the ladies sampled their wares they would come back to buy more at a later time. Mac claimed it was a win-win and free advertising. Shayla knew she was getting the better deal.

Ten minutes before the reading was to begin Shayla started to worry as the author had still not introduced herself. Another five minutes passed before she found Bailey pushing her way through the crowd, dressed in her best suit. Angel clung to her side in her frilliest dress. The three year old had really blossomed in the prior years.

"There you are," Shayla said, giving Angel a peck on the cheek before properly greeting her partner with a toe-curling kiss.

"Wow, this is a better turn out then I thought," Bailey said. Surprise was written all over her face as she scanned the crowded space.

"I know, except Allura hasn't showed up yet," Shayla said, her eyes continuing to stray back to the front door, even though she still didn't know who she was looking for.

"Yes, she did," Bailey said.

"Where?" Shayla asked. She turned around as if she was right behind her.

"Right here," Bailey stated.

"Where?" Shayla asked and continued to scan the room.

"Standing right where I am," Bailey stated. A small smirk played at the corner of her lips as she pointed at her body.

"Is this a joke?" Shayla asked. She didn't think

her partner was the least bit funny.

"If you don't believe me, call your contact and have her call Allura, let her know she hasn't arrived yet," Bailey challenged.

"You know what, that's a good idea. She needs to show up soon. I haven't been able to open the books yet. I was told I couldn't open them till Allura showed up," Shayla agreed. She couldn't help but be frustrated at the author for cutting it so close. Shayla was excited to meet her but couldn't help but be disappointed about her unprofessionalism. The author would be keeping her customers waiting.

She forced her way through the crowd until she finally arrived at the counter with her girlfriend close behind. With a slip of paper in hand, she dialed the publisher's number.

Bailey sat Angel on the counter. The toddler smoothed down her pretty dress. Pudgy little feet kicked the counter as blue eyes scanned the large crowd. Bailey bent down, showering little girl with kisses on chubby cheeks before tickling her.

Shayla watched the interaction, waiting for the line to pick up. She couldn't help but smile at the interaction between her girlfriend and her niece. When the phone was picked up, it didn't take but a few words before she was placed on hold. Seconds passed before she watched her partner pause and pick up her vibrating cell phone.

Bailey picked up the phone with one hand as she continued to tickle the little girl with the other.

"Hello?" She said into the phone. Eyes sparkled with glee as Shayla's eyes grew to the size of saucers. Bailey laughed into the phone.

"Thanks, I'm here. We're good," she said and

hung up.

"You, but how, when?" Shayla asked. She clicked off the phone and it slid from her hand as she slowly walked to her lover, in disbelief she had been dating her favorite author.

"For a few years now. When I was in the military, I started reading more, well mostly Romeo and Juliet, just thinking of you. When I went to get my degree, I minored in English. I found I loved to write and here we are," Bailey said and took Shayla's hands in hers. "I'm sorry I never told you. I just didn't think you would ever believe me."

"Then why tell me now?" Shayla asked.

"I promised Morgan I would. I told her I would do this. But I wanted to see you when you read the new dedication."

Bailey pulled the box of books to her and sliced into it with her keys. She pulled out one book and flipped it to the dedication and handed it to her partner.

Shayla read the new dedication. 'For my Angel, my Grandmother, my Sister, and my One True Love.'

"You've always been the love that the dedication was about. My guardian was my grandma and my rock was Morgan. They knew. They found out when a box of books turned up on our doorstep. I had just returned home and received my author copies and I wasn't there when they arrived. Grandma had opened them and I had to admit why I was getting a box of books," Bailey explained.

"But your stories have all been about unrequited love, then them coming together. They felt so real," Shayla said, never taking her eyes off her lover. She bent down and kissed the hands that still held hers.

"They felt real because for years I've been in love with you and never thought we would be together. My first book didn't have a happy ending and the publisher made me change it, but each time after that when I wrote the happy ending, for just one moment, I was able to feel what it would be like if we were able to be together. It felt real because it came from someplace genuine. Now I know that happiness. But this book is different. It's not about unrequited love; it's about something different. It's about soul mates. One thing I learned about in school was about writing about what you know. This is what I know. You're my soul mate," Bailey said. "I love you, Shayla. I've never loved anybody as much as I love you."

Shayla tore her hands from Bailey's and hurried around the counter as fast as the crowd would let her. She flung herself into Bailey's arms. "I love you too. More than you'll ever know."

"Hey, you two, get a room," Morgan kidded as she pushed her way through the crowd. "I'm here to grab my daughter and take her over there to get something with chocolate in it. Do you want that?" Morgan asked the little girl whose eyes sparkled when they set on her mother.

Dark curls bobbed as Angel smiled with delight. Morgan scooped the little girl off the counter with her strong arms and carried her to the other older women who doted on her as if they were her grandparents.

Shayla watched Morgan heft her daughter on her hip and walk her to the table as if she weighed nothing. It was less than a year ago that Morgan could not even get out of bed. She didn't know what had happened but six months ago they had all cheered when they were told that they could not find cancer in her body. Even though they feared the cancer would return, everybody celebrated every day Morgan had with her daughter. She had even been able to go back to work. Life was full of gifts and she was looking at two of them.

Bailey pulled Shayla close to her and kissed her, not caring about the stares that came their way. It had taken years to get the woman in her arms back in her life and nobody else was going to pull them apart. Her life was not perfect. Nobody's was. She had the woman she loved in her arms, her sister was cancer free, and she had the family she never thought she wanted.

Bailey knew she needed to get to the front of the room to begin the reading but before she started to fight the crowd she pulled her partner close once more. She needed the silent strength that only Shayla could give. The past few years had been hard but with her family surrounding her she was able to face it knowing she was not alone. Another quick kiss from Shayla and she was ready to thread her way through the crowd. Bailey squeezed Shayla's hand and knew that no matter what life threw their way they would make it, hand in hand.

About the Author

Sandy Dugger can be found asking people to hold and reboot their computers by day. But at night she can often be found at her computer writing. Originally from Oregon, Sandy now lives in a small town outside Phoenix Arizona with her partner Stacy and their three furry pets. At almost thirty she went back to school and received a Bachelors degree in computer sciences. She was honorably discharged from the U.S. Navy under DADT. Even though she is now unable to re-enlist she still supports her military brothers and sisters. She enjoys spending quiet days at home with family and friends. Sandy loves to read, play games (all sorts), catch up on her DVR, and travel to new places.

You can reach Sandy at
SDAuthor@yahoo.com

Lightning Source UK Ltd.
Milton Keynes UK
UKOW02f1145300316

271169UK00003B/105/P

9 781939 062796